Sabbath

Modern Jewish History

Henry L. Feingold, Series Editor

Sabbath

Josef Erlich

Edited and with an
Introduction by Hana Wirth-Nesher

Foreword by Dov Sadan

Translated from the Yiddish by
Shmuel Himelstein

Syracuse University Press

English translation copyright © 1999 by Syracuse University Press
Syracuse, New York 13244-5160
All Rights Reserved

99 00 01 02 03 04 6 5 4 3 2 1

This book was originally published in Yiddish
as *Shabbes* in 1970 by Hamenora Publishing, Tel Aviv.

Permission to publish the English language version has
been granted by the author's widow, Cilla Erlich.

The paper used in this publication meets the minimum requirements
of American National Standard for Information Sciences—
Permanence of Paper for Printed Library Materials, ANSI Z39.48-1984.∞

Library of Congress Cataloging-in-Publication Data

Ehrlich, Joseph.
[Shabeṡ. English]
Sabbath / Josef Erlich ; translated from the Yiddish by Shmuel Himelstein ;
edited and introduced by Hana Wirth-Nesher ; with a foreword by Dov Sadan.
p.   cm.   — Modern Jewish History
ISBN 0-8156-0590-0 (cl. : alk. paper)
1. Sabbath Fiction. I. Himelstein, Shmuel.
II. Wirth-Nesher, Hana, 1948– III. Title. IV. Series
PJ5129.E45S513 1999
839'.134—dc21
99-20732

Manufactured in the United States of America

To the pure and holy ones
who perished in the Nazi Holocaust

Josef Erlich was born on 14 December 1908 in the *shtetl* of Wolbrom in Chszhanow, Galacie, Poland. He lived in Wolbrom until 1933 when, at age twenty-four, he emigrated to what was then Palestine. Working in agricultural settlements and towns, he wrote about both the life he had known during his youth in Poland and the experience shared by immigrants from various places. Josef Erlich died in 1982 in Tel Aviv. His other publications include *Tuv Haaretz* ("The Best of the Land") and *Harariim* ("The Mountain-Folk").

Hana Wirth-Nesher is coordinator of the Samuel L. and Perry Haber Chair on the Study of the Jewish Experience in the United States at Tel Aviv University and former chair of the Department of English. She is editor of *New Essays on "Call It Sleep"* (1996) and *What Is Jewish Literature* (1994), and she is author of *City Codes: Reading the Modern Urban Novel* (1996).

CONTENTS

FOREWORD

A Good Sabbath

Dov Sadan

I

THIS IS THE THIRD TIME that I am privileged to write an introduction to a book by Josef Erlich. The first was when I translated his work *Tuv Haaretz* ("The Best of the Land") from the manuscript, thus bringing an original author to the attention of the Hebrew reader, one who had written in Yiddish but was, strangely, to be printed in Hebrew. In particular I sought to indicate his roots, both conscious and unconscious, and his orientations, both in life and in literature.

As for his life, he was raised in the small Polish *shtetl* of Wolbrom. At a young age he became involved in the *halutzik* enterprise, immigrated to what was then Palestine, worked in agricultural settlements and the towns, and, being possessed of a sharp eye, immersed himself deeply in the details of the process of human transplanting that was going forward as we returned to our old-new land. Erlich experienced this process not only in himself and through others who shared his own background, but through the lives of different types

This preface appeared in the original Yiddish and Hebrew language editions of the book.

of people—new immigrants from all sorts of places, each with his own style and nature. This power of entering the lives of different sorts of people is notable in *Tuv Haaretz*, where the characters are new immigrants from eastern and central Europe, and in his book *Harariim* ("The Mountain-Folk"), where the people come from the Orient. The struggle is the same, however, in both works—the struggle with man and with the land itself—and is a source of dramatic tension and revelation.

As for Erlich's literary affiliations, he has a feeling for the elementary forces at work beneath the everyday scene, and he evokes this feeling so as to make the forces accessible to us as part of our perception of man and the world. In this respect he somewhat resembles the writers Isaac M. Weissenberg and Abraham M. Fuchs. We also find in all three writers, however, a transaction in which everything is both realistic and surrealistic, both natural and supernatural. Indeed, if you examine the total outcome carefully, you will see that the coexistence of these features is more than inference—it is the basis of the whole enterprise.

II

This impression is clearly reinforced by *Wolbrom*, a book published both in the original Yiddish of the author's home and *shtetl* and in the Hebrew translation of Shammai Mandel. In my introduction to that book, I discussed the special novelty in this author's life and work, namely, that his *shtetl*, as it were, demanded of him that he speak in its voice and address not only his own pen but his audience, too, in the accents of his father and mother. At that time it was clear to me that this slight volume, a living memorial erected on the ruins of Wolbrom, was the crack in the door; that door would yet open to its full width. I was thus not surprised when I heard that Josef Erlich was working on the book that we have here in front of us, in which Wolbrom figures not as an insignificant dot in the geography of Poland, but as the epitome of Jewish history at large, in its profound faith and culture, as represented by that greatest of achievements of the Jewish People, namely, the Sabbath as it found form and expression in the life of the community.

This book offers an epic, graphic account of the one-and-only day of the week, honored above all other days, with its wealth of expressions and ceremonies. It is more than a report, however; it also hints to us that we should seriously reflect and consider what we may have lost in the towns and villages of our land where the Sabbath is so far from being what it was in the world of the living Jewish community as we knew it: that is to say, a day utterly different from the six working days of the week, a day that wonderfully combined rest and sanctity. Do we truly understand this paradox, that there in an alien land we achieved such greatness? Should not the like of it, at least, remain ours now that we are in our own home?

III

Maybe such was not the author's intention. But good books have the habit of being stronger than their authors' intentions, and the glorious yesterday of the Jewish Sabbath, which we see portrayed for us here, seeks for itself a tomorrow as great and fair as itself, and perhaps greater.

PREFACE

Josef Erlich

I

THE MUNICIPAL ARCHIVES of Wolbrom state that already in 1562 ten Jewish families came to the forest area north of Cracow and established their homes in what would become Wolbrom. One of the ten was my ancestor Wolf Erlich. Throughout the generations, the *shtetl*, or township, developed and took root and evolved its Jewish lifestyle, customs, and beliefs.

II

Over the course of generations, the *shtetl* became firmly entrenched on Polish soil. They were craftsmen: tanners and weavers, tailors, hatters and cobblers, wheelwrights and shingle carvers, smiths, soap makers and lamplighters, wagon drivers and porters. There were Jews who spent whole days and weeks wandering about the different villages—buying a calf, a bundle of wheat, a few chickens, or eggs from a farmer. They made a minute profit, with which they supported their families.

There was practically no occupation in which Jews were not represented. One might say that the *shtetl* was divided into two groups: merchants on the one hand, and peddlers and artisans on the other. The merchants would travel to the large cities to buy their goods and would get to know the language of the country. The peddlers for their part were to be found in the narrow streets of the *shtetl*. They would set up booths in the *shtetl* square on Thursdays, the local market day. On all the other days of the week, except for Friday, they would travel to the neighboring villages to sell their wares. A majority of the artisans were born and died in the *shtetl* and never stepped outside its boundaries. They maintained their faith and their customs and their own distinct Yiddish dialect, which their forefathers had brought with them to Wolbrom six or seven hundred years earlier. They barely eked out a living, but they always lived with faith and hope. They prayed and recited psalms, and they waited for the time when they would return to that Holy Land from which they had been driven.

At first, the Jews built themselves wooden homes with thatched roofs. Later, they erected brick houses with tin roofs. They established *cheders* for the education of the young and *yeshivas* for the older students, built *batei medrash* and synagogues, a *mikveh*, and a hostel for itinerants. Each of them contributed anonymously, based on his means, to the charity for the indigent. People arranged circumcisions for their sons, married off their children, and then lived often to a ripe old age. Evidence of this longevity was to be found in the two cemeteries, especially the old one with wooden tombstones that dated back to a time when either the Jews were unable to carve stone or could not obtain stone for this purpose.

III

My family was of the wealthier, merchant class, with branches not only in Wolbrom, where they had lived for countless generations, but also in the surrounding *shtetls* and in Warsaw, Cracow, Lodz, Kielce, and Bendin. As part of that family, I received, unlike most Jewish youngsters, a more or less normal education. But I was always in close contact with other Jews—the simpler folk.

I would spend all my free time with them. I would enter a tailor's store, where the stifling smoke of the pressing irons filled the room, making it difficult to breath. I could hear only the noise of the machines and see only the shapes of the owner and his assistants as they sewed clothes for the fairs. But in those close circumstances one could hear the singing of a lullaby.

I would stand in amazement at how Jews with long beards would sit chipping away at roof shingles, all the while humming to themselves the song "There Is None Like Our God" as they wiped the beads of sweat off their faces. I would stand and, together with them, breathe in their longing and their faith.

That is why, when years later I studied at the technical high school in Silesia and saw how Christians lived in the larger cities, I lived, nevertheless, with the memories and folkways of the Jews in my *shtetl*.

IV

I found my professional work as a technician very interesting and was employed in various companies and different cities, but I felt cut off from my background—from my family and from the tailors and cobblers, from our common customs and identity. I lived at the intersection of two cultures and two faiths. I struggled with myself. I had no material problems, but felt uprooted from my spiritual sources. The result was that I was not able or willing to renounce my own identity.

V

Together with other Jews, I dreamed of an independent Jewish life in the Jewish land, and so, at the beginning of the 1930s, I moved to Eretz Israel—Palestine as it was called in those days. At that time, the land was half waste, and it needed laborers. I went to work in the orchards and fields as an agricultural laborer and, later, in construction; still later I became an office worker.

I lived with the joy of creating and building and with the knowledge that Jews from throughout the world were gathering together in Eretz Israel and building their independent life here. I was especially proud of the young Jewish generation in Israel. I was drawn to the Sabras, young proud Jews no longer subject to the fear of being strangers in other nations of different customs and beliefs.

But the young Jews had moved away from their traditions. They were involved in working and building the land, and in the process they had distanced themselves from the spiritual values of their people. I had the conviction, however, that as they became more deeply rooted in their Jewish land, they would begin to turn back to their tradition.

VI

Meanwhile, the Nazi era had arrived. The world underwent a cataclysm. We Jews lost a third of our people—six million. The Jews in Eretz Israel and throughout the world mourned their brothers who had been killed and recalled with longing the spiritual values of those who had perished, who had been so filled with faith.

I, a Jewish writer, born in Poland, writing about the Jews living in their land, where they have rebuilt themselves physically and spiritually, felt urged to turn back and bear witness. It was then that I decided to write *Shabbes*, an account of how Feivel and his family observed the Sabbath, the holiest day of the week, in the Polish-Jewish *shtetl* of Wolbrom. By doing so, I have raised up a memorial not only for Feivel and his family, but for all the Jews who were killed.

I wrote the book for our own generation, for their children and grandchildren, so that they should appreciate the worth of their ancestors. I also wrote the book for every human being who might wish to know something of this enduring folk culture, its heights, and its depths.

ACKNOWLEDGMENTS

WITHOUT Cilla Margarit Erlich's devotion and insistence, *Sabbath* would not have been available to English readers. This translated edition has been her dream since Josef Erlich's death in 1982, and it is dedicated to her.

I am grateful for the help, in its various forms, that I have received from Daphna Cohen-Mintz, Harold Fisch, Evelyne Goldblatt, Robert Mandel, Michael Kramer, Zippi Rosen, Ilana Shiloh, and Sonia Weiner.

INTRODUCTION

Hana Wirth-Nesher

SABBATH is a memorial book for a time, a place, and a way of life. Its lyrical and meticulous chronicling of the Sabbath as Josef Erlich remembers it from his childhood in Wolbrom aims to convey on paper the sacred time that the theologian Abraham Joshua Heschel described—"Eternity utters a day." Despite Erlich's reaching for a tender account of a Sabbath that could serve as a monument to the Eastern European Jewish civilization annihilated by the Holocaust, the book's power springs from its historical resonance, from the traces of the era in which it was created. What was Josef Erlich remembering and for whom?

In the early 1930s, Erlich left Wolbrom, the *shtetl* that his family ancestors had founded almost four hundred years earlier, for Eretz Israel to work the soil. He began writing *Sabbath* immediately after the War of Independence and in the shadow of the Holocaust. "I wrote the book for our own generation, for their children and grandchildren, so that they should appreciate the worth of their ancestors." To this he added, "I also wrote the book for every human being who might wish to know something of this enduring folk culture." Insofar as *Sabbath* documents the most minute details of religious observance and folkways, from the order of communal prayer to the preparation of meals, it is a rich archive for readers unfamiliar with Orthodox religious traditions as they were practiced for centuries in Europe and as they continue to be practiced among pious descendants of these communities today. Insofar as the concept of the Sabbath in Jewish civilization is transhistorical, an attempt in every generation, in every place where Jews gather, to transcend material and mundane concerns, the book captures this spirit. Yet, over and over again Erlich's descriptions, intended to convey a representative Sabbath in a representative family of the "folk," reveal the motivations and artistry of a particular mind in a particular time. *Sabbath* tells us almost as much about Josef Erlich's generation in Israel in the first two decades of the state as it does about the world that he portrayed so reverently.

The book opens on a Thursday evening in mid-winter at the close of the fair in the market square in Wolbrom. Although the first character to appear is the family patriarch Feivel, the first recorded speech is that of the non-Jew Mordoch, who is shoveling horse manure into a box: "Scum, and I have to sweep up the square after them." In sharp contrast, Feivel's first words are the prayer for handwashing, uttered in Hebrew (*"s'oo yada'im"* — "Stretch forth your hands in holiness . . . "). His wife Yachet's first comment apart from her greetings is in the Yiddish vernacular, a grievance about her husband's hard lot: "A whole week among the *goyim* without a bite of hot food." The frame of reference for the impending Sabbath, the sacred departure from daily travail, is the boundary between the Jewish and Gentile world, their mutual mistrust and hatred. Whereas Mordoch feels beleaguered and resentful, the Jews rehearse their hardships at the hands of the Gentiles. Their dread of that outer world is echoed several pages later in a conversation between Feivel and Shloime, the leather merchant. In a warning to Feivel about the hazards of his trade outside the *shtetl*, Shloime informs him, "'The *goyim* caught Zanvel and beat him up,' 'Really?' said Feivel, frightened. 'If not today, then they'll certainly beat him tomorrow,' added Zelig, the confectioner. 'Jews have to leave here and go to Eretz Israel.'" Thus Erlich's elegy for both the *shtetl* and the traditional Sabbath is framed by anti-Semitism, by fear of the Gentiles, and by hindsight—he is writing the work only a few years after the Holocaust, and in Israel. Even the children's concept of the Sabbath is affected by this perspective: Rivkele observes, "On Shabbes the Jews stay home and the *goyim* don't beat them."

Ethnographic writing, whether it is cast in the narrative mode of *Sabbath* or not, always bears the imprint of the author in selection and arrangement of material. Erlich's artistic choices are felt on every page, as they sharpen the contrast between the Diaspora world of Wolbrom and the author's new home in Tel Aviv. His Sabbath takes place in mid-winter, with the trodden snow on the first page recurring as a striking motif. Every foray outside the home is through "frozen mist" and over "frozen mud" and every transaction occurs with "frozen fingers" and with "breath freezing in the frigid air." The men make their way to the synagogue as "the town lay in deep snow"; the windows of the prayer hall are all covered with ice. Feivel's wife, Yachet, braves the snow to bring back hot *cholent* from the baker's oven and finds her children huddled under the feather quilt. The frigid temperature not only underscores the difference in climate between the Diaspora and Israel, but also affords a greater contrast between it and the warmth that emanates from the practice of the Sabbath, from the crowded prayerhall to the raisin wine and stew (*tzimmes*) that stave off the cold at home.

Erlich's choice of ritual is equally compelling and pointed. Although the order of the Sabbath service and the benedictions recited at home is prescribed, the Torah readings vary according to the calendar. The Jews of Wolbrom trudge through the silent snow on the Sabbath of *Yitro* ("Yisro" in the Yiddish pronunciation) to read of Mt. Sinai aflame and the sound of the shofar heralding the voice of God. Erlich exalts his poor villagers with the recitation of the Ten Commandments: nothing less than the theophanic moment, the giving of the Law, the founding of the nation. Furthermore, the haftorah portion of the Sabbath of *Yitro*, Isaiah, chapter 6, tells of the cleansing of the prophet's mouth with a hot coal so that he can speak the word of God. Most significantly, Isaiah prophesies the coming of the Messiah and the end of days. Thus, embedded into Erlich's Sabbath are the foundational stories of the Jewish people, from Mt. Sinai to messianic redemption. For Erlich, Zionism was the secular redemptive vision, yet he was saddened by the young Sabra's estrangement from Jewish tradition. "I, a Jewish writer, born in Poland, writing about the Jews living in their land, where they have rebuilt themselves physically and spiritually, felt urged to turn back and bear witness. It was then that I decided to write *Shabbes*." The deep ideological rifts between theological and secular visions of Zion are elided in this portrait of pious Jews drawn by the secular son whose return home also felt like exile from home. The book emits the chill of separation that marked Erlich's immigrant generation.

Even among the women, who are depicted only in their roles as wives and mothers, the return to Zion is a felt undercurrent. When the children clamor for a story, Yachet recounts that of the exile and the return. "The Jewish land is full of sun. Oranges grow there, as well as grape vines and pomegranates . . . When the Messiah comes, he will gather together all the Jews from the entire world and lead them back to their land." The domestic sphere in *Sabbath* serves as the arena for the rich and patient detail of life in Wolbrom. As Yachet's husband lays *tefillin*, she places a cutting board with a fish on her lap and begins chopping with a small black iron knife. The ingredients and procedures for the entire meal are rendered so methodically as to be captivating. Later, Yachet scatters woodshavings on the wet floorboards to lend the room an odor of freshly sawed wood, washes and kisses each of the children in turn, removes and replaces her wig at appointed times, carefully avoids squeezing the dripping washcloth or lathering with soap during the Sabbath, and arranges the vegetables in the *tzimmes* with precision, "a cube over a slice, a slice on top of a cube." When she serves the *cholent*, even the large potatoes, "like pyramids and trapezoids," partake of the Exodus. Although the arrangement of the food has a spiritual dimension, Erlich does not lose sight of the flesh, of the labor that goes into the making of the Sabbath, of "the sharp pain in her back" that she shared with no one. Nor does he omit the sensual dimension of the Song of Songs as Feivel gazes at Yachet's round arms as she dresses for the Sabbath.

Despite his devotion to the Zionist dream and its revitalization of Hebrew, Erlich wrote in Yiddish, the language of the Jews of Wolbrom. Although he knew that only in a Hebrew translation would it reach the younger generations for whom he was writing, the first putting of pen to paper had to be in the language of the world he left behind. Translation cannot always provide the exact equivalent if the concepts are not available in the target culture. For example, Feivel silently places a coin in the hand of Reb Avraham, the *melamed*, who is referred to in English as both teacher and rabbi, neither of which can capture the exact role of this well-known figure in Jewish education. In the original Yiddish text, Reb Avraham's response to Feivel's generosity is to express his gratitude with the phrase, "Yeshar Koach," an idiom invested with religiosity (May God strengthen you). He is indeed thanking him, but in the words that transform social exchange into ceremony. Although the multilingual features of the original Yiddish text cannot be conveyed in an English translation, a remnant of this aspect of Eastern European Jewish culture can be found in the retention of "Shabbes" (the Ashkenazi pronunciation) for social interaction within the *shtetl* (dialogue between characters) and the translated "Sabbath" for the liturgical, religious, and symbolic meanings of the word (in the narration).

The characters in *Sabbath* are all familiar Jewish types: the good-natured laborer who values education; the self-sacrificing, modest, and industrious wife and mother who saves the best morsel of meat for her husband; the elder son who excels in Talmud study; the younger girls who romp with their father and learn from their mother to care for the baby brother. It is an idyllic household of simple folk whose story wavers between elegy and sentimentality. With jagged roofs, moonlit snow-covered lanes, and horsecarts, Erlich's landscape has much in common with the canvases of Chagall. With its close-ups of street life and routine activities, it is reminiscent of the photographs of Vishniak. Yet despite its insistence on the distress of life in a hostile Gentile environment, it eschews the brutality of Babel; and despite the references to superstitions, it is not populated by the demons of Singer. It is Erlich's Wolbrom, treated with the nostalgia that comes of grief, with the caress born of hindsight.

I HAVE CHOSEN to include the author's preface and the original introduction by Professor Dov Sadan (which appeared in both Yiddish and Hebrew editions) to provide a historical context for the English translation. The illustrations were chosen for this edition, and I believe that they are self-explanatory with, perhaps, one exception—the high school pupils' performance near Lublin. It demonstrates that, as early as 1923, traditional religious life as described in *Sabbath* was already relegated to folklore and stylization for less observant Jews, as was the case for Josef Erlich himself.

Sabbath

1

FEIVEL rushed across the threshhold of Moishe's barn. He almost fell through the battered door, right into the market. Finally standing still, he looked about him.

The fair in Wolbrom had ended. All that remained were a few empty carts in the market square; the unfettered horses stood with their heads deep inside feed bags hung from their necks; all over the square lay trodden snow.

Mordoch, a tall, broad-shouldered non-Jew, was busy cleaning the square; his long, thick moustache hanging from both sides of his mouth like pigtails. Using a broad wooden shovel, he collected the horse manure from the square into a box. Mordoch wore a long, threadbare, army uniform, the trousers of which were held up by a piece of string tied round his waist. His full cheeks showed evidence of one drink too many. A lazy man, he took his time shoveling, all the while talking to himself: "Scum, and I have to sweep up the square after them."

The snow on the inclined roofs had begun to freeze. Jews with long beards, fur hats, long coats, and high boots gathered the wares that had been hanging on the walls and over the doors of their stores with red, half-frozen hands—a remnant of cloth, shoe soles, an iron file, a wooden dish. The bakers at their stalls collected up the left-over bread.

The cross on the church at the corner of the market square, between two alleys, seemed to dominate the square. The temperature kept dropping, frost forming on every exposed area; night finally fell.

The sky over the village was a deep blue shade, like a thick, heavy cloth. Feivel walked through the alleys, the snow crunching under his feet. The narrow paths seemed to lead him.

Stepping over the wooden threshhold, he felt hard, packed earth under his feet. He stretched out his hands, as if groping in the dark, took a few steps, and grasped the door handle. The door, swollen with moisture, seemed to spring

The marketplace of a Polish town in World War I, c. 1916. The photograph was taken by George Anker, then a lieutenant in the German army. Courtesy of Beth Hatefutsoth Photo Archive, Tel Aviv, and George Fogelson.

away from him. Dense, clammy heat struck his face and he hurriedly closed the door behind him. "Father!" the voices of three children shouted together. Zlotele, Rivkele, and Yossele ran to him. They had been sitting on the floor near the bed in the corner, and had been playing. Feivel's black eyes sparkled. The red hair of his eyebrows was stiff with frost.

"Hush!" Yachet his wife, a tall, strong woman, said to the children. She folded her hands over her stomach. "Good evening Feivel!" she greeted her husband. Immediately she added, "Sit down." Feivel returned her greeting, moving a bench from the table and sitting down.

Yachet stood staring at Feivel; her large, black eyes seemed to be examining him closely. Feivel, exhausted, remained sitting.

The children went back to their game, buying and selling things in their "store." "Come and eat!" Yachet exclaimed. Feivel did not answer. He merely looked up and shook his head.

Yachet went back to her to work at the stove and stirred the contents of the pot that stood on the small fire. She added a few pieces of tinder to the fire; these caught and the fire flared up.

Yachet placed a whole black bread on the table, along with a tin spoon and a kitchen knife. She put down the salt shaker, took out a soup bowl from the cupboard, and filled the bowl with potato soup. The steam from the pot condensed on her face. "Wash!" said Yachet, as she placed the soup plate on the table. Feivel stood, went over to the water basin, and filled a mug with water. Stretching out each hand in turn, he used the other to pour water over it. "Stretch forth your hands in holiness . . . ," he said loudly in Hebrew; the rest of the words he mumbled, as if swallowing them. He dried his hands on the kitchen towel tied to the adjacent table. He pushed the bench away and slowly sat down, as if unloading a heavy bag of grain. Picking up the bread with one hand and the knife with the other, he pushed the knife into the bread and turned the bread around along the knife edge. He then cut himself a slice. "Blessed are You . . . who brings forth bread from the earth." "Amen," said Yachet loudly.

Yachet went over and sat down on the edge of the bed, opposite him. She pulled her gray flannel dress, which was a little tight on her, over her knees. Her body was outlined by the dress. Feivel bent over the bowl, pouring each spoonful of soup into his mouth, enjoying the taste of the boiled potatoes.

Yachet sat looking as Feivel ate with pleasure. At one point, she shook her head and said, "A whole week among the *goyim* without a bite of hot food." A little later, she added, "But you're not the only one." It was quiet in the house, the only sound being the spoon striking the bowl, like a rooster pecking at its food. Feivel scooped up the last spoonful of soup in the bowl and swallowed it noisily. He placed the spoon on the table. He felt full. Swaying to and fro over the table, he recited the grace after meals. For a while, Feivel sat at the table, his eyes sparkling. Suddenly, he blurted out, "Enough!" and raised himself from the bench as if to stand up. But he remained seated, looking up at Yachet.

Feivel placed his broad hand under his leg, raised his head, and gazed stealthily around his home, as if he wanted to be sure that no one could see him. Afterwards, he stretched out the fingers of his right hand and began counting: "One, two, three." The banknotes totalled only a few gulden, and he counted them as if turning the pages of a book. When he reached fifty, he lowered his eyes, sighed, and exclaimed, "This is for new merchandise." He placed the few remaining banknotes on the table, returning the fifty gulden to his wallet, then picked up the remaining bills from the table and started counting again. He counted aloud till eight. Feivel remained seated with his mouth open, amazed that he did not have any more bills to count. Shocked, he said, "Yachet, there are two gulden missing for Shabbes!" "Feivel, don't worry. God will help next week," and she jumped up hurriedly from the bed.

Yachet took the few gulden from the table and placed them inside her bosom. She threw her brown and green decorated shawl over her shoulders, took out a folded bag from behind the cupboard, placed it in a basket, and moved to the door. A cold gust of wind forced its way into the house, and the air in the house was no longer as damp. The children hunched down, all three of them shivering from the cold. It became even quieter in the room. In the corners of the long, low house, shadows began to fall. Feivel pushed away the bench and slowly stood up. He was tired—for a full week he had been traveling through the villages of the area. He walked to the window and rubbed the frost away with the tips of his fingers. Afterwards, he went over to the corner where the cupboard stood. He remained standing there, his hands covering his eyes, and swayed back and forth in prayer. Finishing, he stepped backward and swayed to the right and then to the left. The children went on playing. Feivel's shoulders shook once. The heat in the house seemed to smother him. He sat down on the edge of the bed and pulled off his boots and socks. His feet were red, as if scalded in boiling water. "What do you want to buy?" Zlotele asked her sister, her voice echoing through the room. "Sugar," Rivkele answered in her thin voice.

Feivel stood up and glanced at his children. A while later his head fell forward, his eyes closed, his weary shoulders relaxed, and he dozed off. Rivkele remained with her hand stretched out, not taking the paper bag from her sister. She heard her father snoring and was frightened.

"I also want to sleep," she said to her sister. "So get into Daddy's bed," Zlotele said as she stood up. She lifted up Yossele, her two-year-old brother, who had been sitting watching his sisters play, settling him down in the corner of the bed, while the four-year-old Rivkele climbed into the bed by herself. Zlotele sat down beside Yossele. "Sleep, children," she said, imitating her mother.

The two children cuddled up next to one another and were soon asleep. Zlotele, the eight-year old, felt lonely in the big house. She cuddled up next to the other children and also fell asleep. The home became darker and darker. The father and children all slept.

2

YACHET remained standing on the street in front of the door. She pulled the shawl over her head, and for a short time looked around; then she suddenly darted down an alley, the fresh snow crunching under her feet. She walked diagonally across the market square, as if cutting off the left, snow-covered corner. She went from one street to the next, finally reaching the butchers' alley; there she breathed in and smelled the raw meat. All about there were dogs, their tails between their legs, waiting for scraps or a bone from the butchers.

For a while, Yachet hesitated, but between the open shutters of one of the booths she saw the head of Dobeh the butcher, covered with a shawl, her hands inside the sleeves of her thick fur coat. Yachet dared not go any further, and entered the store. "How are things?" asked Dobeh, not removing her hands from her sleeves. Her only movement was to nod her head to Yachet. "Let there be no Evil Eye," Yachet answered, and moved closer to the chopping board. The little booth was quite dark; it had no windows, and all the light inside came from the open door. One could smell the congealed fat.

Yachet removed her hands from underneath her shawl and looked around at the meat hanging on the hooks. The sharp edges of a long cutting knife and an axe glinted in the little light of the booth. She turned away, feeling a twinge of anguish in her heart. Dobeh, a broad-shouldered woman, waited patiently.

Shmuel, a tall man, was busy boning a piece of meat on the cutting block. He interrupted his work to look up at Yachet and asked, "Nu, Yachet, what can I give you?" Yachet did not answer him; she had not yet decided. Shmuel pulled out the whetting stone and began to sharpen the knife. "Yachet, take the neck. It was a fat animal," Dobeh suggested. "Can it be cut up into portions?" Yachet asked. "This meat is very cheap," Dobeh answered.

Shmuel put away the whetting stone. With one hand he picked up a slab of meat that had been hanging on a hook and threw it onto the chopping block. "How much?" he asked. Yachet's eyes watered. Quietly and briskly she answered, "Two pounds." She put her hands into her bosom and took out the money.

Shmuel spread his feet apart and turned the blade of the knife away from him to cut the meat. "You will have a fat soup out of this," Dobeh said to Yachet. Shmuel threw the cut of meat onto one side of the scale; in the other he placed the weights. "More than two pounds!" he said. "Enjoy it," said Dobeh.

Yachet placed a gulden in Shmuel's hand. He crushed the banknote in his fist. With his other hand he took out a few coins from his pocket and placed them on the table, Yachet's change. Yachet placed the package of meat in her basket and with frozen fingers picked up her change.

"Be well!" she said as she walked out the door, the change clenched in her hand.

"You too!" Dobeh called, not moving from her place.

The intense cold assaulted Yachet's face and stabbed underneath her fingernails. She again pulled her shawl over her head, only her forehead and eyes remaining visible. She walked through a long alleyway that was the communal property of those living around it. The frost-covered windows of the huts looked like lamps. She took a shortcut, pushing through the fresh snow and shivering in the cold. As she walked, she placed the change, which she had been holding, in the pocket of her dress.

Yachet came through an open space between two huts, emerging on the mountain road. It was a narrow road with a steep incline. She slipped into Yaakov's store, a low, large building that looked more like a barn. The air inside the store was oppressive, like frozen mist. A smell of frozen mud assailed the nostrils. Yachet caught her breath as the vapor from her breath froze in the frigid air. She looked around. "Hello!" she finally exclaimed, her voice echoing in the store. The women in the store turned their heads and looked up. Yaakov, the short storekeeper, nodded his head. A wet, semifrozen sack was tied around his waist; his short fingers were red from the cold and the damp.

A few women stood by the table examining fish. Yaakov stood on the other side of the table and barely spoke: "How much?" "Which?" He took the fish, weighed them, packed them in old, crumpled newspapers, and checked the money.

A woman stuck her head, bound in a black kerchief, through the door. "Do you have any live carp?" she asked. "Only dead hake. The rivers are all frozen," Yaakov answered, going back to his work.

The woman who had asked about the carp left. The other women bought fish, checked the weight, and paid. Yachet remained silent throughout, gradually moving closer to the table. When she reached the table, Yaakov raised his eyebrows. "Take these," he told her, pointing to a basket of fish at the side. Yachet turned her head and looked at the broad, silver-gray fish. Yaakov did not wait for Yachet's agreement and never asked her how much she wanted. He took a thick piece of paper and weighed her a pound of fish, just as he

Water pump in the fish market in Otwock, 28 kilometers southeast
of Warsaw, Poland, 1920–1930. Photograph by Alter Kacyzne.
Courtesy of YIVO Institute for Jewish Research, New York.

did every other week. "A quarter," he said, wrapping the fish. Only later did
he add, "of a gulden." Yachet took out the coins and laid them on the table.

The cold penetrated her body as she went back into the street, this time one
of the town's main streets, which led to the only paved road. Yachet hurried
to Zerach the baker. She went down to a cellar, and with her hand through
the shawl, pushed the door. The warmth of the oven used to bake the bread
surrounded her.

Zerach had dozed off, his head propped on the counter, but as Yachet came
in he woke with a start. "I've brought you what we owe this week," Yachet said.
Zerach shook his head from side to side to wake up properly and pushed up

his cap. Yachet's hands reached below the shawl. From her bosom she pulled out two banknotes. "Two gulden, like every week," she said, laying the money on the counter.

Yachet went over to the shelf on the left. On the shelf lay a few loaves of bread. She bent over, took a loaf of bread, and placed it in her basket. She looked to make sure that Zerach had noticed; he nodded his head.

Yachet closed the door after her and climbed the four steps to the street. Again the cold attacked her. Two houses down the street, at a low hut, she stopped again. The doors were open; Yachet crossed over the wooden threshold. In the corner by the window, on an upturned crate near the counter, sat the storekeeper, his long white beard tucked into his belt. He stopped studying the holy work that lay before him, glanced at Yachet, and again resumed his studies. Yachet removed two guldens from her bosom and called out, "Reb Asher, my debt!" She laid down the two bills. Asher's thick, gray eyebrows arched. He glanced at the money, picked up the bills, and placed them in his wallet. "Nu, nu!" he muttered, and returned to his studies. "Reb Asher, I'll serve myself."

In the corner stood a barrel filled with potatoes and covered with straw. Opposite it, by the wall, was a barrel with pickled cucumbers and another with sauerkraut. Yachet took out a small bag she had in her basket and sat down. She did not bend over, lest Asher see her knees. She filled the bag with potatoes and placed it on the scales. "See, Reb Asher," she said, "twenty pounds." She selected and weighed two pounds of onions and added three carrots to the potatoes. She tied the bag of onions and carrots with string that was attached to it and picked up the potato bag in her other hand.

Yachet left the vegetable store, and as she stepped out she pushed her way through the half-open door right next to it into Sarah Leah's store. "Yachet, how are you? How are the children?" "Thank God," Yachet answered. She sat down on a crate. Her shawl slid off her shoulders. "Sarah Leah, how are things?" she asked. Sarah Leah nodded. "God will provide," she suddenly said. Sarah Leah was a widow. Her son, who had married early, was now serving in the army. Her daughter-in-law had just given birth. "A beautiful baby?" Yachet asked. "Would that all Jewish children were like this one," Sarah Leah answered.

For a while both sat silently. Suddenly, the wind blew into the open door; a smell of kerosene wafted into the store.

"Could you please prepare my order for me?" asked Yachet.

"Yes, dear child," Sarah Leah answered, and turned to her again.

Sarah Leah was considerably older than Yachet. She wore a kerchief over her head and a brown, sleeveless, fur jacket. With the edge of the kerchief she dabbed at the corners of her mouth. She placed a package of sugar on the table, tore off a thick, gray piece of paper and spooned red beet jam into it, weighed it, and announced: "A quarter of a pound." She broke off a piece of chicory and laid it on the table; then, taking a piece of newspaper, she poured some unground coffee beans into it and weighed the whole package. She wrapped some yeast in another piece of newspaper. Her thick, small fingers worked expertly at all these tasks.

Yachet, watching Sarah Leah, suddenly burst out, "Sarah Leah, don't forget the children. Give them a Shabbes treat."

Sarah Leah filled a small bag with various hard candies, along with some peanuts. "How much do I owe you?" "One and a half gulden plus another five groszy," said Sarah Leah. Yachet wrapped herself in her shawl, tying its two ends around her throat to make sure that it would not come loose as she walked. Then, clutching the bag of potatoes to her stomach with one hand and carrying the basket in the other, she went over to the door.

The bag and basket were heavy. She did not have to walk far—only the distance of three houses to Michoel the miller. For the last few steps, she hurried through the open door into the mill, as if breathless. She bent down, put down on the floor all she had been carrying, sat down on the potato bag to catch her breath, and checked to see that nothing had fallen out of the basket. Her *shaitel* shifted slightly, and her black, short hair could be seen underneath it.

Sabbath

At the right side of the store lay sacks filled with corn meal, ready for the bakers. On the wall opposite was a great weighing machine. The window of the mill had an iron bar across it. In the corner, under the window, stood a table with a pair of scales, and next to it sat Michoel. Behind him were a few sacks of flour, one of which was open. Yoske the porter, a short, broad-shouldered man, went over to the sacks. He moved his feet apart and bent down, with one hand grabbing the corner of a sack as he swung it over his back. Yachet looked about, then eventually took a bag out of her basket. She walked over to Michoel. "Reb Michoel, a gulden worth of flour," she said, laying the bag on the table along with the money. Michoel stood up, took the little bag from her, and went to the open sack of flour. Using a scoop, he half filled the bag with flour. "Blessings on you!" She took the bag with flour from his hand, folded down the top, and laid it down in her basket. Yachet went into the street. Far away, on the horizon, a pale moon began to shine intermittently through 'the clouds, which covered a good part of the night sky.

The night was frosty and windy, and the roof tiles groaned as they scraped against one another. Yachet walked fast, her cheeks red with cold. When she finally came to the small street where she lived, she walked even faster. The steeply sloping roof of the hut seemed to rest on the ground; the path trodden in the snow lead to the porch.

The porch was dark. The air inside its wooden frame was freezing cold and damp. She walked carefully, so as not to bump into anything. When her shoes accidentally hit the door, she stood still for a while, put her hand to the door handle, and pushed the door open.

It was dark in the house as she tiptoed over to the stove, putting the potato bag down next to it. She pulled the shawl off her head and threw it onto the bed.

3

YACHET put out her hands and groped about in the darkness like a blind woman, moving toward the cupboard. Finding the matches, she lit one, and a tiny flame erupted as shadows flitted about in all the corners. Yachet hurriedly took the glass cover off the lamp and turned up the wick. A strong smell of kerosene filled the room. She replaced the glass on the lamp and turned down the wick. The flame fluttered a few times, making the shadows in the room dance about. Finally, it took hold and lit up the entire room. All the contents of the room—the benches, the stove in the corner, and the cupboard across from it—emerged from the darkness. In the corner, under a bench, stood a basin, and next to it a pail filled with water. The knapsack and staff that Feivel carried as he tramped from village to village seemed to be waiting for him to leave any minute.

Yachet looked at her sleeping family and the crumpled bedding. She went over to the stove, opened the doors, threw in a few logs from the pile behind her, and again closed the doors. The fire in the stove flared up anew.

Feivel woke up and immediately sprang out of bed. Yachet began to unpack and put away the things she had bought. She remained standing with the meat in her hand, pushing the bag of potatoes with her foot so that it would not be in the way. Then, going over to the water pail, she picked up the basin from underneath the bench, filled the basin with water, and soaked the meat.

"You can tell Shabbes is on the way," said Feivel. "Thank God for that!" "Mommy," called out the sleepy Zlotele as she opened her eyes. She tried to block out the light from the lamp with her elbows. She was surprised, because when she fell asleep the lamp had not yet been lit. Soon afterwards, both Rivkele and Yossele woke up.

Yachet wiped her hands with the towel that hung by the side of the table. "Children, time to eat and then to go to bed." As she spoke, she felt that she was rushing them. The little girls looked at one another, neither saying a word.

Yachet went on with her work: she cut three slices of bread and smeared them with jam, cutting off the crusts of one of them. She then moved to the stove, poured three tin cups of *bavarke*, a mixture of hot water, milk and a sweetener, and placed the cups on the table: "Daughters, time to eat!"

Feivel also sat down at the table, with his young son on his lap. He held the child between his arms, leaving his hands free. Feivel pulled the crustless slice over to himself, preparing to feed his son. He tore small pieces from the bread and with two fingers placed them in the child's mouth. With his other hand he held the cup tightly to prevent it from spilling, and put it to Yossele's lips.

Yachet went over to the bed, pulled off the feather quilt, and arranged the bedding. She picked Rivkele up under her arm; the child did not resist. She then wiped Rivkele's mouth and hands with the hand towel hanging above the bench. She took off the child's dress, shoes, and socks, and placed her in the bed. After that, she took Yossele, undressed him and laid him next to Rivkele, covering both children with the quilt.

Feivel sat slouched over, his head resting on his hands, while Zlotele stood at the window, drawing designs in the frost on the glass with her finger. Every so often she tried to peer out to the dark night—darkness frightened her.

Yachet pushed the bag of potatoes over into the middle of the room, filled the pail with water, pulled a stool out from underneath the bed, and filled a basket with the potatoes. "Zlotele," she called out to her daughter. Zlotele turned to her. "Peel the potatoes," she said, and handed her the basket. Zlotele's eyes sparkled with joy; she grabbed the knife from her mother's hands and sat down on the stool. "Feivel, you should also go to sleep," said Yachet. "I'll wait until our *kaddish* comes home," he answered.

Yachet looked at Feivel with her big dark eyes. "Go and lie down. When he comes, you'll wake up."

Zlotele sat peeling the potatoes. Her small hands were barely able to hold the potatoes and the knife, but she peeled well. As each was finished, she threw it into the basin; each time, the water in the basin splashed her.

Feivel tugged at his beard with both hands as he read the *shema*. He pulled out a bench and sat down slowly, taking off his boots and his trousers. He finally lay down next to the children. The warmth of the bed made him sleepy; though he did not want to doze off, his eyes closed by themselves.

Yachet pulled out the salting board from beneath the basin and laid it over the basin. She took coarse salt and began to salt the fresh meat; she salted all six sides of the meat and then placed it on the salting board. She took out a bowl and placed it on the stove; she then scooped out a quantity of flour into a sieve and sifted it into the bowl. The flour formed a heap in the bowl; she scooped out a hole in the flour, and in it she placed the yeast, adding some sugar and a pinch of salt. Then she beat in two eggs, poured in a little warm water, and used a fork to beat the mixture. She put the bowl aside and covered it with a cloth so that it would rise.

Yachet took the kitchen knife and walked toward her daughter. Seeing the peeled potatoes, she said, "Peel thinner!" "Look!" Zlotele answered her mother, and pointed to the peels. Zlotele moved away a little, and Yachet sat down in her place.

Yachet sat by the greenish light of the kerosene lamp. In the corners around the bed, the cupboard, and the table, shadows danced about. From a distance, Yachet and Zlotele appeared to be no more than moving shadows. Both peeled together. All that could be heard was the periodic splash of water as another potato was thrown into the basin.

Suddenly, the door creaked and opened. Feivel opened his eyes. Yachet raised her head from the potatoes. "Dovid!" shouted Zlotele.

The ten-year-old boy closed the door. The collar of his coat had been turned up so as to cover his ears and prevent them from freezing. "Daddy!" he cried out, and ran over to his father. Dovid bent over the bed as if he wanted to lie down beside his father. Feivel took Dovid's hand and placed it on his chest. With his other hand, he patted Dovid's round, cold face. The son stared into his father's eyes.

"Dovid, come and eat!" his mother said, and stood up. Feivel let go of his son's hand. Dovid got up, took off his coat and threw it on the bench, took off his hat, and rubbed his hands together.

He had large, black eyes like his mother's. His red sideburns were curly and clung to his wet cheeks. He went over to the table and waited. His mother pushed his food over to him: bread with jam. She went over to the stove and checked to see how hot the water was. Feivel placed his *yarmulke* on his head and remained sitting on the edge of the bed, his feet on the ground. Yachet placed a warm cup of *bavarke* before Dovid. Afterwards, she picked up his clothes and hung them on a hook on the wall.

Meanwhile, Zlotele sat quietly, busily peeling potatoes, glancing up from time to time. She was afraid to make herself conspicuous, lest her mother send her to bed. Dovid placed the empty mug on the table. He slid off the bench, stood up and moved a short distance from the table, and remained standing in the middle of the room.

"Feivel, take the boy and go to sleep," said Yachet. Feivel stood up and went over to Dovid. He placed his hand on the boy's shoulder and led him away. The alcove off the main room was small, its walls wooden and its roof made of wooden boards. High up on the wall that lead to the outer courtyard was a little window. In the winter, the window was boarded up with a wooden shutter. On the two opposite walls, facing one another, were two iron beds. On the wall that contained the door there stood a wide, two-door cupboard, topped by a cornice. There was no lamp in the alcove, and whatever light it had came from the open door.

Feivel went over slowly to one of the beds. He looked at his son. Dovid had already undressed and was shivering from cold. "Crawl in!" Feivel told him. Feivel undressed swiftly and lay down next to his son. The son's body was warmed by the father, and the father's by the son.

Yachet went over to her daughter. She stretched out her hands and took her in her arms. The peeling knife fell out of Zlotele's hands. Yachet pulled off her blue flannel dress, her shoes and socks, and put her to sleep next to the other children. It was warm in the house. Yachet sat on the stool and peeled potatoes. She worked quickly, and every so often there was the splash of another potato being tossed into the water. The illumination in the room had a greenish tinge. The cupboard upon which the lamp stood seemed, from afar, to be in flames. Yachet peeled and listened for sounds.

"Did you understand the lesson?" Feivel asked his son. Feivel had to wait a while until his half-asleep son answered, "Yes." "Did the *rebbi* go over it with you?" But Dovid did not answer; he was already asleep.

Yachet stood up. She looked under the bed, where various pickled vegetables were stored, and again sat down. Suddenly, she felt alone, with everyone already asleep. From time to time, she turned her head and looked at the children; all she could see were vague forms in the light of the lamp. Her fingers were stiff. She worked quickly peeling carrots, the pile of peels getting bigger. Finally, she stopped and placed the knife on the window ledge.

Yachet stood up, shook off the peels that had fallen onto her dress, and went over to the stove. She removed the cloth cover, looked at the rising dough, and went over to a basin of water. Then she washed her hands, took out the dough, and began kneading it.

The lime-coated stove, which had room for two pots, also served as a table. Yachet stood up, her back bent as she kneaded the dough. She kept adding small quantities of flour, firming the dough until it could be twisted and shaped. She put some of the dough aside to be used later on. As she kneaded the dough over and over, she tested it with her finger, afterwards scraping off the dough that had clung to her fingers. Then she took a small tablecloth out of the cupboard and covered the dough, and finally placed a pillow over the tablecloth.

The frost outside pushed its way into the house through the cracks. Yachet remained standing with her hands at her sides. For a short time, she listened attentively; it was quiet in the house, the children breathing rhythmically and Feivel snoring. She went to the water basin and washed her hands again. Now she bent over to work on the fish, which lay on the floor in the corner. She carried the fish to the basin, placed a red porcelain pot on the floor, and took the knife from the window sill. She got down on her knees and set to work, taking each small fish individually, raising its head, and looking under it to check that it was a fresh red color. She then removed the scales, slowly slit its belly, and removed the gall, taking care not to pierce it. She then cut off the head and cut each fish into pieces, which she placed in the pot. When she finished, she moved the pot aside, straightened out, and stood up. She washed the knife and her hands, put the knife back on the windowsill, and put the pot of fish alongside the other pots standing beneath the window, each containing a different dish at some stage of preparation. She then covered the pot with a towel.

Yachet placed her hands under her armpits, trying to get a little warmth into her cold fingers. She could just make out the objects in the house in the half-light. She recited the *shema* and began to undress, her teeth chattering with cold as she removed her dress, shoes, and socks. Barefoot, she went over to the lamp and put it out, and in the dark removed her *shaitel* and placed it on the bench. She did not remove her slip, but, exhausted after the day's work, crawled under the blankets next to Zlotele, feeling the warmth of the children seeping into her body.

The house was cold and dark. Everyone slept.

4

YACHET opened her eyes. It was still dark, but the contours of the various objects in the house could be made out more clearly. She sprang out of bed, shivering in the cold, and swiftly put on her shoes and socks, drew on her dress, buttoned it, ran her fingers through the hair on her *shaitel* to straighten it, and placed it on her head. She then went over to the basin and poured water over her hands, rinsed out her mouth, and washed her eyes. She wiped her hands and quietly recited *moydeh ani*. She did all this quietly, not wishing to wake anyone in the house.

Yachet bent over and looked through the window; the glass was covered with frost. Looking around, she saw that all were fast asleep. Pulling her kerchief over her head, she went to the cupboard and took out a white enamel milk canister. With her other hand she took the bag of peelings, which lay by the door, and quietly opened the door. The cold thrust its way into the house. Yachet ran through the outer passageway. When she reached the street, she caught her breath. With one hand she pulled her shawl more tightly about her head as she ran on until she reached an open area. Even when she was still some distance away, she could sense a warm, sour smell wafting out of an open stall.

Zashke, a fifteen- or sixteen-year-old Polish girl, was sitting on a stool waiting to milk a cow. She had red, round cheeks and straw-blonde hair. The cow was standing on a layer of straw and was eating out of a feeding trough.

"Good morning," said Yachet. "And to you, too!" Zashke replied. She smiled and showed her large white teeth. Yachet showed her the bag of peels, put it aside, and handed Zashke the milk canister. Zashke took it, placed it between her knees, and began milking the cow. A stream of milk gave a sudden thud as it hit the empty pot. "Two quarts!" Yachet said in Yiddish, and held up two fingers. Zashke nodded her head to show she understood. She kept milking and looked into the pot, making sure not to exceed two quarts. The measure she used was her eye. "Take!" she said in Yiddish, and handed Yachet the pot. Yachet wrapped herself tightly in her shawl and left the stall. As she left, she shouted out, "Zashke! I'll pay you after Shabbes," and she hurried on.

No sooner had Yachet closed the door behind her when Feivel woke up. He remained in bed with his eyes open; the little room remained in semi-darkness, like a place where the light of the morning has been blocked out. Feivel felt his son next to him. It was warm, but his shoulders felt cold. They were outside the covers. He got up, glanced at his son, and saw that the child was sleeping.

Feivel went over to the bench and put on his trousers and shirt. He sat down on the bench, put on his socks, and then pulled his boots over his feet. He left the alcove and went to the basin in the living room. He poured some water over his hands, washed his face, rinsed out his mouth, and wetted his beard. The hair on his beard now looked longer and redder. As soon as he had wiped himself dry, he recited *moydeh ani*. He then went to the stove, threw in a few pieces of tinder, and lit them. Soon a little fire burned in the stove. The smoke burned his eyes, and the fire flickered.

Yachet came back into the house; placed the canister with milk on the stove, and stood on guard to make sure the milk did not boil over. Feivel also stood by and watched as the milk was heated up. When the milk began to boil, Yachet grabbed an edge of her dress, and clutching the pot handles through the dress fabric, moved it off the fire. She put the pot aside.

It was beginning to get light in the house; the light of day shone through the frosted window glass. The house was already warm. Now Feivel clutched his hands behind his back and began pacing back and forth.

Feivel earned his living traveling through the different villages. Day after day, throughout the week, he went from one village to another, his staff in his hand and his sack on his shoulder. Each day at dawn, he would leave his home. Being able to remain at home right now, he felt contented.

Yachet filled the teapot with water and put it on the stove. Then she bent over and took an onion from underneath the bed. She peeled the onion and took out the peeled carrots. She cut up the carrots and the onion and threw them into a pot of meat. She filled the pot with water to the brim, added a little salt and placed it on the second burner. Now she took another pot, containing white cheese, from the cupboard, along with two loaves of bread. She used the knife to cut thin, even slices of bread. She cut the bread slices in half, making two slices of each one. She cut only half a loaf and put the remaining half aside. She smeared a thin layer of cheese on the bread and placed the slices with the cheese on the table. Two of the slices were smeared with a thicker layer of cheese, and were then covered by other dry slices of bread to make sandwiches.

She bent over the table and pulled the two loaves of bread over to herself. Feivel's shoulders trembled as he noticed the cleavage between Yachet's breasts. He turned away and went into the bedroom. The second loaf was not black bread. Yachet took from underneath the cupboard a tin and zinc bowl, which she filled with water. She then cut the bread into pieces and soaked it in the water.

Dovid sprang down from the bed and began to dress. He stretched out a foot to push it into the trouser leg, but lost his balance. Feivel caught him and tried to help him. "I can do it myself!" he said sleepily and testily as he slipped out of his father's hands. Dovid poured water over his hands, wiped them, and remained standing in the middle of the room. His linen shirt peeped out over the top of his trousers. He stood and said out loud "*Moydeh ani lefonecho*—I thank You, eternal King, who has mercifully returned my soul within me—great is Your faithfulness." He knew that this would please his mother. "Sit down and eat!" Yachet told him.

Zlotele sat up in bed. The two younger children also woke up. Dovid sat down to eat. He knew that the two sandwiches were his portion. "Eat slowly," his father said. Dovid did not answer him. He ate with a healthy appetite. His mother brought him a cup of hot *bavarke* that had been sweetened with saccharin.

Zlotele hurriedly put on her thick black stockings and laced up her shoes. She pulled her dress over her head and went to wash up. After that, she picked up the comb and went over to her mother, who buttoned up Zlotele's dress at the back, took the comb, and combed her hair.

Yachet poured three cups of *bavarke*. She handed one cup to Zlotele and the second, along with bread and cheese, to Rivkele, who was still in bed. Yachet then went over to the table and took one of the slices of bread, from which she cut away the crust. She took the third cup and the bread without a crust to Yossele and sat on the edge of the bed to feed him.

Dovid pushed away the empty mug, stood up from the table, put on his coat, and walked to the bed. He bent over, pulled out a worn piece of wood, his whetting "stone," which was tied with two pieces of twine. He speedily pushed the whetting stone under his coat and pulled one side of the coat over the other.

"Start cutting the carrots," said Yachet to Zlotele. Zlotele placed an old iron pot on the ground, picked up the basket in her hand, and sat down to cut the carrots. Meanwhile, Yachet cut up the radishes. She filled a large pot with water, and placed it on the stove. Next she took down the chopping block, which had been hung behind the stove, wiped it off, and placed it on top of one side of the stove. She went over to the window and checked the temperature of the fish pot. "Ice cold," she said. She placed the fish pot on the stove and began to prepare the fish within the pot. She took out each piece of fish and placed it on the chopping board. She then brought over all the other necessary ingredients and placed them on the stove. She also brought out a small, black, iron chopping knife from underneath the cupboard. The handle of the chopper was short, no larger than a person's fist. Yachet pulled over a bench and sat down, placing the cutting board with the fish in her lap, and began chopping up the fish. The odor of the various dishes on the stove began to fill the house.

By the time the fish had been half-chopped, Yachet began adding the other ingredients. She broke an egg and added it to the mixture, and then some of the bread that had been soaking in water, some salt and pepper, and two onions. As she cut the onions, she turned her face away to prevent her eyes from watering; still, they became red. When all the other ingredients had been added, she continued chopping the fish.

The house was already warm and quiet. Suddenly, a heavy tread was heard from the alcove, the sound of feet sliding on the ground rather than walking on it, and Feivel appeared in the open doorway. One of his *tefillin* was suspended on his forehead by means of a leather strap, and his head was covered with his *tallis*. The left sleeves of both his jacket and his shirt had been pushed up beyond the arm muscle, and his other *tefillin* box was on the muscle, its retaining leather strap wrapped seven times around his arm. The leather strap cut into the flesh of the arm, raising the flesh between the strap. "Praise the Lord, call upon His name," Feivel had begun reciting the morning prayer, addressing the living room in general.

Feivel turned around and returned to the alcove. Zlotele cut the carrots, from time to time glancing down to see how many whole carrots still remained. Suddenly, she exclaimed, "I'm almost finished," and went on cutting. Yachet turned to Zlotele and smiled. She went over to her daughter, gathered the few remaining carrots, and added them to the potatoes. She then took the pot with carrot slices from Zlotele, rinsed off the carrots, carried the pot over to the stove, and then, pouring a little warm water into a plate, dipped her hands in the water, and began shaping the fish balls. It became quiet in the house as Yachet worked on. Only the pots could be heard simmering on the stove.

Suddenly, Feivel's deep voice echoed through the house as he recited the prayer "*Ahava rabba*—With a great love You have loved us . . ." Yachet finished preparing the fish and twirled the pot around so that the fish balls would settle. Then she smoothed down the fish balls with her fingers, counting how many portions she had. She cut a carrot into long, thin strips, which she placed on the fish balls, filled the fish pot with water, and put it aside. She left the cutting board as it was, merely rinsing the chopping knife and her hands.

Seeing that Feivel was finishing the morning service, Yachet went over to the stove and with both hands tested the warmth of the pot filled with water; it was hot, so she moved it aside. She then lifted the lid of the soup and smelled its contents. "It smells fine!" she said, replacing the lid, and moved that pot off the fire as well. From beneath the stove she pulled out a hard faggot of peat and added it to the stove. The flame soon caught it. She placed the fish pot on the fire while she placed the pot with radishes on the other fire.

Feivel pushed himself through the door and was immediately struck by the delightful smell of the different dishes. "Enough! Go and wash for the meal! I need the fire," Yachet said. Feivel went over to the basin and poured water on his hands. He wiped his hands and went over to the table. Breaking off a piece of the bread, he recited the blessing, " . . . Who brings forth bread from the earth," dipped the bread he was holding in salt, and took a bite. Now he cut himself a thicker slice of bread and smeared it with white cheese. Yachet brought him a mug of sweetened *bavarke*. Suddenly, she sprang up from the table. "Oh, why am I wasting time here?" she asked rhetorically. With her foot, she shoved the stool under the bed, and bending down, pushed the chamber pots to one side. Using a rag, she wiped the liquid that had spilled on the floor. As she got up, her back bumped into the bed, and the two children woke up. Zlotele ran over and crawled onto the bed and began to calm the younger children. Yachet pulled a sugar cube out of a cup lying in the cupboard, broke the cube into thirds, and gave each child a third. Zlotele put hers into her mouth at once, and said to her little brother, "I'll wash you up, comb your hair, and dress you in your Sabbath clothes. I'll take you for a walk in your carriage, just like the commandant's wife with her child."

Yachet took the lid off the fish pot and looked inside the pot. "It's done!" she said, and replaced the lid. "It smells delicious," she murmured as she carried the pot into the alcove. Yachet waited for Feivel to finish eating; she needed the table. Meanwhile, she prepared the Shabbes afternoon special, the *cholent*. She stood bent over the pot of potatoes on the floor and with one hand threw the potatoes into the water. The bigger potatoes were cut in half, while the very largest were cut into quarters. Suddenly, she stood up straight and sighed, feeling a sharp pain in her back. Her face became flushed as the blood flowed to her face. She walked over to the table, picked up the leftover bread, and bit into it.

Yachet swallowed the last bite of bread and began clearing off the table. She took the mug off the table, went over to the stove, swiftly drank down the remaining *bavarke*, and rinsed the mug and put it away. Then, seeing that the dough had risen, she removed it from the bowl and placed it on the table, pouring a little flour on the table as well. She brought over the rolling pin and kitchen knife, placed the dough on the loose flour, and began kneading it. She kept pounding the dough with her fists in order to harden it. Zlotele swallowed her sugar cube and said, "Mommy, I want to do the kneading as well!" "Yes, yes," Rivkele added. Yachet stood up straight, glanced at the dough, and divided it into three parts. Feivel stood by the door holding his bag tied around his staff—the tools of his peddling trade. Yachet tore off a piece of dough, placed it on a tin plate, and gave it to Zlotele. Zlotele took the plate with both hands. "Rivkele, come! We're also going to bake," she said to her younger sister. "Don't dirty the bed," Yachet cautioned them.

Feivel pushed the staff and bag underneath the bed.

Yachet took a part of the dough, divided it into fifths, and then divided each piece into thirds. The children played while Yachet kept working. She rolled the pieces of dough into strips, and plaited the strips together to form *challah* loaves. Zlotele followed what her mother was doing. Seeing her plait the strips together, she said, "Now it's my turn," and she began plaiting her bits of dough.

Yachet took the first *challah* and put it aside. She moved away a little to see the *challah* from a different angle. Feivel came over. He was holding the four corners of a patched-up sack full of peat for the stove. He bent over and shoved the peat into a bin near the stove. He left the small pieces at the front for kindling.

Yachet ended her work with the *challah* loaves, five of them now lying on the table. She took out a blackened baking tray, washed it off, and placed it on the table; then she picked up a handful of flour and sprinkled it on the baking pan. Next she arranged the *challah* loaves on the baking pan.

Feivel sprang to his feet and leaned his back on the wall where the stove stood. His boots looked like two props supporting the entire house. From his belt he withdrew a penknife and began cutting shavings from a piece of wood. The shavings would later be used by Yachet as kindling.

Meanwhile, Yachet dissolved a few pieces of sugar in a plate of warm water and then dabbed the liquid all over the *challah* loaves. She then placed the baking pan on the floor near the stove. "Mommy, Mommy," the children soon called out. They had become bored with playing with the dough. "Quiet, quiet. Be good children, and I'll give you a treat," Yachet told them. She was afraid that they might disturb her work. Yachet went to the cupboard, took out the remaining half loaf, cut it into three parts, and spread each part with red beet jam. She gave each child a piece. The house was again quiet, everyone was busy. Suddenly, Feivel said, "Enough!" He closed the penknife, replaced it under his belt, took a few steps, and remained standing in the middle of the house. The frost on the windows had been dissolved by the steam from the pots, "It's time to go out," said Feivel. Yachet raised her head from the table. "Don't be late. It's a short Friday," she said, and went back to work. Feivel pulled his hat over his ears, took his coat off the coat hook, and put it on. The long, heavy coat made him seem bigger than he was.

"Be well!" "Take care!" Yachet answered, not raising her eyes from her work. Feivel opened the door and swiftly closed it behind him. "Where did Daddy go?" asked Rivkele. "To the market," her mother answered. Yachet went back to preparing *kichlach*, a dough that is baked very flat. She divided the dough into two parts. Half of the dough was left unsweetened for Yachet and Feivel. The other half was for the children. She poured a little sugar on each of these *kichlach*, and added a raisin to each. When she had finished, she placed the tray of *kichlach* next to the tray of *challah*. From the cupboard she took out a low, broad iron pot, which she rinsed off and then filled with water. She rinsed the carrots in the water they had been sitting in and then placed them in the pot, along with a little salt, a few saccharin tablets, and a little oil. She then placed the pot on the stove.

Yachet picked up the small portion of dough she had put aside earlier and threw it onto the table. She used both fists to glue it to the table and then began rolling out the dough; it kept getting thinner and thinner. From time to time, she would place the dough on the rolling pin and pick it up. It remained hanging on the rolling pin. Then she would flip it over so that she could continue rolling it from the other, thicker side.

She cut the dough into quarters, rolling up each quarter by itself. She pushed three of the pieces to the side, took the remaining piece and spread it out over the table, and began to cut *lokshen*, or noodles.

It was quiet again. The children were asleep in bed. All that could be heard was a sound like the pecking of a woodpecker—the sound of the knife cutting the dough into strips. Yachet kept cutting. Whenever a quantity of *lokshen* had accumulated on the knife, she would move the batch aside and separate the strips; the pile of *lokshen* kept growing. Finally, there was a heavier thud, as Yachet cut the last, thick edge of the dough. "Enough," Yachet said, and straightened up. She rubbed her hands clean of the dough and then shook off the flour that had accumulated on her dress. The house was now comfortably warm. Yachet, too, felt warm; her cheeks were red. She bent down to the window, trying to estimate from the light outside what time it was. There was no clock in the house.

"I must finish in time for Shabbes," she said, and continued with her preparations. She cut up the rest of the potatoes, rinsed them, and placed them in her largest double-handled saucepan. She covered the potatoes with water and added salt; she then went over to the cupboard and took down an iron pot containing rendered fat. She also took out a clay pot. Returning, she brought with her the bowl with the rest of the bread that had been soaked. She placed everything on the table. She divided the fat into two, adding half of it to the *cholent*. Then she squeezed the water out of the bread she had soaked and placed the bread in a pan. She took the rest of the fat and added it to the bread, and then added a little sugar. Placing her hands in the pan, she kneaded the mixture. When it had all been formed into a single lump, she used the knife to scrape off whatever had stuck to her fingers. After that, she shaped the lump with her fingers. This would be the *kugel*, a pudding cooked within the *cholent*. Taking the *kugel* from the pan, she pushed it into the saucepan together with the potatoes, taking care that the water did not overflow the edge. She covered this saucepan with a cloth, and then, taking out a few old newspapers, packed them around the top of the saucepan, tying the improvised lid down with string. The *cholent* was ready. Next she took down a one-eared jug, which she rinsed and then filled with water. She threw in a few saccharin tablets, a third of a package of chicory, a few spoonfuls of ground coffee that she stored in a can, and then a little milk. She tied this jar, too, with paper and string, and put it on the floor where the *cholent* stood. From her *shaitel* she removed a hat pin and used it to pierce holes in the paper lids.

Yachet went over to the bed. She gently shook Zlotele's arms. Zlotele remained in bed with her eyes open. "I have to go to the baker," Yachet said to her daughter.

Yachet threw her shawl over her shoulders and tied the two ends under her throat so that the shawl would not fall off her shoulders. She placed the tray with the *challah* loaves on top of the tray with the *kichlach*. A dry cold penetrated into the house through the open door. Yachet took the two trays, propped them up against her stomach, and hurried out of the house.

Zlotele stood by the bed. With both her hands she clutched the blanket. Yossele and Rivkele were still asleep. Zlotele was afraid to look around, because she alone was in charge of the house, which seemed enormous. She stood and spoke to herself quietly: "Mommy will soon return. Mommy will soon return." Yachet did not take long. Zerach's bakery was nearby. As soon as Zlotele saw her mother, she jumped back into bed, snuggled into the blankets, and soon fell asleep.

5

FEIVEL stood on the street near the hut. The cold bit through his clothes. He took a deep breath, the intense cold searing his nostrils and lungs. He placed his hands in his pockets and snuggled his head into his collar so that it seemed to be lying directly on his shoulders. There was snow on the ground underneath the windows. He pulled his hands, already in his pockets, deeper into his sleeves to try to gain a little more warmth.

Feivel raised his feet high each step, following the path that had been trodden out in the snow. The snow crackled underneath him. The short street appeared to him like a sack that had been pulled apart. There wasn't a human being on the street. Only a small, black and white calf, which had escaped from the stall, was about, moaning desolately. Then along came a gray-haired dog with a mangled tail, which began barking, trying to drive the little calf away from the street. The calf drew back in terror, moaning piteously.

When he reached the end of the second street, Feivel slowed down. Here, the snow had not been touched. Feivel had to raise his foot high each time in order to be able to tread out a path with his high boots. Here, the huts were lower and more scattered, and the snow reached almost to their roofs.

"Feivel! Feivel!" a voice echoed back and forth in the dry, clear air.

Feivel stopped in his tracks at a low, decrepit hut with a high, sloping roof. In front of the hut stood a man with a long black beard.

"Feivel!" he shouted again. With his hand he gestured that it was he who had called out, and he then hurried back inside the open door. He was not wearing a coat. Feivel knew him. Entering the hut, Feivel was greeted by angry barking, as if the brown dog inside were furiously angry at him. The hut was not used as a home, but as a warehouse for furs. Feivel walked slowly and carefully through the corridor, warily watching for the dog, which was standing on its hind feet, its teeth bared, evidently wanting to attack Feivel. But the dog was chained down and was unable to get closer.

The door, with an iron bar attached to it, creaked as it opened. Aaron, the man who had called out, opened the door and asked Feivel to follow him. It was dark in the warehouse. The single window was frosted over and had metal bars across it. The air inside the hut was pervaded with the odor of drying carcasses. Feivel remained standing by the door. Aaron clapped his hands together a few times; the sound seemed to come from far away. Aaron then sat down on a bale that had been tied up with wire and stretched out his feet. He, too, wore high boots, as well as a flannel shirt and a sleeveless fur jacket. Feivel sat down opposite Aaron on another bale. They sat in the light of the open door.

Aaron used both hands to stroke his beard. When he reached the corner of the beard, he looked at Feivel and asked, "Do you smoke?" Feivel shook his head no. Aaron put his hand in his pocket and took out a cigarette paper. He filled the paper with tobacco. With a practiced twist, he rolled the cigarette; then, with the tip of his tongue he licked the cigarette paper to ensure that it stuck together. From another pocket he took matches and lit his cigarette; a thick cloud of smoke enveloped his face.

Aaron closed an eye. With the other eye, he squinted at Feivel. Feivel sat with downcast eyes, his hands on his knees, waiting. "Feivel!" said Aaron. Feivel nodded his head and looked at Aaron. His look was strained. "Business is bad," said Aaron. Feivel looked at him. He was not sure what Aaron wanted.

Aaron kept him in suspense for a while longer, as he spat out a little tobacco that had stuck to his tongue.

"I have lots of merchandise. That's not a problem. It's a hard winter. The local farmers are slaughtering their horses, but they can't export any furs." Feivel stretched out his head and looked about him. He shook his head, as if asking himself a question—he didn't know what "export" meant. "The Germans and the British have stopped buying," Aaron added. "Buenos Aires is flooding the market." Feivel looked about him. Aaron's warehouse was packed with bales of furs. "But that doesn't matter to you. You will still get your commission," he said. He put his hand in his pocket and brought out a clenched fist. "Here," he said. Feivel placed his hand under the fist. For a while the two stared at each other, silent and deep in thought.

"Have a good Shabbes!" Feivel said. He stood up and began to go. "A good Shabbes to you! Keep well!" answered Aaron. Aaron bent down and started work again on his furs.

When he came out of the hut, Feivel remained standing. Only now did he open his fist to see how much Aaron had paid him; then he shook his head as if in a daze. He picked up the half gulden in his hand and thrust it in the pocket of his coat.

Feivel walked diagonally through the fields to the other side of the town. The huts on that side were even lower and larger, and were arranged neatly. Each had its own fence enclosing a snow-filled yard. There was some distance between one hut and the next. Under the snow, which covered all, they seemed identical, but Feivel knew exactly where Mordechai lived.

Feivel stamped his feet at the door to remove the snow from his boots. The entrance to Mordechai's home was in the front. He pushed at the door latch, which had swollen because of the moisture it had absorbed; the door sprang open. A warm mist hid everything from view. "Close the door!" a hearty voice called out. Feivel hurriedly closed the door behind him. "I just dropped by to see how things are," said Feivel hesitantly. "Welcome!" said Mordechai. Mordechai Tandeiter, a short, broad-boned man, stood with a coal pressing iron in his hand. He was careful not to damage the garment he was pressing. His jacket was open, its sleeves unbuttoned. His long black beard was curled at the end.

"How are you?" he asked Feivel. "Thank God, as long as we can see each other from time to time," answered Feivel. His shoulders shivered and he moved closer to the table where Mordechai stood. He felt the damp heat envelop him. The small, narrow room, almost nothing but a corridor, was as warm as a bathhouse; the air was full of moisture, both from the garments and from the heat of the pressing iron. Mordechai sewed suits for various merchants who traveled from fair to fair. This was his workshop—he lived in the courtyard.

The two workers who had been crouched over sewing machines straightened out. Each looked at the other. Both were singing the Yiddish lullaby *Oifn pripechik*. The apprentice joined them; his cap was on backwards. He sat on a crate in the middle of the room sewing buttons on a jacket, his feet crossed. "Quiet, someone has just come in," Mordechai told his workers. Both workers turned to one another, as if confiding a secret. Across from them hung a kerosene lamp, its glass dirty with soot.

"How was your week?" Mordechai asked Feivel curiously, sticking his neck forward, his head hanging down.

"The same as with everyone—there's always something lacking," he answered, "but my wife is an excellent housekeeper." His black eyes sparkled for a moment. "And how about you?" Feivel asked.

"One cuts, one sews, and one eats potato soup. One has to ask for lots of strength—that the ten fingers hold out," added Mordechii.

One of the workers, who was tired of remaining quiet, started singing a Yiddish song. He had a strong tenor voice. Soon, however, he stopped. The apprentice buried his head even deeper in his work, as if wishing to hide in the jacket he was working on.

"Come," said Mordechai, "have you heard any news from our town?"

Feivel did not answer him. He merely shook his head indicating that he knew nothing. Both came from the nearby town of Zharnovtze, an even smaller place than Wolbrom. They had both studied in the same *cheder* with Wolf the Redhead. Both had married in Wolbrom. Mordechai had married the daughter of Ozer the tailor, and later Feivel had married and had returned to Zharnovtze, but Mordechai had brought him back to Wolbrom. "Neither had any relatives in Wolbrom. Mordechai's father was the fishmonger of Zharnovtze, while Feivel's mother, a widow, along with her two daughters, made butter and cheese so that the Jews of the town would be able to obtain kosher products.

"We should visit," Mordechai said, and he looked at Feivel. The distance between the two towns was about nine miles.

"By my life, that would be a good thing," Feivel said, and immediately added, "But every day I travel through the different villages."

"Well, then," proposed Mordechai, "how about after Shabbes, when the stars come out?"

"And to leave Yachet and the children alone at night?"

"Oh, oh," exclaimed Mordechai, and punched one hand with the other.

There was a short silence, and then Mordechai asked, "How are things in your home?"

"Can't complain. And by you?"

"Thank God," Mordechai answered.

Feivel stretched out his neck, as if he wanted to get closer to Mordechai, whispering to him, "And what about the match you spoke of?" He nodded toward the worker who was deeply engrossed in his work.

"God is good," Mordechai answered him, and shook his head. A little later, he added, "The girl is with her grandfather in Zharnovtze, taking care of the small children in the house—they should live and be well."

"I'm keeping you from your work," said Feivel, and he looked out the frosted window again. "It's time to go."

"At least we talked a little."

"Have a good Shabbes." Feivel went over to the door.

"Have a good Shabbes," all answered.

When he came outside, Feivel paused for a moment. He closed his eyes and then reopened them. The pure white snow, after the dingy interior, blinded him.

He walked through the snow-covered fields. They seemed to go on forever, although in reality the distance was quite small.

When he came to the first two huts, Feivel stopped to gain his breath. He could see the market square in the distance.

The heavens were overcast, dark, seeming to press down on all the roofs. The market square looked like a frozen crate. In the main street, beneath the walls of the local church, stood an empty sled. The pair of brown horses that normally pulled it had been unhitched from the sled and were eating from feed bags. The horse on the right was standing sideways on the street, blocking it. A few houses further on, standing at a large glass door that had five steps leading up to it, stood Motl Shenker. His head of silvery white hair seemed to be framed by the door. Even though the door was closed, one could hear the shouting of drunks.

The stores were empty: Friday, before Shabbes, none of the merchants displayed their wares. Every so often, a person appeared at the door of one of the stores—a Jew bundled up in a heavy coat, his hat pulled over his ears, or a Jewish woman in a sleeveless jacket with her hands thrust into socks that she was using instead of gloves.

In the middle of the market square, leaning on a wall, stood Chaiml the porter. He was staring at the sky and not moving. His face was expressionless. At the well, which from a distance looked like a block of ice, stood a wagon on which were a few bales of straw. The horse stood with its neck extended, its head down to smell the snow.

"It's free for all," said Feivel quietly, and he broke off a stalk of the straw, which he chewed on as he walked.

On the further side of the well stood a few Jews. "Good morning," he said to them from afar, and looked at them as it he wanted to stop for a while, but he kept walking. As he walked, a tall non-Jew crossed in front of him. The man wore a long, thick coat and had wrapped a scarf around his hat. In one hand he carried a package of some kind, while with the other he drove a pig in front of him. The pig ran and snorted.

"Tfu!" Feivel spat out as he jumped to the side. In the corner of the marketplace, near the bell that was used to sound an alarm when there was a fire, Leibl the wagoner was leaning on a wagon. He was getting ready to meet the daily train, which arrived from Katowitz at 10 A.M. bringing passengers from Sosnowiecz and Bendin. Leibl stood, holding his whip in his hand. He was not waiting for passengers to the train station, because on Fridays no one left the town. He had to drive to pick up a few Jews who were coming to Wolbrom for Shabbes.

Feivel went to the edge of the market square and looked around. As he walked, he peered about to see what was happening in the large, open area. Soon he again came close to the group standing by the well.

"Good morning," he said.

"A good year!" answered Velvl, a tall, thin man. His elongated, gaunt face was surrounded by a small black beard, which was already flecked with gray.

The others looked up. They had just realized that Feivel was standing there.

"How are things with you?" Baruch asked Feivel.

"Let there be no Evil Eye," Feivel answered him. Baruch was an expert in setting dislocated limbs.

Moishe the egg preserver asked Feivel, "The *goyim* don't drive you away?"

Feivel seemed to be struck dumb, and merely stared at Moishe.

"The *goyim* caught Zanvel and beat him up," said Shloime the leather merchant.

"Really?" said Feivel, frightened.

"If not today, then they'll certainly beat him tomorrow," added Zelig the confectioner. He craned upward, and his sparse beard seemed to come to a point. He squinted, and said, "Jews have to leave here and go to Eretz Yisroel." His angular head rested on his shoulders.

"As long as all the non-Jews did was to beat up Jews, we could somehow go along with them, but now that they are going into trade, opening up co-op stores in every town and village, things are quite different," added Velvl. The expression on his gaunt face froze, as if he had donned a mask.

"We have to rely on the Almighty," said Shlomo, and stretched his hands to the sky.

Feivel began to walk faster. At the edge of the other side of the market square, where the two-story homes stood, he stopped. The road here was very steep. The path that had been trodden through the snow was icy. Feivel continued on, one hand holding onto a wall. Inside the courtyard, the snow was white, untrodden. Only in one spot was it stained yellow, where someone had emptied waste.

Feivel's boots left deep holes in the snow. He went from one courtyard to another, taking shortcuts. The courtyards were all open, with only the houses themselves demarcating the lines between them and defining the yards. He finally came to a hut that stood deep in the snow. The snow, which had reached up to the windows, had been shoveled away from them to allow light in. Feivel ran into the courtyard. It was dark in the front passageway. He sensed the moisture in the soil under his boots. He felt his way to the inner door and pressed the door handle. The door sprang open. The clammy warmth assailed his face.

The boys who were sitting at a table looked around in amazement. They forgot about their teacher's presence. Dovid, Feivel's son, looked down.

Yitshkok Erlich, the Belfer (helper of the Melamed) carrying
children to cheder in Staszow, Kielce Province, Poland, 1920s.
Photograph by Avram Yosi Rotenberg. Courtesy of
YIVO Institute for Jewish Research, New York.

Pupils' performance at the Jewish high school. Zamosc, near Lublin, Poland, 1923. Courtesy of Beth Hatefutsoth Photo Archive, Tel Aviv, and Esther Hering, Tel Aviv.

An angular head, sitting on top of rounded shoulders, looked up. A long gray beard hung down from the elongated face. The man's eyes were black and deep. "Welcome!" the teacher said, smiling. He turned his back to the students, looked at Feivel, and waited.

Finally, he shook Feivel's hand and then pinched Dovid's cheek.

The child looked down again.

The home consisted of a single room, where the children studied, and a kitchen. At one side of the room, opposite the door, stood a long table with benches on each side. Above the table hung a kerosene lamp. The children sat at the table and studied. Opposite them, in the corner by the door, stood the stove, and on the other wall was a basin of water. The windows were frosted over. A small fire burned in the stove.

"We have a guest!" said a hoarse voice. Inside the open door, which was partitioned off with a curtain, stood a woman in a gray, loose dress and an unbuttoned coat. On her head she wore a brown cloth hat, wrapped like a turban.

"Ha, ha, ha," laughed one of the boys.

"Quiet, urchins," shouted the teacher, and stamped his foot on the floor.

The children swayed back and forth over the open Talmud tractate they were studying. Their young voices reviewed the text in a singsong fashion: "If one's ox kills another person's ox, the person must pay."

The children swayed, but each glanced up periodically at Feivel.

Feivel looked up. He sensed that he was being watched. He lowered his head, put his hand in his pocket, and pulled out the half gulden.

"Reb Avraham," he said quietly, and handed the rabbi the money.

The rabbi put out his open hand, looked at the coin in his palm, nodded at Feivel and said, "Thank you!"

"God should only give you double," the rabbi's wife said to Feivel, and returned to the alcove.

The rabbi placed the coin in his trouser pocket.

The children began swaying even harder. The sound of their study echoed through the room. A thin voice recited a few words of the Talmud, and then the students in the room repeated it together.

"Reb Avraham," said Feivel, "I'd like to take my son with me."

"Dovid, go with your father."

Dovid kissed the volume he had been studying, closed it swiftly, and got up from his seat. On a bench to one side lay a pile of coats. Dovid went over to the pile, pulled out his coat, and put it on. Feivel pulled his hat over his ears. Dovid took the volume he had been studying under his arm and walked to the door.

"Have a good Shabbes!" both the father and son said.

When they were outside, Feivel looked around. He looked for his son, who had dived into a snow drift and was kicking the snow with his feet.

"Get up, you'll catch a cold!"

Dovid grabbed the Talmud volume, which he had rested on his stomach to keep it dry, and jumped up. He looked to see if his father was about to catch him.

Feivel really wanted to play with his son, but his face suddenly became stern and he exclaimed, "Here you're already studying Talmud, and you act like a *shaygetz*. Come."

The snow on that particular street had been trodden down. One could see various footprints in the snow. The street was semicircular. Feivel looked around and then turned right. He walked in the direction of the town rather than of the small *beis medrash*. His son followed him. They walked around a little hill on which the night's snowfall still lay untouched. The ruins of the old *beis medrash*, which had burned down twenty years earlier, poked out of the snow. The synagogue, the *beis medrash*, the *hekdesh*, and the *mikveh* had all been built around the little hill. Baile the Lame stood by the blank wall of the *hekdesh*. She was wrapped in numerous shawls. Only her old, weary eyes and her nose could be seen.

Feivel took a groszy out of his pocket and looked at his son. The child took the coin and gave it to the beggar. Feivel walked up an alley between two tall buildings.

The father and son came to the *mikveh*. The brick walls under the tin roof were a dull red. Long, narrow windows had been set into the walls. The rectangular panes were covered with steam and drops of water ran down them. The lower wall of the *mikveh* building had been built at the edge of a pool. Feivel took his son by the collar and led him through the open door. The entrance lobby was narrow and long. The air was damp and hot.

Dovid pushed the closed door of the attendant's home with his head. He laid his Talmud volume on a small table near the door, closed the door again, and looked at his father.

Henia, the tall female attendant, stood by the little brooms. She had an apron with a large pocket tied around her waist.

Feivel gave her five groszy, which he had been holding in his hand, without looking at her. She took the money and handed him a little broom. She did not look at him either.

It was dark in the entrance to the bathhouse and steambath, almost as dark as a windowless room. The only light came from the open door. Feivel examined the little broom from all sides. He then bent down and picked up one of the basins lying on the floor. Using his other hand, which clutched the little broom, he pushed his son through the door and then followed. The door closed by itself.

The large, square room was cold, like an empty warehouse. The walls were wet with steam, In the corners, the steam had frozen into gray ice, as if moss grew there. The stone floor was covered with soaking wet wood planks. The benches attached to the wall emitted a foul odor. Naked and wet, the bathers trembled with cold and hurriedly dressed. Half-undressed figures moved about, jerking their arms and legs as though doing gymnastics. Some took off their clothes; some put them on. Drops of condensed steam seemed to pour from the ceiling. The doors on both sides kept opening and closing. The door to the front entrance added to the cold every time it opened, while from the door of the steam bath a cloud of steam blew in each time it opened. The cold and heat were inseparably mixed.

Feivel undressed hurriedly. Dovid hung back, looking about him at the naked figures.

"What are you waiting for?" Feivel asked him.

Feivel was already naked, trembling in the cold. He began to undress his son. Dovid helped him. His father removed his shirt, and gave him a playful slap on the behind.

Dovid, who was also trembling from the cold, smiled.

"Come on!" his father called out. Feivel bent over, picking up the basin and little broom with one hand and pushing his son forward with the other. With his naked knee, he pushed the door open. He let Dovid go through first and then followed. They went into the steam bath.

Both father and son remained standing by the door. The acrid smoke assailed their noses and blocked their vision. They could not see anything, but could hear the cries of pleasure: "Oy, ah, oy, oy, ah!"

Soon they began to distinguish shapes in the semi-darkness—hands, feet, and beards that moved. Feivel bent down and filled his basin with water from a wooden barrel, and father and son sat down on the first steps.

Dovid stopped and looked, sometimes at his father, sometimes at other people who were beating themselves with the little brooms to bring on the sweat. The steam curled overhead, and the ceiling looked like a cloudy sky. The small window panes were wet; the heat was stifling. Men lay prostrate on the wooden ledges and moaned; their bodies were red. Some people were beating themselves with the little brooms. There were those who were not satisfied with the heat and called out, "Moishe Yosef, more steam!"

Moishe Yosef the bath attendant, a tall, broad-shouldered man, was wearing a cut-down pair of pants. From time to time he poured cold water on the boiling hot bricks. A fresh burst of steam spread throughout the room.

"Very good!" Feivel sighed contentedly as the warmth penetrated every organ of his body. He plunged his hands into the water basin and poured water over Dovid. Dovid shivered.

Feivel dipped the end of the little broom into the basin of water. He placed one hand on his son's shoulder to hold him, and with the other hand rubbed his back with the broom.

"Wait, don't move!" Feivel ordered Dovid.

Feivel took the basin and little broom and began scurrying down the steps. At the fourth step he stretched out his neck and squinted. One step higher, with his back up, lay the rabbi, sighing happily. Zisha, the town *shammes*, a short, thin man with a sparse beard, was rubbing down the rabbi's back.

Feivel went up to the sixth step. He moved to the side, poured the basin of water over himself, and began beating himself with a broom. The steam choked him, the beating hurt. From time to time, he dipped the broom into the remaining water and sprinkled the water over himself. The water drops failing on him burned his body. At first he found it hard to breath, but a little later he began beating himself again with the little broom. When the basin was empty, he threw away the little broom. He ran down to the cold *mikveh* and immersed himself in it. Three times his head went down under the water and emerged dripping each time. He climbed the steps again, streaming with water. His skin was fiery red and his wet hair stuck to his forehead.

Feivel looked at his son and nodded his head. Dovid ran over to him. The father and son stood opposite one another. Feivel dried the water off Dovid.

They both left the steam bath. Dovid's teeth were chattering from the cold. Feivel drew him close. Each felt the nakedness of the other. Feivel brought his son to where they had left their clothes.

Feivel squeezed the water out of his hair and beard. They both dressed swiftly.

"I'm ready," said Dovid after he had finished dressing.

"Come on and don't forget the *gemara* volume you left at the door to the bathhouse!" said Feivel, as he started walking.

Dovid walked alongside him and then went out of the door first.

Feivel kept his mouth closed, breathing through his nose. His wet hair became stiff with the cold. The frost outside became sharper.

6

WHEN they reached home, Shabbes was already at the doorstep. The special Shabbes dishes were all ready. Yachet's cheeks were red. The wrinkles in her face all showed sweat from her hard work. It was warm in the long, low home, damp and airless. The warmth was permeated with the odors of the dishes that had been cooked. Yachet could smell the sweetly sour odor of the radishes.

Yachet went into the alcove and came out with a basket of clothes to be washed. On top of the laundry lay a towel. With the hem of her dress, Yachet wiped off part of the table top and placed the wash on it. The clothes were all cream-colored. She took down a tin basin and a bottle of kerosene. She placed the basin on the bench and the. bottle of kerosene on the floor nearby.

"Drink, drink, child, and you'll feel better," Zlotele, worried, told her doll as she pushed her finger into its mouth. The doll was made of rags that her mother had sewn together. The face was made out of a black stocking.

Rivkele looked at her sister. She picked up her own doll, a plain piece of wood that her father had carved.

Yossele sat between his two sisters and looked first at one and then at the other. The children sat on the floor in the corner by the bed on a cloth blanket that had been laid down for them.

Yachet poured off some hot water from the pot that stood on the stove into the basin. She got up on her tiptoes and took down a comb. Then, with the same hand, she took a piece of soap that lay by the basin. She bent down, and with her other hand picked up Yossele at the waist. The child remained hanging in the air. Both sisters turned to see what was happening. Only now did they realize what their mother was doing. Right then Zlotele began scolding her doll: "You have to be clean for Shabbes."

Yachet sat down on a stool near the basin. She placed Yossele on her lap, clamping him between her knees, and undressed him. She unbuttoned and took off his little green suit. The trousers and jacket were all one piece. Both the sleeves and the trouser legs were broad and shapeless. The trousers had an opening at the back. Yachet herself had sewn the little suit from an old undergarment. The child threw himself about in her hands. Yachet wet a hand, soaped it, and began to wash the little boy. Yossele began to shout. "Quiet, quiet," his mother calmed him as she continued washing him.

When Yachet finished, she took a towel and wiped Yossele. Yachet hurriedly took apart the bundle of clothing that she had washed and which she was now holding in her hand. She wanted to dress the child as quickly as possible so that he would not catch cold. She couldn't resist, and planted a kiss on the little boy's chest. Yossele laughed because the kiss had tickled him. She placed him in the bed and covered him with a blanket. Yachet added water to the basin. Now she took Rivkele by her hand and picked her up. The doll fell out of her hand. Yachet undressed Rivkele and sat her down on a bench, soaped her neck and ears, and washed her. Rivkele sat with her eyes shut. Drops of water dripped from her feet onto the floor. The air in the room began to smell of the soap.

Yachet poured a little kerosene and began to rub it into Rivkele's scalp. The smell of kerosene was added to the other smells in the house. Yachet combed her hair. "You're having your hair combed," Zlotele teased Rivkele. "Yes, but I've already been washed," Rivkele answered her sister. Yachet put Rivkele in bed. The child crawled under the blanket and snuggled close to Yossele. The brother and sister held one another. Each was warmed by the other. Zlotele stood looking at both. "Mommy, wash me as well," she asked. She also wanted to crawl into the bed. "A big girl washes herself," her mother answered. Yachet's tired face broke out into a smile.

Yachet picked up the blanket on which the children had been playing and pushed it underneath the straw mattress. She checked to see how Zlotele was washing herself and went to the stove. She moved the pot off the fire, added another log to the fire, and returned the pot to it.

She poured some kerosene and rubbed it into Zlotele's head. Again the powerful smell of kerosene filled the house.

Yachet combed her hair and spoke to her.

"I already have a big daughter." Her eyes were red from the kerosene smell, but they smiled. Zlotele took off her dress and her other clothes. Yachet stood and waited. Zlotele remained naked. Her mother looked at her. She bent over and kissed her shoulder. Rivkele squealed with delight and began dressing in fresh clothes. She pulled a shirt over herself and felt the linen on her body. The shirt was short on her, for she had outgrown it. She finished dressing in a skirt that her mother had sewn her for the winter. The skirt was too large. Yachet took her by the hand as well, and Rivkele moved her cheek to her mother's lips. Yachet kissed her, picked her up and put her in the bed. Zlotele pushed herself between the other children. Their mother covered them with a blanket. The three children lay crossways on the bed. Each warmed the others. It was quiet in the house. Yachet gathered together the dirty clothes and pushed them under the bed. Each Sunday she would do the wash, so that all would have a change of clothing.

The children sat up in bed and listened to Yachet speaking: "Soon it will be dark, and we will make Shabbes. I will light the candles. Your father will come home from the prayers. We will eat fish and meat, and your father will sing." Yachet used a bucket to scoop some water into the basin and then added the water that she had used to wash the children. She carried a brush to the basin, dipped the brush in the water, and began scrubbing the floor. The straw at the bottom of the brush had already been worn away, and the handle was short. Yachet, bent over, kept dipping the brush in water, and scrubbed board after board. She kept moving closer to the door. The boards absorbed the water. Each board that had been washed was more wet than clean. The level of the water in the basin kept going down.

The pace of Yachet's work kept increasing. She wanted to finish the floor as soon as possible. Her face was red with exertion, and she now appeared younger than her age. When she finished washing the last board near the door she straightened out, dipped the brush in the last bit of remaining water, and shook out the brush. She bent down at the stove and took out a bag of wood shavings. With one hand she held the open bag and with the other she spread the shavings on the ground.

The children bent over the bed to see better how their mother was spreading wood shavings all over the floor, like a farmer sowing seed. The wet boards soaked the wood shavings and soon the odor of freshly sawed wood was added to the room. The floor was now cream-colored.

Yachet sighed and with both hands patted her face. She had finished all her work. She removed the pot from the stove. She then poured the remaining water into a basin and placed the pot in a comer under the stove. She took a piece of soap in her hand, threw the towel over her shoulder, picked up the stool with the basin of water and walked away slowly, tiptoeing, taking care not to spill any water or to push aside the wood shavings. She entered the alcove.

Yachet closed the door, but she was more embarrassed for herself than for the children. She removed her *shaitel* from her head. Pitch black hair fell on her shoulders. She placed the *shaitel* on the bed and hurriedly began to undress. She remained in her shift. Her arms were full and round. Her large breasts were visible through the open undershirt. Yachet, embarrassed, looked around the alcove. She put her hands through the undershirt and pulled it over her head. It fell on the ground. She began to wash herself. Running over to the closet, she took out a clean shift and a pair of socks, put on the undershirt, and sat down on the bed so that she could put on her shoes and stockings. She stood up and put on her underpants and dress. She swiftly buttoned up, gathered her hair, and placed the *shaitel* over it.

Yachet looked at the beds and began to make them. She smoothed out the sheets and puffed up the down quilts and pillows. She remained standing at Feivel's bed for a moment. As she made his bed, she imagined that she sensed the smell of Feivel's body. She licked her lips and breathed heavily. Now she arranged the bedding for the night. She turned around, opened the door of the closet, and took out the two mens' shirts, which she laid out on the bed. She picked up the towel from the floor and went back into the other room. She threw the towel under the bed and glanced at the children. She had a blank look on her face, as if staring into the distance. She had the feeling that the children knew what she had felt. She looked down and called out, "Children, I'm going to give you something to eat soon, a little fish sauce." And she began working.

With one hand she picked up three slices of bread and with the other a deep, round, tin bowl, and she went into the alcove. The children accompanied her with their eyes. She soon came back. She walked slowly, her shoulders hunched up. She was careful not to spill anything.

"It's already Shabbes!" shouted Zlotele, and sat on the bed, ready to eat.

Yachet brought the food over to the bed. First she straightened out the bedding and then placed the bread on it. She took her time putting down the bowl, holding it with her fingers. "Take care not to spill anything," she said, holding the bowl firmly. Yachet carefully seated the children at the edge of the bed. "Little boy, you're hungry too," she said to Yossele.

The girls ate with gusto. They broke off pieces of bread, dipped them in the fish sauce, and then ate them. Yachet fed Yossele. From time to time she wiped off his mouth. Finally he turned his head away, not wishing to eat any more.

Suddenly, the door creaked loudly and opened wide. In the open door stood Feivel with his hand raised up to allow Dovid to come in.

Dovid ran into the house. Feivel pushed his way through the door and closed it.

"Daddy, Daddy!" the children sang out in a chorus.

Feivel stood surrounded by his family. His cheeks were red, as was the tip of his nose. His hair and his beard clung to him, frozen. Outside, it was bitterly cold. He finally unbuttoned his coat and took it off.

Dovid ran over to the table as soon as he came into the house. He pulled out a drawer and placed his Talmud volume inside it. He unbuttoned his coat and remained standing with the coat in his hands. His eyes sparkled. He looked at his sisters. His mouth was open, his cheeks rosy with cold. He threw down his coat on a bench and then ran over to his mother. He snuggled up to her and threw his hands around her neck.

Yachet turned her head, feeling his cold hands. She placed the last morsel into Yossele's mouth and then stroked Dovid's hair. His hair was stiff with the cold and ice.

"I want to eat!" said Dovid, as if on the verge of collapse. He grabbed a bite from Zlotele and swallowed it.

Yachet put away the bowl and picked up two soup plates and two spoons. She took off the lid of the large pot, and the delightful odor of cooked radishes wafted through the house. With a spoon, Yachet ladled the cooked radishes onto two plates and then put a spoon in each plate. She covered the pot and pushed it aside. She then carried the two full plates and put them on the table.

Yachet moved to the side, remaining standing by the stove. She clutched her hands behind her back, as if warming them at the stove.

Dovid was already busy eating. He kept moving the spoon rhythmically between the plate and his mouth. The two girls sat up and looked. "Mommy," Zlotele called out, but she soon became silent. "We will have radishes at night as well," said Rivkele to Zlotele, as if to comfort her. As she spoke, she shook her head. "I'm going to run over to the baker," said Yachet.

She threw a shawl over herself, with its ends under her arms so that her hands would be free. She went over to the stove, placed the coffee pot on top of the *cholent* pot, picked up both together and, resting them on her stomach, walked to the door.

Yachet pressed the door handle with her elbow. The door burst open. She pushed herself through the door. Using her knee to help her, she pushed the door closed.

"Mommy went to take the *cholent* to the baker. She will soon bring us *kichlach*," said Zlotele.

Feivel pushed the plate aside and straightened out. He pushed the bench away and stood up, stretching his hands and feet to limber up.

"Daddy, Daddy!" both girls shouted, seeing what Feivel was doing but not understanding it.

Feivel put his hands down and glanced to the side.

"Little doves," he said, and went over to the bed. He walked slowly, ponderously, as if climbing a hill. For a while he hesitated, and then climbed into his bed. "My dear little doves," he said as he embraced the children.

The children began to tug at his hair, his ears, and his nose. His eyes were closed, his breathing regular. Suddenly, he sprang up.

"Daddy, Daddy," the children cried out to him and ran over to him with outstretched arms.

"Mommy will be back soon," he said as he turned and walked away.

"It's already late," said Feivel as he took out the shoe brush and shoe polish. He dipped the brush into the polish and began shining his boots. When he had finished, he put the shoe polish aside for a while. He stooped over and brought out the children's shoes from under the bed, lining them up neatly. Then he began polishing the shoes.

The small shoes, which he held with two fingers, looked like toys. He brushed the shoes vigorously, as if working hard, but still the shoes did not shine — they were worn and discolored with sweat. Feivel turned around, wanting to see what his son was doing and why he was so quiet.

Dovid stood hunched over, some of the wood shavings in his mouth.

"Your mother worked very hard, and you are destroying her work. Come here, and I'll polish your shoes," Feivel told Dovid. Feivel lowered his hand, and the shoes that had been held by his two fingers clattered to the ground.

Dovid went over to his father, as if guilty.

"Lift up a foot," said Feivel.

Dovid placed a foot on the edge of the stove. Feivel dipped the brush in shoe polish and began to polish Dovid's boots.

Dovid lost his balance and had to hold on to his father to prevent himself from falling.

"Stand still," said Feivel, and he polished the boot with the brush. Dovid's shoes could not shine, because they were made of horse leather.

"Lift your other foot up," his father told him.

Dovid clutched at his father's trousers with both hands. He put his first foot down and raised the second.

Feivel looked down and dipped the brush in the shoe polish again. He did not want the polish to rub off too soon. Again he started polishing the boots.

Feivel put his arm around his son's shoulder so that Dovid would not disturb him, and kept polishing. Although the boot still did not shine, it looked better than before.

"Enough," Dovid said, and put his foot down.

He ran to his sister and pulled her hair.

"Daddy, he's hitting me!" shouted Zlotele.

"Dovid, you're already studying the Talmud," said Feivel, in feigned anger.

Dovid threw himself into the bed, and his sisters moved away, making room for him.

Zlotele covered him with a blanket. Dovid pretended to close his eyes, but was still able to see how Zlotele fussed over him.

Feivel gathered together the shoes. He placed each on a different finger, the way one picks up empty glasses, and carried them to the bed. He walked slowly, staring at the shoes, as if he was carrying eggs. He put the shoes down and arranged them in a row underneath the bed.

A little later he went over to the stove, moved the pot off, and checked the fire.

He bent down, picked up a few lumps of coal lying nearby, and placed them in the fire. He placed each lump of coal individually, one on top of the other, building up a pyramid so that the fire would give warmth for an extended period. The smell of the burning coal was added to the air. The children, with balled fists, rubbed their stinging eyes. Feivel's nose smarted; he couldn't stand the smell of burning coal.

The door opened and Yachet, bent under the baking pans she was carrying, came through the door. The pans contained the *kichlach* she had baked earlier.

The children both jumped off the bed and began to shout: "I want a *kichl!* I want a *kichl!*" Even Yossele clutched Yachet's dress and looked pleadingly at his mother.

Yachet's face was frozen with cold and the hair on her *shaitel* had become matted into knots; it was covered with a thin layer of snow. She was breathing heavily but did not put down the trays. Feivel went over and closed the door tightly.

"It's for Shabbes," Yachet told the children in a stern tone as she pushed her way into the alcove.

"Please, Mommy, a *kichl*, a *kichl*," begged the girls.

Yachet returned to the main room, carrying a single *kichl*.

49

"Hooray," the children shouted, and clapped their hands.

Yachet took the *kichl* and carefully broke it into four pieces.

Dovid jumped off the bed, slithered under his mother's arm, and went into the alcove.

Yachet handed the first piece of *kichl* to Yossele. He grabbed the piece and stuffed it into his mouth. The girls stretched out their hands. Yachet handed each a piece of the *kichl*. She looked around, searching for Dovid. She smiled and did not say a word. She realized where Dovid was. Yachet took the last piece of *kichl*, broke it in half, and gave the halves to the little girls.

Dovid came out of the alcove and looked uncertainly at his mother. He went over to the stove and began to eat the *kichl* to which he had helped himself. Yachet pretended not to see.

Feivel stood rubbing his hands, as if trying to warm them. Dovid started drumming with both hands on the edge of the stove, as if beating time to a song.

Yachet went into the alcove and returned almost immediately. Her hands were full. In one hand she carried laundry and in the other clean clothes. She placed everything on the bed.

Yachet dressed Zlotele in a flannel dress and buttoned it up. Zlotele stood stroking her dress. The dress went up to the throat and had a round, lacy collar. It was basically straight, but at the back it spread somewhat. Yachet turned Zlotele around, and began buttoning the buttons at the back.

Yachet stepped into the alcove, stretched out her hand, and from a distance reached for the comb in the cupboard. She soon returned and began to comb Zlotele's hair. She made a part and arranged Zlotele's hair into two braids.

Next, Yachet went to Rivkele and pulled a dress over the child's head. Feivel helped Yachet pull the dress over her head. The dress was already a little small on her. As they both pulled on the dress, their fingers met. Yachet blushed. Feivel's eyes became misty. When Yachet finished, she turned Rivkele around and closed the snaps at the back of the dress.

"My Shabbes dress," said Rivkele, and she looked downward to see the dress. "It's beautiful," she said quietly. This dress also had a straight cut, but the waist was taken in a little. The dress had been cut down from a larger one, and the old stitching could be seen.

Feivel went over to the basin, washed the tips of his fingers, and dried them.

"Come!" he called out to Dovid, and went into the alcove. Dovid stood up and followed his father.

"Let's play Etl-Betl," said Zlotele to her sister.

"Include Yossele," Yachet told Zlotele. Yachet picked up Zlotele and placed him at a bench near the table. Zlotele sat down next to him and gave him a little pinch on the cheek. Yossele turned around and with his hand shoved his sister away.

"Rivkele, look after him. I'm going to bring the pieces," said Zlotele as she went away.

Zlotele raised herself on her tiptoes and barely reached the pieces, which stood on the closet. She threw the five small metal pieces on the table. Originally, the pieces had been cubes, but the edges had been worn away with time. She pushed four of the pieces into the middle of the table and threw the fifth into the air.

Yachet was not standing about idly. She collected the children's dirty clothes and pushed them under the bed. She gathered the dolls and placed them in a drawer in the cupboard. Then she fluffed up the pillows and rearranged the feathers in the quilts to prevent lumping. As she made the bed, she slowed down for a while. She wanted the linens and blankets to be placed properly. Finally, she covered the bed with a bedspread made of red cloth with a green border.

Zlotele kept separating the pieces on the table and throwing one in the air. While the piece was in the air, she would attempt to scoop up another piece on the table in time to use the same hand to catch the cube in the air. Her hand was too small, and she was not able to hold two pieces in one hand at the same time. The piece she had tossed up kept falling on the table.

Rivkele saw how her sister was not able to master the game. Each time the piece fell on the table, Yossele tried to catch it himself. Zlotele kept pushing his hand away but remained silent.

The door to the alcove opened. Dovid came out. His father followed him with his *siddur* in his hands. His pace was restrained, a Shabbes pace, even though he was still wearing his heavy boots. Feivel remained standing behind his son. The girls turned their heads. Their hands remained resting on the table. They looked at their father and brother.

Yachet felt more than saw that the men had come into the room. Feivel was already dressed in his Shabbes clothes. He wore a velvet hat with a brim. Underneath the hat, one could see part of his velvet *yarmulke* sticking out. His black silk jacket, which already had the green shine of age, was still unbuttoned. He had combed his beard, and it seemed longer. His red hair shone.

Dovid, too, was already dressed in his Shabbes clothes. He wore a round velvet cap. Around the edge of the cap was a silk band with two buttons. Dovid wore a gray suit that was too large on him.

Feivel put his foot forward as if ready to leave but did not move from his place. Instead, he pulled the bench away from the table, flipped up his coat, and sat down. He opened the *siddur*, laid it on his knees, and turned a few pages.

Dovid went over to the table. He put his hands in his trousers pockets, took out two handfuls of buttons, and laid them on the table.

Zlotele stopped playing with the pieces. Both girls looked at Dovid. He counted the buttons, wanting to know how many he had won during the week.

"Yachet," said Feivel.

Feivel closed the *siddur*, stood up, and placed the siddur on the table. He reached into his jacket and took out his money bag. He lifted the straw mattress and placed the bag there, making sure that Yachet saw where he had put it.

"Seventeen. I won three," said Dovid as he started sorting the buttons on the table by size.

Feivel pushed the bench on which he had been sitting over to the window. He picked up the *siddur* and sat down, his back to the bed, with the light from the window opposite him. A little later, his fingers rested on the open *siddur*. He swayed back and forth and sang, "*Shir Hashirim*—The Song of Songs, which is Solomon's . . . "

Yachet went into the alcove. The door swung back but remained half open.

When she entered the alcove, Yachet began to dress for Shabbes. Feivel looked through the door and saw how Yachet pulled off her dress, and underneath noticed her ample bosom and round arms. He began swaying from side to side and continued singing: "You are beautiful, my love, as Tirzah, comely as Jerusalem . . . " His voice became deeper and he sang more quickly: "There are threescore queens, and fourscore concubines, and maidens without number." But one could only hear the melody and not the words.

Yachet came out in her Sabbath clothes. She wore a long, light red dress that reached to her ankles. The dress was cut straight at the front. At the back, though, the cut was broader. The buttons of the dress extended up to her neck. The fabric was heavy. Her *shaitel* had been combed out. She walked slowly, her hands under her neck. She carried the tablecloth, its whiteness reflecting on her face. She appeared slimmer and taller than she normally looked.

Yachet unfolded the tablecloth and spread it on the table. The color seemed to be reflected on the walls. The house became lighter; the empty, covered table caught the children's attention. They stood and waited. Yachet placed a nickel tray on the table, and on the tray she placed the brass candlesticks.

She raked the fire in the stove, shut the stove tightly, and put the pots on to warm up.

Feivel kissed the *siddur* and closed it. He stood up, looked at the children and at Yachet, and placed the *siddur* on the table. He went over to the cupboard and took out a lamp and matches. He placed the lamp on the table next to the candlesticks, and put the matches on the nickel tray.

Yachet brought two *challah* loaves from the alcove along with a rectangular cloth to cover them. At the head of the table, opposite the door, she placed the two loaves next to one another and covered them with the cloth. The cloth was cream-colored, round, and hemmed with a green silk thread.

Embroidered in the middle were two Hebrew words, *Shabbes Kodesh*, the Holy Sabbath.

Feivel took a match out of the match box and struck it. It flamed up, and he removed the glass and lit the lamp wick. The lamp began to give light, as if calling out, "Shabbes."

"Yachet, light the candles," he said. He moved to the side, in the process coming close to Dovid. He stretched out his hands and embraced his children, who were standing and watching.

Yachet approached the candlesticks. She struck a match and lit the candles. The candlelight radiated throughout the room. Even the corners became light. The children snuggled up to their father, and he held them more tightly in his embrace.

Yachet placed the used match on the tray, raised her hands, and waved them before her eyes three times. Then she covered her eyes with her hands and recited the appropriate blessing: " . . . Who has sanctified us with His commandments and commanded us to light the Shabbes candles." Her voice was unsteady. Warmth filled the entire room. For a short time she stood with her hands over her eyes, swaying back and forth. Afterwards, she slowly removed her hands from her face. She squinted because she needed to adjust to the sudden exposure to light. With the tip of her finger, she wiped away a tear from the corner of her eye and then, placing her hands on the table to support herself, she began to sway back and forth as she recited a supplication: "In honor of God, in honor of our prayer, in honor of the beloved holy Shabbes, which our great God has given us—the beloved holy Shabbes, and the beloved commandments which He has commanded us. May I be able to fulfill it along with all the 613 commandments of the Torah given to the Children of Israel. Amen, and may it be Your will."

The house became brighter. One could smell the linen and the fresh clothing that everyone wore, mixed with the smell of the chicken soup that was warming on the fire. Yachet stood away from the table, looked at her family, and said, "Good Shabbes, children! Good Shabbes, husband!"

Blessing of Sabbath candles by Haya-Zipa Slep, Nee Chatzkel,
Dusetas, Lithuania, 1935. Courtesy of Beth Hatefutsoth
Photo Archive, Tel Aviv, and Sara Weiss, Israel.

"Good Shabbes, Mommy," all answered.

Yossele stretched out his hands. Yachet picked him up, kissed him, and placed her head next to his.

"Time to go to pray," Feivel told Dovid.

Both father and son got up. Dovid went to the bench where his coat lay, and Feivel to the hook where his coat hung. They put on their thick warm coats over the Shabbes suits.

Dovid took his *siddur* from the table and ran after his father. Feivel turned around and called into the home, "Good Shabbes!"

"A good Shabbes to you!" Yachet answered.

Feivel opened the door. The dry cold of the evening pushed its way through the open door.

The window panes were all covered with a white hoarfrost. In the short time that the door had been open, the house had become colder than before. The mother and daughters stared at the candles, each little flame with a yellow aura around it.

With her foot, Yachet pushed a bench from the table and moved it closer to the stove. She sat down, along with her daughters, and placed Yossele in her lap. The child placed his head on his mother's breast.

"Mommy, tell us a story," Zlotele asked her, and rested her elbows on her mother's knee.

Yachet wiped her lips with the tip of her tongue, and began to speak: "Once there was a great lady who had the best of everything. She had lots of money and jewelry. She lived in a mansion, where she had many servants. She was a very generous and very beautiful woman. She gave to charity, both directly and secretly. Whenever there was a person in need, she helped him. If a poor man needed to marry off a daughter, she would bring the cloth for the bride's dress and would pay for the wedding. If any person, heaven forbid, became sick, she would send him food to help him recover. If an orphan girl was to be married, she would come to help her celebrate. She was wealthy and happy and lacked nothing.

"Once, the town water carrier was about to marry off his only daughter. As usual, the lady came to join in the celebration. Everyone present cleared the way for her. But she was sad. The young bride, who was dressed in the wedding dress that the wealthy woman had given her, was more beautiful than she. The visitor was offered a seat of honor, and all danced around her and served her. But she sat in silence. Immediately after the wedding ceremony itself she left the festivities. She didn't wish the bride *mazaltov*, she didn't taste a thing, and she went home. The bride's and groom's families were saddened, but they went on with all the festivities.

"From that day on, the lady did not rest. She would wander from store to store in the town, and whenever she found a beautiful silk or velvet fabric that she liked she would buy it. She swamped the seamstresses of the town with work so that they had no time for anyone else. Every few days she would come for another dress. Her cupboards were stuffed with dresses. She was always putting on a different dress and would spend hours in front of the mirror trying to see if she was as beautiful as the water carrier's daughter.

"The wealthy lady was so engrossed in her clothes that she forgot that a person who has money must help others. One morning, as had been her custom in recent times, she went to her closet. It seemed as though colored butterflies were dancing before her eyes; she became dizzy and almost fainted; all her precious dresses had been torn up into pieces, and a pile of rags lay at the bottom of the closet. 'Who did this?' she screamed furiously."

"Well, children, who did it?" Yachet asked her daughters, and immediately answered, "Those who had control over her—tfu! tfu! tfu!" and she spat three times to drive away the demons.

Yachet remained sitting. Throughout the time she had been telling the story, her voice had been loud and clear. She herself was enthralled by the account. In her little home, she could see another world.

The little girls stood openmouthed. The light of the candles flickered. "Ah!" shouted Yossele as he suddenly clenched his fist. He wanted to catch one of the flames.

7

FEIVEL remained standing in front of the house, Dovid behind him. Feivel looked down the alley where he was standing. Dovid jumped across the frozen threshhold. He began to mark time with his feet to keep them from freezing as he waited for his father. The snow in all the streets was deep. The sky over the town was a turquoise blue. A dry cold wind blew in from the outlying fields. On the horizon, the sky was filled with clouds. The houses were covered with snow, only their roofs visible. The window panes reflected the candles burning inside each home. The light of day was beginning to fade. Shadows settled down into the corners.

"Good Shabbes, Feivel!" A hoarse voice pierced the cold.

"Good Shabbes, Gedaliah! How are you, neighbor?"

"Can't complain as long as I stay well!" Gedaliah answered, and walked on.

At the corner of the alley they turned left into the next street. The street was short and wide and looked like a sack that had been torn open. The houses here, too, were low and wide. The chimneys emitted thin, gray smoke into the fierce cold. The windows in the houses were larger and wider and were blocked off from the casual eye by curtains. The light of the candles through the curtains was dimmer. Almost every home had four candles burning. In the middle of the street, between two houses, stood wooden pillars upon which hung lanterns. The lanterns had not yet been lit.

It was already Shabbes out-of-doors. Bearded Jews wearing thick coats kept coming out of the different houses, the lapels of their coats pulled one over the other to keep them warm, their hands thrust deep into their sleeves. Seldom did a person emerge from a house alone—they came out in twos and threes. Here walked a gray beard, accompanied by another whose hair had begun to gray. They were followed by a few younger men and these, in turn, were accompanied by children walking alone and by others holding their elders' hands. The Jews were going to "welcome the Sabbath Queen," but their pace was leisurely. When they met, they wished each other "Good Shabbes." The sound of the words echoed through the cold air, like an echo from afar.

Witzek, a tall, thin Gentile wearing a long coat and high, well-cared-for boots walked into the street looking like a person who had lost his way. He walked quickly and looked around to see if the Jews had noticed him. The ends of his mustache flapped about. He wanted to get out of the Jewish lanes and alleys as fast as possible.

Feivel looked all about him: He wanted to be sure that he did not accidentally overlook anyone with his Sabbath greeting. His "Good Shabbes" assumed two forms: when he passed one of the store merchants, he uttered a quiet "Good Shabbes," while he gave a louder "Good Shabbes!" to the peddlers, who travelled from one market to another, and to the craftsmen.

Feivel speeded up his pace. Dovid had to work hard to keep up with his father—he did not want to lose sight of him, this area frightened him.

Dovid grabbed the flap at the back of his father's coat and held on, but he soon put his hand back in his pocket. It was too cold to leave the hand outside for any length of time without his fingers freezing.

Dovid did not want his shoes to be soaked through on Shabbes. Deep ruts ran through the snow-covered streets where heavy wagons had been driven. The snow in these areas had been compacted to slippery ice, criss-crossed by the ruts. There were places where the snow was still fresh, untouched by man or beast, and reflected any light that hit it; elsewhere the snow had been trodden or driven and was now blackened, as though salt had been strewn in the road.

A little later, they began to walk more slowly. They were coming close to the town hill. The road to the hill lay between two rows of long, narrow houses. The wooden tiles on their roofs lay at an angle and reached down almost to the snow. The candle flames, which could be seen through their frost-covered windows, flickered up and down, as if beckoning. The hill had a flat top and looked like the arched back of a cat about to pounce. The snow on the hill itself was deep, thick, and untrodden. They walked through one of the back paths that cut diagonally across a field and led to a small *beis medrash*.

The one-story, red brick building with a flat tin roof stood opposite, at the side of the street. It was at the very edge of the town.

Dovid let go of his father's hand and began to run. For a second, he lost his balance and put out his hands to try to regain it. He clutched the *siddur* tightly in his hand throughout, afraid that it might fall. The puddles in the yard in front of the *beis medrash* had frozen into ice.

Feivel put down his heavy boots one at a time, as if walking on glass. Father and son approached the *beis medrash* from the rear. The ice on the semicircular windows had melted somewhat, and the windows were wet on the inside. Rivulets of water streamed down them. The light that was reflected in the water was yellow and seemed to have been embedded in the glass itself. The three alleys leading to the *beis medrash* were full of Jews. The snow all around was trodden down and was a dirty color. The worshippers pushed themselves through the open entrance.

Dovid ran through the entrance. His father followed. In the entranceway, it was dark and cold. The stone floor was wet with melted snow that the people had brought in on their shoes and boots. In the corner hung a long, thick icicle, like the beard of one of the elders. The water in the basin was frozen.

Feivel stamped his boots on the floor and pulled the door to the *beis medrash* open. The sudden light blinded him.

The *beis medrash* consisted of a long, high hall. The walls dripped with moisture, the white lime coating shimmered. The circular holes at the top, made to admit light, had been boarded up with wooden shutters that crisscrossed one another. The rust-colored wooden ceiling reflected the light. The wood, brown with age, had been mortised, one board into the other. The black knots in the wood seemed to be staring down at the people like eyes. The candles in their brass holders dripped, their flames reaching upward. The light in the two kerosene lamps flickered. Their glass covers kept turning darker with soot. The warm humidity seemed to make everything shine. In the middle of the wall, where the door was located, stood a tall, narrow stove like a tower.

Men with their coats buttoned up stood by the stove, warming their hands behind their backs. Further along, by the same wall, stood a wide, low bookshelf. The covers used to bind the different volumes were soiled and tattered; a goodly number of the books had torn spines. In the corner, between the bookshelf and the wall, lay a box for discarded holy books. The approach to the raised *bimah* in the middle of the *beis medrash* was near two sets of four steps each, on each side. The wooden steps were worn from much use. The table on the *bimah* was overlaid with a green, velvet cover with gilt tassels.

On the wall facing the east, toward Jerusalem, stood the Holy Ark: a brown, glossy closet with two dark-covered tablets with the Ten Commandments engraved over it. The letters of the Commandments shone a fiery yellow. The Holy Ark had a blue velvet *paroches* in front of it. The *paroches* was embroidered in gold thread in the form of the Shield of David. Inside the shield was the word "Zion." The shield of David was guarded by two lions standing on their hind feet and with bared teeth. To the right of the Holy Ark stood the *amud*, where the *chazan* led the prayers, and above it a decorated panel called a *Shivisi* with a message in Hebrew that read, "I have placed (*Shivisi*) the Lord before me always." On each side stood a large brass candlestick, and their light lit up the panel.

Tables and benches, black with age, were everywhere. At the tables sat men with their legs under the benches and their elbows resting on the tables. Some of them swayed back and forth, and others rubbed their hands together. The crowd grew larger from minute to minute.

Close to the stove stood a rather large group of individuals. They were all broad-shouldered and had short beards. Their fingertips showed signs of the tar that had eaten its way under the skin. They also wore boots, but not the heavy ones worn by the others; their boots were relatively short. Their hats were tilted to the side.

Another group of men, short and broad-shouldered, stood in a circle between two tables. They stood with their feet apart, as if working. They had short, curled beards and their fingernails seemed red. They looked at each other and remained silent. These were the tanners. Their eyes were red from the lime in the troughs where they soaked animal hides.

Near the *bimah* was a larger group. These men had short hands and bruised fingers from the needles with which they sewed the cloth. Their caps were shoved to the backs of their heads. Their trousers were long, covering their boots, so that they looked as if they were wearing high shoes.

Feivel drew close to a group standing not far from the door.

"Good Shabbes, my friends!" he greeted them, while still some distance away.

"Good Shabbes!" they all answered together. These were the men who made their living peddling from village to village. Their fingers looked frozen, red. All spoke fast—they wanted to meet their friends and catch up on everything as soon as possible.

8

"Praise the Lord for He is good, for His mercy endures forever," a hoarse voice suddenly pierced the air, and the atmosphere in the *beis medrash* changed immediately.

"Praise the Lord for He is good, for His mercy endures forever," the worshipers repeatedly loudly, as if trying to out-shout one another. They all began swaying back and forth, their lips murmuring; each prayed quietly, but they all swayed to the same rhythm.

A few loud bangs were heard. Pesach the *shammes*, the caretaker of the *beis medrash*, or Pesach the Lame as he was known in the town, banged on the table and then moved aside. His shoulders were straight, so that he had an angular look about him. He had been wounded in the Russian-Japanese war, and that was why he limped. His wife, Pesia, was the breadwinner in the family, being the wig maker of the town.

The Jews prayed, swaying and murmuring, at the same time checking to see if their sons were paying attention. Feivel bent over to his son and leafed through the *siddur* until he found the right page.

The lights flickered. Each little flame burned at its own pace. There were those that spluttered and gave off sparks, as if calling out; others had elongated flames, as if mourning; yet others would flicker alternately higher and lower, as if laughing. From time to time one heard a sharp "crack" as someone snapped his fingers. At other times, the prayers would be interrupted by a sigh or a groan, as if someone were in pain.

Suddenly, the murmuring stopped. Now the worshipers swayed more slowly. This was the silent prayer, or *amidah*, the main act of devotion. After a little while, only a few men remained standing, like figures in a chess set. One by one the men stepped backward with a jerk and looked around them, as if they had just woken. Only the *chazan* was still praying. Feivel ended the silent *amidah* and looked at Dovid's *siddur* to see where his son was up to.

Now the *chazan* alone remained standing. He pulled his *tallis* over his head, for it had slipped off during his silent recitation of the *amidah*. He grabbed the sides of the *amud* and looked around at the assemblage and, bending down, he began the public repetition of the *amidah* prayer that all had just said silently to themselves.

"Blessed are you O Lord, our God and the God of our fathers, the God of Abraham, the God of Isaac, and the God of Jacob—great, mighty and revered, the supreme Being," he began, and the Jews echoed his last words, as if arguing with the entire world. Now they stood without swaying back and forth, listening to the words as recited by the *chazan*. They alone knew the fear of God.

The window panes were wet. The ice on them had melted. The night looked in through the windows. The air inside the *beis medrash* was oppressive, hot, and muggy. The children began to sneak away from their fathers, chasing one another and playing hide-and-go-seek, but they did it all quietly, as if on tiptoe, so as not to anger their parents.

A boy with blonde earlocks remained standing opposite Dovid. His large, fiery black eyes stared mischievously at Dovid. Dovid stretched his head forward. For a short time, the two children looked at one another, then Dovid suddenly jerked his body to the side; he wanted to run off with the other boy. But Feivel saw what was happening, and blocked the way. The boy who had teased Dovid ran away.

"Return to Jerusalem Your city in mercy," the *chazan* intoned, seizing hold of both ends of the *amud* with his hands. His shape, wrapped in the *tallis*, seemed to hover over the *amud*. He threw his head backward; his *tallis* slipped off his head, and he shouted toward the heaven, "Let our eyes see Your return to Zion in mercy." The Jews swayed, as if suddenly hit by the hot desert winds and the cold of the Judean mountains. All the Jews joined in with the *chazan* as he concluded the paragraph with the blessing, "Blessed be You, O Lord, who returns His Divine Presence to Zion." When they finished, they all remained standing silently, fearing that any action might break the spell.

The *chazan* continued with the afternoon service, ultimately uttering the words, "He who makes peace in His high places, may He make peace for us and for all Israel, Amen!" All responded loudly, "Amen!"

The *chazan* remained for a few moments, caught up in the prayer. Then, bending over slowly, he began, "*Yisgadal veyiskadash*—May His great name be exalted and sanctified . . . ," and finally concluded with the words " . . . and let us say Amen." A little later, the words were repeated by those in the first year of mourning for a parent, who recited the "mourner's *kaddish*." The congregation seemed to rouse itself from its torpor, and at the appropriate time all responded fervently, "Amen, May His great name be blessed from now and until all eternity." The men's faces all took on a somber look. Unrest and awe could be seen in their eyes. Slowly, as if in great fear, they turned their heads and looked around. The fathers laid their hands on their children. Only after the different mourners had concluded their recital of the *kaddish*. to be greeted by a chorus of "Amens," did the Jews venture to move.

The chanting stopped as this part of the prayer came to an end. It became quiet in the *beis medrash*, the air inside became even more muggy; the worshippers began to move about. Their sad eyes began to look cheerful, their toil-lined faces were at ease, their look one of innocent relaxation. They were happy that they were again together in the *beis medrash*, their weekday cares behind them. Now, they could rest the hands that had labored throughout the week. They all waited expectantly for the psalms that would be recited to welcome the Sabbath bride.

The children made use of the opportunity. In the brief interval they played hide-and-seek as well as tag, chasing one another around the *bimah*, they hid behind the stove or stopped for a second with their hands stretched out and looked around to see who would be the first to touch the other. They ran under the tables and between the men's feet. They ran away and did not allow themselves to be caught. Their eyes sparkled, their cheeks were aflame. They ran everywhere in the *beis medrash* but kept their distance from the Holy Ark.

The lamps flickered, their flames a bright yellow. The light reflected off the windows, as if the sun were setting there and hiding the darkness of the night outside.

The *chazan* turned around to look at the people for a moment, pulled his *tallis* over his head, and placed his hands on the *amud.* He closed his eyes, shook his head back and forth a few times, and sang out the Opening verses of Psalm 95: "*Lechu neranena*—Let us proceed to acclaim God, let us sing to the Rock of our salvation . . . " He continued the rest of the psalm in an undertone, the people all reciting it along with him. As they prayed, they swayed back and forth like wheat in a field, their chant filling the *beis medrash*.

The children stopped playing. Each went back to his own father.

The *chazan* moved a little away from the amud and remained standing upright. He pulled his *tallis* over his head and drew his head back. Placing his left hand behind his ear, he sang out, "*Lecha Dodi*—Come my beloved to meet the bride—let us welcome the coming of the Sabbath."

The people turned their heads upwards, and raising their voices, sang along with the *chazan* word by word. The lamps began to flicker more fiercely, the flames dancing up and down—they, too, were singing along with the Jews, welcoming the Sabbath bride.

The worshippers were engrossed in their prayer. Later, the light in the lamps began to grow dim as the service drew to an end. Here and there a man took three steps back as he completed the silent *amidah*, waited a while, and moved back to his original place.

The *chazan* stood up straight and took a deep breath. With the fingers of one hand he wiped his lips, while with the other he stroked his beard. He rubbed his forehead, as if trying to remember something he had forgotten, and looked at the congregation.

"*Vayechulu*—The heavens and the earth were completed . . . ," he sang out, his voice trembling. "The heavens and the earth were completed . . . ," the congregation repeated after him, drawing out the words. The rest of the words were said by each worshiper to himself, but they all seemed to be flow up in harmony.

Suddenly, it was over, and everyone seemed to move at once. They were all trying to move forward, but there was very little movement. It was as if they were marking time. Feivel held Dovid tightly by the hand and pushed. He made his way to the table where the coats had been laid. Everyone was intent on reclaiming his own coat. They shoved the pile of coats back and forth, each one pulling out his own.

The lobby was cold and dark. "Good Shabbes," the Jews wished one another, not able to see much in the dark. They all hurried home.

Feivel buttoned his son's coat. The ice on the windowpanes did not allow the light to shine in. The windows were green. From the outside, the *beis medrash* looked like a lamp that was slowly going out.

Feivel wrapped his scarf around himself tightly. He felt the cold.

"Come!" he said to Dovid, and began to walk briskly. Dovid ran along behind him.

It was a dark night. Feivel and Dovid walked in silence, the snow crunching under their feet.

9

YACHET sat with Yossele on her knee, her hands around him, while at the same time holding the *siddur* written specially for women. Yossele's head rested on his mother's breast. He sucked his thumb and stared at the light. He saw a golden aura around the flames. On both sides of Yachet were her daughters, leaning against her; they listened to her.

Yachet held the *siddur* close to her nose. Her cheeks were flushed, her eyes strained at the effort to make out the words. She read slowly, stressing every word, as if speaking to herself: "I wandered about like a lost lamb. I asked: 'Favor your maidservant and show me the way to go, for I have not forgotten Your commandments.'" Yachet's eyelids fluttered for a while; her eyes were moist with tears. She raised her head from the *siddur*, her large black eyes shiny as she looked around the room, as if just having woken.

The lamps shone brightly. The long, low room was bright, but the alcove was dark. The ice-covered window panes were all white as milk. The house was warm, the air fresh.

"Now?" asked Zlotele.

Yachet kissed the *siddur* and closed it. Taking the *siddur* in one hand, she held her arm under the child with the other. Then she raised herself slowly, and placed the little boy where she had just been sitting. She then laid the *siddur* on the cupboard.

"Look after the child. I want to set the table." Her voice was mellow, as if she had just drunk something.

Yachet took a number of forks and spoons from the cupboard and placed them in the middle of the table. She wiped the long kitchen knife, checked to be sure there was no rust on the cutting edge, and placed it underneath the cloth that covered the *challah*. She went into the alcove.

When she returned, she was carrying a small white glass bottle over which an upturned goblet lay. In her other hand she held a kitchen towel. She placed the bottle on the table. The bottle had once been used for perfume and was now the wine decanter for the *kiddush* ceremony.

Once a month, Yachet would ferment a few raisins to make raisin wine. Right now, there was very little wine in the bottle. Yachet returned to the alcove and brought back a short bench, which she placed next to the table. She took the plates from the cupboard on the stove so that they would be ready. She turned her head, listening.

"Mommy, tell us about 'Etzisro'el' (Eretz Israel)," Zlotele begged her.

"Your father and Dovid will be here any minute," Yachet answered.

"Tell us, tell us," said Zlotele eagerly, and Rivkele helped her along by chiming in, "Yes, yes!"

Yachet moved to the wall, her back against it and her palms touching it, as if the wall supported her. She stared at the frozen window panes, as if looking through them, and began speaking to the children.

"A long time ago, the Jews had their own land and their Temple." Yachet wiped her lips and continued, "The walls of the Temple were of gold and with precious jewels. The floors and stairs were of the finest marble. The ceilings were of ivory. In the middle of the Temple stood an altar. On the altar, the priests would offer sacrifices to God for His goodness to the People of Israel. On the altar burned a fire, which never went out. All the vessels of the

Temple were of gold. The clothes of the priests were woven of gold thread." Yachet's eyes sparkled, and the two little girls gazed in astonishment. Yossele sat quietly. He looked at his mother's lips. For a while, Yachet remained silent, and then she suddenly exclaimed, "Yes," as if she had just remembered something. She continued with her story: "When the Jews had a land, they also had soldiers. Every soldier had a coat of armor and rode a horse." As Yachet spoke, her neck stretched upward, as if she were riding a horse. The children stared at their mother, fearing to move or say a word.

Yachet's eyelashes fluttered. She bent her head down and continued, "The emperors and their soldiers gathered and attacked the Jews and chased them out of their land." Her voice trembled. Zlotele moved closer to her little brother. "The Jews became a wandering people, atoning for their sins. But the land belongs to us." Yachet remained sitting silently. A little later, she added, "The Jewish land is full of sun. Oranges grow there, as well as grape vines and pomegranates." Then she went on happily: "When the Messiah comes, he will gather together all the Jews from the entire world and lead them back to their land." The thought overwhelmed her, and she remained silent, deep in thought, for a time.

The door creaked. Yachet hurriedly turned her head to the door. She had not heard the footsteps of her husband and son.

Dovid, followed by Feivel, pushed himself through the door. Feivel immediately closed the door after him. He turned toward all those in the house and said heartily, "Good Shabbes!"

"Good Shabbes, husband," Yachet answered.

Dovid placed his *siddur* on the table. He pulled off his coat and tossed it carelessly on the bed. His eyes were red with cold. Dovid rubbed his ears, trying to warm them.

Feivel slowly took off his coat. He loved the warmth in his home. He picked up both his coat and Dovid's and hung them on a clothes hook.

Dovid went over to his sisters and with each hand playfully cuffed them on the ear.

"Oh!" both girls screamed, and clutched at their ears.

"Son, it's Shabbes!" Yachet reprimanded him.

The little girls sprang down from the stool where they had been sitting. They went to the table and sat down on the bench there. Yachet lifted Yossele over their heads and seated him between them. Yossele began banging on the table. Zlotele embraced him to calm him down. Rivkele hurriedly smoothed out the tablecloth where Yossele had crumpled it.

Yachet moved the other benches from the stove area and placed them by the table. She leaned on the table, the tips of her fingers touching it. She stood and waited.

The light in the lamps began to move about. They contracted and expanded. The intensity of the light in the home kept changing. Sometimes it was lighter, at other times darker. The white of the tablecloth reflected the light.

Feivel raised his head, as if he had seen someone. "*Sholom Aleichem*— Peace be to you, O ministering angels," he began to sing, and started pacing back and forth. He clutched his hands behind him and continued, "angels from on High, from the Supreme King of Kings, the Holy One, blessed be He." Feivel sang as if he saw the angels before his very eyes in the room before him. When he approached the wall at the end of the room, he stopped.

Dovid sang along with his father, "Peace be to you, O ministering angels, angels from on High, from the Supreme King of Kings, the Holy One, blessed be He." His alto voice trembled.

Feivel thrust his hands into both sides of his belt and continued singing the other verses of the song, finally coming to the last verse, "Leave in peace, O angels of peace, angels from on High, from the Supreme King of Kings, the Holy One, blessed be He." He seemed to be personally addressing the angels. Feivel contemplated the words in the *siddur,* not stirring from his place.

He finally straightened up and recited a chapter in Proverbs: "*Eishes Chavil*—A woman of valor, who shall find?" Yachet modestly lowered her eyes as he seemed to address her personally with the words. Her cheeks were flushed. The light in the room reflected off her face.

Feivel walked over to the table and reached over the two *challahs* to pick up the wine bottle. After checking to be certain there was enough wine in it for *kiddush*, he poured wine into the special goblet reserved for *kiddush*. The silver goblet, engraved with the picture of a tower, was dented; it was an heirloom that had been handed down in his family for generations. Feivel slowly poured the wine to the very brim. There was still a little wine in the bottle, and he corked the bottle to save it for another time. He stretched out his right palm and carefully placed the goblet on it.

The little girls stood up. Both together began to lift up Yossele. Yossele remained standing on the bench. Dovid stood at his father's side. Yachet adjusted her *shaitel* and smoothed down her dress. It was quiet in the house. Feivel closed his eyes and began reciting the *kiddush*: "*Yom Hashishi*—The sixth day, and the Heavens and the earth and all their hosts were completed . . . " He said each word slowly and carefully, the words echoing in the quiet of the room.

Feivel brought the goblet up to his lips and drank half the wine in it. He looked at Yachet and handed her the goblet. Yachet bent down and took a sip. After the sip, her lips remained pursed to preserve the taste of the wine. She moved the goblet to Dovid.

"Dovid, only one sip," she cautioned him, holding the goblet in her hands as he drank. Dovid took a sip.

Yachet moved the goblet from him, leaned over the table, and gave the wine to Zlotele. Then she went to the other side of the table and handed the cup to Rivkele.

Yachet placed the empty goblet on the table and went into the alcove. She came back with the pot of fish and placed it on the stove at the side.

Feivel filled a mug with water, stretched out his right hand, and poured water on it. He transferred the mug to his wet right hand and poured water on his left hand. He laid down the mug and raised his hands up high.

Meanwhile, Yachet took a small tin plate out of the cupboard, placed it on the stove, and arranged the fish portions on it.

Feivel put aside the towel he had used to dry his hands and went over to the table. He uncovered the two *challahs*, folded the cloth cover in half, and put it aside. He placed his hands on the *challahs*, closed his eyes, and recited the blessing over bread, " . . . Who brings forth bread from the earth." He raised up both *challahs* and replaced them on the table.

He pushed the bench away from the table, slid in between the bench and the table, and sat down. Picking up the bread knife in one hand, he took one of the *challah* loaves in the other. He cut the *challah* in half and then sliced it up. Dipping the end of the *challah* in salt, he took a bite of it. Taking the cut up *challah*, he set aside a piece for Yachet and gave one to each child.

Yachet brought over two plates of fish, for Feivel and for Dovid. She gave Feivel two fish balls and Dovid one. Then she came back with pieces of fish for the little girls. They each received half a fish ball.

Yachet soon returned with the last two plates of fish. She hurriedly placed them in front of her seat and sat down. She mashed the small piece of fish she had brought for Yossele and placed it in front of him. Yossele dipped the edge of his *challah* slice in the fish broth.

Feivel pushed the piece of *challah* he had set aside for Yachet over to her, and only then did he begin to eat. He had waited for Yachet to come to the table.

Everyone around the table became preoccupied with eating. The light shone on the table. The shoulders of those eating were all in the shadows.

"Shabbes fish, a real treat," Feivel said, seemingly addressing his plate.

Yachet raised her head and swallowed the bite in her mouth. "Thank you. Enjoy it," she said happily, and went on eating.

Feivel finished his fish, pushed the bench away from the table, and with a hurried pace went into the alcove.

Yachet stopped eating and went back to the stove. There was still a little of her *challah* on the table. Yachet raised the lid of the pot and checked the soup. Reaching into the cupboard, she took out the deep soup bowls and arranged them on the shelf.

Feivel returned. He walked slowly and deliberately. In his hand he carried a white, square bottle. He remained standing at the table and bent down to examine the bottle before placing it on the table. The bottle was half full. He pulled the cork out of the bottle and began pouring its contents into the goblet. When he had filled half the goblet, he replaced the cork, pushing it down with the palm of his hand to ensure that the alcohol in it did not evaporate. Sitting down at the table, he raised the goblet. Seeking Yachet with his eyes, he exclaimed, "*Lechaim* — to life!"

"*Lechaim*," answered Yachet and the children. Yachet returned to the table.

Feivel raised the goblet to his mouth, threw his head back, and tossed down the drink. One could hear him swallow. The children remained silent, with bated breath. Feivel held the empty goblet in his hand. He shook his head to clear it. "Ha!" he exclaimed, and he remained with his mouth open wide. All the others looked at him. The children sat and waited. Feivel replaced the goblet on the table and rubbed his hands together. The warmth penetrated to his very bones.

Feivel got up from the bench, stretched his hand across the table, and picked up the *siddur*. He turned a few pages until he found what he was looking for, and began singing one of the Shabbes songs, "*Kol mekadesh* — Whoever honors the seventh day as is proper . . . " He sang the verses to a Chassidic melody that he had learned in his childhood at home, but after the first two or three verses he began to sing only the melody, swaying back and forth as he sang.

Dovid, too, sang out loudly. His alto tones could be heard clearly above his father's bass. The house was full of song. Three-quarters of the Shabbes lights had already gone out. One of the remaining candles began dripping, the tallow pouring over the brass candlestick.

The children's faces were radiant. Both little girls banged on the table in time to the beat. Yossele kept getting up and sitting down, as if riding a horse.

Yachet came over to the table. She carried two bowls of soup. She bent over and placed a bowl of chicken soup with noodles before Feivel. The second plate she placed in front of her son, and she went back for more. Feivel bent over the plate, savoring the delightful smell of the soup. His face was covered with the steam from the plate. A layer of fat floated on the soup. The noodles stuck out in the bowl, like the tip of an iceberg. In Dovid's bowl, the noodles barely covered the bottom. His soup, too, had circles of fat floating on top.

All sat hunched over the plates, eating. The table and those sitting around it seemed to be enveloped in a fog. The steam from the plates hung over them. From the back of the room, the shoulders of those in the room appeared to be shivering. Yachet ate together with Yossele. She took some soup and noodles and fed the little boy. She gave him only part of a spoonful each time. Yachet ate speedily. Feeding Yossele, though, she took her time. Before each bite, the little boy opened his mouth wide and pushed himself closer to the spoon.

Feivel picked up the *siddur* again and opened it. He cleared his throat, closed his eyes, and again began singing: "*Menuchah Vesimchah*—Rest and joy, light for the Jews." This, too, he sang to a Chassidic melody, this time a lively march that seemed to rise to a crescendo. He sang each word separately and paused after every verse. Dovid beat time with his fist and tapped his foot under the table. "May all those who take delight in the Sabbath day be granted blessings, and may they witness the coming of the Messiah and the life of the World to Come," Feivel ended. He closed the *siddur* and pushed it to the side.

The plate of meat on the stove was steaming hot. The flame in the lamp dipped down, flared up into a point, and emitted smoke. The room became momentarily lighter. Yachet's face took on a yellowish hue in the light of the lamp.

Yachet pushed her stool back with her foot. She then placed the plate of meat on the table. She collected together the plates on the table and began to divide up the portions, taking care that everyone got his or her share. The small pieces of meat were red and seemed to have shrunk in the cooking.

Feivel slowly pulled his plate toward himself. On it were two pieces of meat and a long, narrower piece as an extra portion. Feivel stretched out his hand, picked up some salt between his fingers, and sprinkled it on his meat. As he ate, he looked at his wife.

Yachet, feeling him looking at her, lowered her eyes. Her portion was a small piece of gristle, which she could not chew. Feivel speared a piece of his meat with his fork and placed it on Yachet's plate. Yachet was startled. Hurriedly, she took it and returned it to Feivel's plate. Now it was Feivel who lowered his eyes. In Feivel's home they ate meat only on Shabbes.

Feivel picked up the *siddur* again, searched for the proper page, and again began singing: "*Yoh ribon olam* — Lord, Master of the universe . . . "

Yachet gathered together the forks on the table and went over to the stove. She did not hurry, as if pacing herself deliberately.

She now brought over the bowl of *tzimmes*. The radish cubes were brown, and the yellow carrot slices glistened with the fat on them. The two vegetables were mixed together, a cube over a slice, a slice on top of a cube. The dish steamed.

Feivel continued to sing the same song, pausing after each line. The singing now became livelier but confused, as he mixed together the first melody with a march that the town firemen played when they paraded.

Yachet looked at the plate of *tzimmes* she was holding. It was full. She placed it before Feivel.

"I don't want any," said Dovid, and he leaned against the back of the bench.

Yachet, surprised, looked at Dovid: "But *tzimmes* melts in your mouth!"

"I also don't want any," said Zlotele.

"And I don't either," chimed in Rivkele.

Yachet remained standing helplessly, with the serving spoon in one hand and the *tzimmes* in the other. It was such a waste of food. Later, though, she said, "Thank God." She was delighted the children were full.

Feivel completed his singing, stretching out each word. The smell of the *tzimmes* was tantalizing. He closed the *siddur* and again laid it aside. He stretched out his hand to the plate of *tzimmes* and pulled it toward himself. He picked up the serving spoon and stuck it into the *tzimmes*.

It was quiet in the house. The people in the house heard the lamps burning. The children were tired and sated. They sat and looked at one another.

The flames started diminishing in size as the candles burned down to the end. Finally, they burned out. One could smell the strong odor of the burnt out wicks.

The house became darker. The corners now showed only short shadows. Feivel placed the spoon in his empty plate and slowly stood up from the table. He lifted his head and looked around at his family. "Dovid," he said suddenly.

Dovid sprang up. He took the goblet from the table and went over to the pail of water.

Feivel tossed his head. His red beard shone in the light of the lamp. Yossele slipped away from the table and clambered on his father's knee.

Yossele began laughing, as his fathers beard tickled him.

"I also want to sit on your knee," said Rivkele. "Sit, sit, Rivkele," said Yachet.

Dovid returned and placed the goblet filled with water in front of his father. He sat down again.

Feivel extended his hands, as if trying to embrace the little boy on his knee, and picked up the goblet. He stretched one hand over the empty *tzimmes* plate and poured water on his fingertips with the other. Then he reversed hands and poured water on the other hand's fingertips.

"I will bless the Lord at every time," he murmured, as he closed his eyes and began swaying back and forth. It became even quieter in the house. The flame in the lamp became elongated, as if trying to burst forth out of the glass cover. Feivel went on: "I am hereby ready to fulfill the commandment of reciting grace after meals."

Yossele was very tired. He sat quietly with his head facing his father and pushed his fingers into his father's mouth. He tried to close Feivel's lips. Feivel kept raising his head higher so that Yossele would not disturb him, and continued reciting the grace.

Yachet bent over. She stretched out her hands toward the little boy. Both Feivel and Yachet held their breaths. Yachet took Yossele from his fathers arms. "Come to sleep," she told the little boy.

Yossele resisted, kicking out with his feet. Yachet moved aside, to make sure that he would not kick her in the stomach. "Children, time to sleep," she exclaimed.

Dovid was dozing.

"Rivkele," Zlotele said to her sister, "we'll sit at the table until late, even after Mommy and Daddy have gone to sleep. O.K.?" A little later she said, "Until the lamp burns out." She talked quietly. She looked into her sister's eyes and said, "I want Shabbes to go on for a long time."

Rivkele looked at her innocently. Her eyes were red with fatigue. She didn't understand her sister's meaning.

Feivel prepared for the night. He removed the red bedspread with green fringes from the bed and folded it up, then placed it on a bench.

"Children, time to go to sleep," their mother said again.

Dovid pointed with his finger to the bed. All three children recited the prayer before sleep, beginning, "Hear O Israel, the Lord is our God, the Lord is one." They continued the rest of the recitation in a singsong manner, their voices echoing through the house. The little girls stood on one side of the table and Dovid on the other. When they ended, Feivel responded, "Amen." Yachet repeated "Amen," and added, "May good angels hover over you."

The lamp gave a last, dying gasp, and for a brief moment flared up. The home was warm. The children hurriedly undressed. Each wanted to be the first one in bed.

Yachet also prepared for bed. She went from one place to the next, putting the children's clothes away neatly. Afterwards, she went over to the bed. The children were already asleep, two on either side of the bed, the girls on one side and the boys oh the other. Rivkele's hand lay on her sister's throat, and Zlotele held her tightly. Dovid lay curled up like a ball; Yossele had his finger in his mouth.

Feivel was almost asleep, his eyes closing each time until he awoke with a start. "Let's go to sleep," he said.

"Go, go, I'll be along soon," Yachet answered. Her voice was mellow.

Feivel covered his eyes with his hand and began reciting the *shema*—"Hear O Israel . . ." When he had finished, he again opened his eyes. He picked up the bottle of brandy and carried it into the alcove.

Yachet gathered together the plates on the table and on the ground, along with the forks and spoons on the stove and on the table. She put the dirty dishes and silverware aside. All that remained on the table were the left over *challah*, the cloth cover for the *challah* and the salt bowl.

The door moved, slowly but forcefully. A tall non-Jew entered the house, and swiftly closed the door behind him. He nodded to Yachet and blinked as the remaining light in the room temporarily blinded him. He was a fifteen-year-old youth, son of the owner of the house, in his boots and cotton waist-coat. His winter hat was pulled over his ears. His hair, straw-colored, hung out at the front. His blue eyes looked at the lamp, the candle holders, and the white tablecloth. With his hand he rubbed his frozen nose.

He went over to the stove, opened it with the metal poker lying beside it, and proceeded to shift around the still burning coals. Then he turned down the lamp.

Yachet stood and waited, and gave him the leftover *challah* from the table. Stach, as was his name, shoved the *challah* into his ample sleeve. "Good night," he said, smiling and showing his even white teeth. He opened the door swiftly, and even more swiftly closed it behind him.

The lamp died out. The room grew darker. The shadows in the corners grew longer and longer. Yachet went over to the door and bolted it shut.

Tiptoeing, she went over to the bed; she glanced at the children and entered the alcove. The lamp gave a last dying gasp. The house was dark, quiet, and warm.

Feivel was already snoring.

10

FEIVEL opened his eyes. The morning light in the alcove was still gray. One could already make out the contours of items in the home. It was quiet in the house; everyone else was sleeping. He had no idea what time it was. In Feivel's home, they lived without a clock. The house felt cool, but Feivel was warm under his blankets. He looked at his wife. Yachet lay with her head to the side, her ample bosom filling the front of her nightshirt.

Feivel felt a dryness in his mouth. He jumped out of bed. "It is Shabbes morning," he said to himself. He pulled on his trousers and hurriedly buttoned them up, and throwing a shirt over his shoulders, quietly left the alcove.

Feivel remained standing on the other side of the door. The light in the front room was brighter than that in the alcove. It was quiet in the house. He heard the breathing of those who were asleep. For a while he listened. Then he turned his head to look at the children. They were breathing easily. A warm feeling encompassed him.

He placed the ladle into the water and withdrew it slowly to prevent the water from splashing. He stretched his hands over the basin and poured water over each in turn. He replaced the ladle, and with his wet hands twice washed his face. Finally, he pulled his fingers through his beard. He again picked up the ladle, poured some water into his mouth, and replaced the ladle. Throwing his head back, he gargled and rinsed out his mouth. Then he took down the towel and wiped his hands carefully, dabbing each finger separately. He murmured a prayer quietly to himself.

Much of the warmth in the house had dissipated, pushed aside by the cold night air outside. The window panes were covered with ice. For a while, Feivel felt that he could sense the cold air outside penetrating right through the window. He stretched out his hand and picked up the *siddur*. Opening it, he flipped a few pages, placed it open on the table, and began his prayers from the beginning.

He glanced at the children in bed. They were all sleeping. He hurried across the room and quickly finished dressing. He opened the door quietly, holding it open with his knee until he was able to push his way through it. He hoped that the door would close silently, but instead it gave out a creak.

All four children in the bed opened their eyes; the gray of the morning hung over them. Yossele uttered a little cry; he wanted his mother beside him.

"Mommy is still asleep," Zlotele said softly, asking Yossele to remain quiet.

"Good Shabbes," the little girls called out from the bed, and raised their heads.

"Good Shabbes, good Shabbes, little children," Feivel answered. His face, red with cold, broke out into a big smile.

Feivel hurriedly closed the door and rubbed together his frozen fingers.

"Today is Shabbes," Zlotele said to her father.

"The whole day until the night," Rivkele went on. She wanted to be sure.

"The holy Shabbes," Feivel answered, and playfully gave Yossele a very light poke in the ribs.

Yossele reached out and grabbed his father's finger. Through his finger, Feivel felt the warmth of his little son's body. Feivel pulled back his finger and moved away from the bed. Yossele remained lying down with a clenched fist, staring at his father.

Feivel put on his silk jacket, took his *gartel* out of the pocket, and wrapped the *gartel* around his waist. His weekday clothes were covered by his special Shabbes clothes.

The door moved and opened as Dovid entered the room. He closed the door behind him.

"There is a frozen crow lying in the courtyard," he said in one breath. It was quiet in the house. "All the roofs are full of crows. They're hungry."

Zlotele turned her head, staring at her brother. One could see fear in her eyes. Rivkele and Yossele looked at Zlotele, not understanding what their brother had said.

"That's what a young man who is already studying Talmud devotes himself to on Shabbes," said Feivel, shaking his head.

He went over to the table, pulled out a drawer, and took out from it the *chumash*. He sat down and placed the *chumash* before him. The *chumash* had been bound many years earlier in brown leather. Feivel opened the *chumash* and turned the pages. The edges of each page were brown from repeated use and turning. Feivel looked around the room, as if searching for someone in the gray morning light. "Today's Torah reading is the section of *Yisro*," he said, and he bent over the volume. His back was curved. He opened his eyes wide and began reciting the text in a singsong fashion. He was no longer in his own home, but with Moses as he took the Children of Israel out of Egypt.

Yachet opened her eyes and closed them again, feeling the gray darkness all about her and the warmth of her body. She lay and listened.

"Jethro rejoiced for all the good which the Lord had done for Israel" (Exodus 18), sang Feivel, filled with pride, for God is good to the Jewish people. When Feivel came to the words, "Jethro, the father-in-law of Moses, took a burnt offering and sacrifices for God," his voice trembled with emotion. In order to ingratiate himself with the Jews, Jethro had brought sacrifices to God. "The next day, Moses sat down to judge the people," sang Feivel. He was overcome with fear as he read this. He had known the story ever since his childhood, but each time he was afraid again of Moses' judgment. "'Why do you sit alone and all the people stand before you?'" Feivel asked, quoting the Biblical text, and was disturbed again. He could not stand the fact that Jethro had come to rebuke Moses. "And Moses said to his father-in-law, 'For the people come to me to seek God,'" sang Feivel. "Aha!" he exclaimed, overcome with the audacity of Jethro. "And Moses' father-in-law said to him, 'This thing that you do is not good.'" "Ay, ay," sighed Feivel, unable to stand the way Jethro spoke to Moses. Feivel made sure to sing the verses according to the *trop* melody, but one could feel his hurt in the reading—Jethro was teaching Moses something. However, when he recited the verse, "Be you for the people before God, and bring their causes to God," Feivel did so in a strong, sure voice.

Dovid stood by the window and used his nail to scrape the ice from it. He wanted to see if the crows were still on the roofs. Soon after he had scraped off the ice, the windows were again iced over. Finding this occupation tedious, Dovid went over to the bench where his coat lay.

Yachet was still half asleep, but her senses were wide awake. Her mouth was dry, but inside she felt a quietness that permeated all her bones.

Dovid buttoned up his coat; he moved around and stood behind his father as Feivel read on.

Feivel felt his son behind him, reading along with him. He put his arm around the boy as they read together: "The Lord said to Moses, 'Go to the people and sanctify them today and tomorrow, and let them wash their garments.'" Dovid's alto voice enlivened the room.

Feivel swayed back and forth over the *chumash* as he sang quietly. Once again he would savor the words of the commandments. From time to time, fragments of verses were heard, as if he were playing with the words: "Do not make yourselves a graven image," or "Do not bow down to them." He again bent over the *chumash* and sang according to the cantillation marks. Now one heard only the melody, but not the words. From time to time he stopped, remaining staring at the text. Then he would repeat phrases aloud: "Honor your father and mother," "Do not kill," "Do not steal," "Do not covet." After each verse, Feivel sat still for a moment, his eyes bright with joy and a kind of pride. He sat joyfully and proudly, thinking of the Jewish heritage. His singing echoed through the house.

Yachet opened her eyes. The alcove was still half dark. There was just a glimmer of light visible through the open door.

Dovid went over to the cupboard. He bent down and pulled out from underneath the cupboard a few folded pieces of paper. When he had finished, he turned toward the stove. These were papers that Dovid had once brought home from his *cheder*. He had traded a button for them. The paper itself was already yellow with age. Dovid bent down and became engrossed in his work. The stove served as a table. He folded and refolded the paper in different ways, eventually coming up with a "horse."

The light in the house was already clearly evident. Feivel began to pace about in the room, his hands clutched together. He used a diagonal course in order to have a longer path to walk. The white tablecloth helped to brighten the room.

From time to time, Feivel heaved a sigh of contentment. After each sigh he stopped for a while and then continued. He took pleasure in the joys of Shabbes. The fringes of his *tallis koton* hung down to his feet, brushing against them, as if urging him to move faster.

"I want to get dressed," said Zlotele, and she jumped out of bed.

Rivkele soon followed her.

Both girls bent over, pulled their shoes and socks out from under the bed, and began to dress.

"Me too!" Yossele shouted, and stretched out his hands. Feivel smiled. He went over and sat at the edge of the bed. With one hand he picked up Yossele and with the other he reached under the bed for the child's shoes.

Zlotele dressed herself, but Rivkele needed her sister's help; she couldn't push her hands through her sleeves unaided.

Feivel took care of Yossele. He struggled to put on the child's socks and shoes. Yossele kept thrashing about impatiently, wanting his father to put him down onto the ground as soon as possible. Feivel's thick fingers did not help matters.

Dovid's paper horse lay ready on the stove. Now he folded a second sheet of paper into a ship.

The open door to the alcove moved on its hinges.

"Good Shabbes," Yachet said from the alcove, and she came into the room.

Elderly Jewish couple. Wolbrom, Kielce District, Poland, 1920s. The woman is wearing a Kupke, a traditional head cover. Courtesy of Beth Hatefutsoth Photo Archive, Tel Aviv, and Yeshayahu Mordecai Zanin, Tel Aviv.

"Good Shabbes, Mommy," the little girls both answered.

"Good Shabbes, wife," Feivel said. The words fell into his beard. He smiled. He went back to his work.

Yachet remained standing inside the door. All the children except Dovid looked at her. Yachet's face was placid, rested; her cheeks were red.

Feivel bit his moustache between his lips. Yachet, shyly, lowered her eyes; her eyelashes were moist. "Good Shabbes, son," she said to Dovid in confusion, and she turned to the stove. Her cheeks were flushed.

"Good Shabbes! Good Shabbes!" Dovid answered swiftly, not lifting his head and continuing with his work.

Everyone in the home went back to preparing for the day. Rivkele stood with her back to Zlotele so that she could fasten the buttons at the back of her dress.

Yachet again lowered her eyes as she passed Feivel. She went over to the cupboard. As she walked, she pulled her dress over her.

Feivel stood up straight, picked up Yossele with both hands, and put him down on the floor. He breathed heavily, as if he had just been engaged in strenuous physical work.

"I'm going to the bakery," he said, and stood up.

"Are you going to bring the coffee?" Zlotele asked him, and looked at him with her large eyes.

Feivel closed the door behind him. Each time the wind howled against the door, it creaked. As the door closed, it rubbed against the jamb and scraped the floor, emitting a sound of protest.

Dovid was busy folding a new piece of paper. The other children looked on curiously. Dovid came to a dead end. He could not manage to fold it the way he wanted. It was quiet in the house; all were silent.

"Come and wash," Zlotele said to her sister, and pulled Rivkele behind her. Both girls went over to the basin. Zlotele got up on tiptoe and drew a ladle full of water. She looked at the water and saw a reflection of herself. She soon lowered herself. She was unable to stand on her tiptoes for any length of time.

Rivkele stretched her hands over the basin.

Zlotele poured water over both her hands.

"With soap," Rivkele begged.

"Today is Shabbes," Zlotele answered. She put away the ladle, and used her hands to wash her sister's hands. Then she repeated the entire process. Only now did she pour water over her own hands. She washed her sisters face and then her own face. Rivkele stood with her eyes closed. Zlotele grabbed the towel. "There you are," she said, giving it to her sister.

Rivkele opened her eyes and grabbed the other end of the towel. Both girls wiped themselves.

Yachet took Yossele by the hand, lifted him up, and said something to him as she carried him to the basin. She held Yossele suspended over the basin; with her free hand she wet a corner of the towel, and using that end of the towel she washed Yossele's face and hands.

Zlotele stretched out a finger, giving the sign. The two girls began reciting in unison, "*Moydeh ani*—I thank You, Eternal King, that you restored my soul within me. Great is Your mercy."

"Amen," said Dovid together with his mother.

"Rivkele," Zlotele called out. Zlotele stretched out her hands. The little girls grabbed the bench at each end and moved it away from the table so that they could sit on it. Yachet carried Yossele over to the table, lifting him over the girls' shoulders. The girls moved apart, and Yachet sat him down between them. It was quiet in the house. Near the walls, one could feel the cold from outside. The children were now dressed in their Shabbes clothes. They sat and waited for the day to begin.

Yachet went over to the cupboard and bent down. She straightened out and came to the table carrying six mugs, each on a different finger. She placed a blue porcelain mug before each place. At the head of the table, where Feivel would sit, she placed a white mug, twice the size of the others.

Yachet took a plate out of the cupboard and went back into the alcove. A little later, she returned to the living room. The plate now contained a few cookies or *kichlach*. She moved over to the table and began to divide up the *kichlach*. Each of the three youngest received a *kichl*. At Dovid's place, she put down two *kichlach*. She placed nothing next to Feivel's large mug. At her place, she put down a *kichl* with burnt edges. The children's *kichlach* had a raisin in the middle.

For a short while, the children sat without moving. They looked, inspecting the *kichlach*. At the table, one could smell the odor of the baked pastry.

Rivkele licked her lips. Her mouth was full of saliva. She stretched out her hand hesitantly, as if ashamed, and pulled the raisin off her *kichl*. She tossed the raisin into her mouth and sucked it, smacking her lips.

"Wait!" said Zlotele angrily. Her anger was her way of disguising the fact that she wanted to do the same.

Yossele grabbed the *kichl* with both hands and bit off a little piece. His mouth was already full. Zlotele grabbed a crumb from Yossele's *kichl* and thrust it into her mouth.

Dovid also smelled the cookies. He hurriedly put away the things he had been playing with and placed them in his trouser pocket; then, shoving the papers under the cupboard, he sprang over to the table.

The door opened slowly. Feivel stood in the entrance, as if he had pushed the door open with his stomach. The children at the table looked at him. Dovid sat down. "We're going to eat!" he announced, and he banged on the table with his fist, as if wishing everyone to be quiet.

Using the toe of his boot, Feivel closed the door. He held a jug by its handle. "Ha!" he blew, and his cheeks filled out. He went over to the oven and placed the coffee jug on it, and then swung his hand about; it was stiff with cold.

Yachet went over to the jug and slowly removed the paper that had been placed on the jug to close it. She took care not to burn her fingers. She lifted the lid and smelled the brew. "It's delicious," she exclaimed, and covered the jug. In the room one could smell the chicory. Yachet picked up the jug and carried it to the table. Feivel took off his coat. His face was moist with perspiration; only his nose and the tips of his ears had been exposed to the cold, and they were red.

Yachet bent over the table, holding the jug in one hand by its handle. The table was covered with a tablecloth. There was a warm smell of chicory.

Feivel stood leaning on the bed, watching the children eating; he took in the smell of the hot beverage. Yachet shook her head, as if she had just reminded herself of something. She looked at Feivel. "Nu?" she asked him. Feivel bent down, stretched out his hand and picked up his mug. His lips seemed to flutter as if he was shivering, and he recited the blessing: ". . . By whose word all was created," and took a sip from the mug.

Dovid wolfed down his first *kichl*. He was hungry. He hunched down over the table, picking up the second *kichl* with one hand and his mug with the other, and went on eating. He took a bite and followed it with a swallow of the hot liquid. Now he ate slowly, as if it would be a pity to finish.

Yachet walked around the table. She bent down, picked up the jug from the floor, and looked inside it. She poured the remaining chicory into Feivel's cup. "Drink!" she said to him, and placed the jug on the floor again.

It was quiet in the house. The pungent odor of chicory lingered on. Although the house still retained some warmth, it was beginning to feel cool.

Feivel went over to the pail where water was kept. He ladled out a little water, poured it over his fingertips, and wiped his hands. Slowly he turned his body, without moving his legs from their place, as if he paralyzed from the waist down. Only then did he begin to walk. After every step, his feet seemed to freeze in their place. As he walked, he buttoned his silk jacket, following which he tied the *gartel* around his waist. He went into the alcove. The children accompanied him with their eyes. None of them wanted to move from the table.

Feivel entered the alcove and came back with his *tallis*. His pace was now regular. When he reached the middle of the room he remained standing. He swiftly spread out his *tallis* and wrapped himself in it.

Dovid sprang off the bench, walked to the door, lifted his father's coat off the hook where it was hanging, found his own coat, which he put on, and picked up the *siddur* from the table. He was ready to go. Feivel put his coat on over his *tallis*; the coat covered it amply. He did not button it, but placed one lapel over the other and held both together with his hands. "A good Shabbes," said Dovid, as he ran to the door. "A good Shabbes! A good Shabbes!" said Feivel, as if singing to himself, and he followed his son. "A good Shabbes! A good year!" Yachet answered, and followed her men with her eyes. Dovid pushed the door open with the side of his body, using his elbow to raise the latch. The door sprang open and a cold blast blew into the house. "Ah!" both little girls sighed, and huddled close to one another.

The house was quiet. The sound of the closing of the door still re-echoed, and the cold that had been let in soon spread through the house. The sisters, who had been huddled together, moved apart. They sat and waited for what was to come as they did every Shabbes. The window panes were frozen, misted over with a white coating like milk, but the light outside shone through.

The floor close to the window was lighter than the floor in the rest of the room. The wood shavings there had already been trampled down.

The door hinge creaked and the door sprang open. Stach came in but remained standing inside by the door. The tall, well-complexioned Polish youngster was dressed as on the previous night, but the collar of his coat was turned up. For a while he stood motionless, as if not knowing what to do. Every other day of the week, whenever he passed the window of Feivel's home, he would yell into the window "Yids!" whether there was anyone to hear or not. But on Shabbes, when he came to light the fire in the stove and he saw the white tablecloth on the table and the brass candlesticks, his impudence evaporated; he looked around at the home and its occupants as if seeing them for the first time, and he smiled. He could not help it.

"Time for you to light the stove," said Zlotele with a nod of her head.

"Now then, my girl, don't say that," said Yachet, and she pulled Yossele close to her.

Stach went over to the stove, spat into his hands, and rubbed them on his trousers, pushed his cap back on his head so as to see better, slid back the oven door, and stirred the ashes with two fingers. He then bent over, took some precious coal from the pile, and threw it into the stove. He placed a few pieces of tinder on the coal.

Yachet moved Yossele from one arm to the other and went into the alcove.

The little girls' eyes did not remain still. They stared at everything Stach did.

Stach took some coal dust and spread it on top of everything else in the stove. He repeated this twice. Now he took matches out of his pocket. He lit one, and a little flame flickered.

Stach slowly moved the match to the tinder until it caught, and closed the aperture. The smell of burning coal dust swept through the room. Yachet came over to Stach carrying a *kichl*. The smell in the room was even sharper. The coal was burning. Stach again wiped his hands on his trousers.

Yachet handed him the *kichl* without saying a word. Stach grabbed it and pushed it into his pocket. He shoved his hair back under his hat and was soon out the door. Under the oven top the red glow of the fire was visible.

11

DOVID ran through the frozen courtyard. He ran with his head held high, as if afraid that he might bump into something. He jumped over the threshold and remained standing in the street. His *siddur* was underneath his arm so that he could keep both hands in his pockets. The cold went through him.

Dovid looked up to see the crows on the roofs. As he looked for the crows, he heard the telephone wires above the roofs shrieking in the wind. "Daddy, how far do the wires go?" he asked.

Feivel did not answer. He didn't know. The cold was stabbing at him underneath his fingernails. His large black eyes were at peace; he stood and looked ahead.

The deep snow on the ground had frozen. The snow-covered roofs seemed to be lying in the snow, and the blue of the sky seemed to be mixed with milk. Dovid strained his neck to look down the little alley. He was curious to see what was happening in the township.

"Come," said Feivel.

The trodden path between the wagon ruts seemed to snake into the distance. Not wanting to step in the snow, they walked carefully, as if crossing a little bridge. The frozen snow crunched under their dry boots.

The few snow-covered huts on both sides of the alley crouched low on the snow-covered ground. Not a single door opened; only the thin smoke curling from the chimneys gave evidence that there were people in the huts.

At the corner stood a tall, broad-shouldered Jew wearing a heavy brown coat with a black fur collar. From afar, he seemed to be bundled into his coat. His hands had been thrust into his sleeves. His black beard lay on his coat like a scarf.

"Good Shabbes, Berish!" said Feivel when he was yet some distance away, and he waved to the man.

Dovid pulled at Feivel's coat. He wanted his father to walk through the streets with Berish, for taking that route would mean passing through the area where Dovid's *cheder* friends lived.

"Feivel, good Shabbes to you!" Berish answered, and turned left.

"Is this the way you are walking?" Feivel asked him. "Why not come with us?"

"Good Shabbes!" Berish said again, and went his own way.

Feivel and his son went alongside the wooden wall of a stable. Feivel wished to see the Shabbes crowd in the *shtetl.*

He walked slowly but with a measured pace. Later, be took a short cut through the market area, right through the snowed-under market square on which there stood but a few houses. The snow in this area had not been trodden down very much. In the alleys and courtyards, the top layers of snow were already black. Here and there, a path had been beaten through it. Every so often there was a yellow or black patch, where people had emptied commodes. The few scattered houses looked from afar like frozen crates, standing upright or lying on their sides. The cold was sharper here in the open area than in the alleys.

Feivel stayed far from the houses, striding through the middle of the market place. The path he had chosen had barely been trodden.

Dovid followed literally in his footsteps, stepping where his father had stepped. This way, it was easier for him to walk. Every step that Dovid took, he swayed, as if carrying a heavy burden. The area where the two were walking was known by the local folk as "the bare patch." The earth here was hard, and nothing grew on it.

Dovid bent down. He picked up a fistful of snow and shaped it into a snowball. He threw the snowball, and a flock of pigeons flew off the roof, fleeing the area. They flapped their wings in fear.

"Dovid, Shabbes," Feivel reprimanded him and looked to see where the pigeons were flying. The pigeons flew about in circles, not wishing to abandon their perch on the roof. Dovid stood looking upward, trying to tell the different kinds of pigeons from their flight. "Those are carrier pigeons," he said excitedly.

Feivel and his son walked on. The street was long and narrow. The huts here were low-built, roofed with wooden shingles. Each hut had a little tract of land around it, with two or three trees growing in front of the door. The snow on the roofs was softer than in the wider streets. The street barely divided the huts on either side. In those places where there was no snow, one could see that the street had been crudely paved with irregular stones. This street had no name. The Jews called it "Village Lane."

Here, on this street, Feivel was able to walk faster. Dovid lagged behind.

"Good Shabbes, Feivel," a voice echoed from the distance.

"Good Shabbes, Itzik," Feivel answered.

Feivel walked over and stopped when he approached Itzik. They looked at one other and nodded. Both their faces were frozen with cold. Itzik's gray eyes sparkled. Dovid finally came up and also stopped. Itzik looked at the boy and pointed at him. Feivel nodded his head, confirming that Dovid was his son.

Itzik, a short, broad-shouldered man, had a round head and a long black and gray beard. The features of his head seemed to have been chiseled in stone. His cheeks were laced with red veins. His glance was sharp, but with a smile. Itzik wore high, soft leather boots, a short sheep fur coat with a collar, and a high astrakhan hat that made him look taller than he was.

The front of Itzik's house was narrow. On part of his land, he had an area for parking wagons; behind his house was a stable for horses. The parking area was fenced in, with a double gateway. The gate was bolted shut, so as to make it difficult to open. Two steps led to the entrance, on which an olivewood *mezuzah* had been affixed. Many Jews made it a point to pass Itzik's home just to kiss the *mezuzah*, the townsfolk believing that Itzik had bought it from an Eretz Israel emissary and had paid a lot of money for it.

From behind the house, on the left where the fence ended, two youngsters emerged.

"There go my jewels," said Itzik with a contented nod of the head.

The young men walked fast. When they came to the stable, the older one looked over the fence.

"Feivel of Zharnovtze," Itzik told his sons. As they reached the street, both said, "Good Shabbes, Feivel," and they remained standing with their backs to the fence. For a while they looked at one another.

"How are you?" the older one asked Feivel.

"Thank God," Feivel answered, and nodded. Dovid also stood by, staring at the young men.

Sholom and Baruch, his younger brother, looked alike. They were both strong-looking fellows with well-shaped limbs; Sholom had the beginnings of a dark beard.

"Baruch, will you let me have a ride on your horse?" Dovid asked. Everyone looked at Dovid. "Will you, Baruch?" Dovid did not let up. Baruch remained silent, looking at his father and at Dovid's father.

Sholom grabbed a single hair on his straggly beard. Both Baruch and Sholom wore well-fitted sheepskin coats. They also wore slim-fitting, fashionable boots. There was heard a long, drawn-out whinnying of the horses in the stable.

"The horse has run away," Dovid said, half asking and half stating it as a fact.

Itzik pinched Dovid's cheek. A blue mark remained on it. Dovid rubbed his cheek.

Feivel took Dovid by the hand.

"We have to go to pray."

Itzik nodded to Feivel. He and his sons followed Feivel. As they walked, Itzik tried to stay in step with Feivel, but his steps were smaller than Feivel's, and he had to hurry to keep up. All the sons followed behind their fathers.

"The farmers are selling out?" Itzik asked Feivel. "Like they do every winter. The rich ones keep their animals, the poor ones sell them," Feivel answered.

Itzik looked around him. The street was empty. Then he stopped in front of a wooden hut two doors from his. Everyone else stopped as well. Itzik looked into the window; later, he went over to the gate, which was closed. He knocked twice on the gate with his fist; it shifted on its hinges. Later, it opened abruptly and a little blonde boy, dressed in dark blue and with boots and a knitted cap, ran out of the house, and after him came a tall, broad-shouldered fellow with a round black beard and large black eyes. "Good Shabbes, everyone," he said. He smiled and looked around. The little boy ran to Itzik. "Good Shabbes, Grandpa," he said, and laid his head on Itzik's leg.

Itzik caressed the little one's head with both hands, and muttered, "Joy of my life!"

Azriel, Itzik's eldest son, the child's father, was similar in appearance to his brothers; he was even taller and stronger than they. When it came to ordering from the local tailors and cobblers, the family would order together.

"Children, time to go! It's Shabbes," Itzik ordered, and began walking.

Feivel followed Itzik and kept in pace with him.

"Shmiel, come," Dovid said to the little boy, and he ran after his father. Shmiel ran after Dovid.

Feivel turned to Itzik, and glancing to the side to be sure no one else was able to hear him, asked, "Are you preparing for any family celebrations?" "With the Almighty's help," Itzik answered. "I have sons to marry," he added proudly.

"Please God, I hope to visit Matye in Obziv tomorrow," Azriel said loud enough for the entire family to hear.

"Shabbes," Itzik reprimanded him for discussing business on the holy day. It became quiet. They kept walking; only the snow could be heard under their boots.

A few huts down, on the same side of the street, Itzik stopped, and everyone else did likewise. Baruch hurried to open the gate and enter a wooden house that was wide and low, its walls already curved with age, as if it were pregnant. The roof sloped down to meet the snow on the ground. The house was one of the first to be built on the street.

Baruch did not remain long. A short, elderly man appeared at the gate, walking with slow but steady steps. Baruch followed behind him.

"Good Shabbes, Father," Itzik said, his gray eyes looking at his old father.

"Good Shabbes, Lazer," said Feivel.

"Good Shabbes, Grandfather," the grandchildren greeted him.

"Good Shabbes, good Shabbes, children," the old man answered them, and the greetings carried down the street. The old man's gray eyes looked curiously as he inspected one after another, his gaze resting on the two children who stood together. The old man had a squat face and broad forehead with a long, pointed beard. The white in the beard had already turned yellowish with age.

"Come here, my children," said the old man, summoning the boys with a crook of the finger. The boys went over to him. Lazer bent over and pinched Shmiel's cheek. His old gray eyes became transparent; they sparkled. Shmiel ran away from him in fear. Itzik followed him with his eyes. Dovid moved to one side. Shmiel ran over to his father, resting his head on his father's knee to keep himself from crying. "Silly boy, Grandpa Lazer loves you," his father said to Shmiel, and took him by the hand. The boy's eyes looked doubtful.

Dovid stood to the side. He waited to see what the old Lazer would do now. "Is this one yours?" Lazer asked Feivel, pointing with his finger at Dovid. "My oldest," Feivel told Lazer. "Fine, fine, may there be many more," the old one said and began walking. Everyone followed him. The old man wore a long sheepskin coat. You could just see the soles of his boots. The coat had a broad black collar and he wore a fur hat pulled over his forehead. The sleeves of his coat were wide and long, much longer than his hands. The sleeves, too, were of fur. From time to time, the old man stopped in his tracks and looked around at everyone accompanying him. His family filled the narrow street, he was the leader of his tribe! The snow crunched under their feet.

"How is Mother?" Itzik asked his father, eagerly stretching out his head for an answer. The grandchildren also listened attentively.

"Your mother wants to invite you for *kiddush*. She has prepared an excellent stuffed *kishke*," Lazer answered his son. The old man walked on, waving his hands about as he went, as if he were in a hurry.

"A fatty *kishke*?" Itzik asked, rubbing his hands in anticipation, as if he could already taste it.

"Of course, of course," Sholom answered his father.

"Feivel!" the old man called him. Feivel went over to him.

"You must also come," the old one said.

"Thank you for the invitation, Reb Lazer," Feivel said. A little later, Feivel added, "But on Shabbes a Jew must be with his wife and children." Feivel slowed down until he was abreast of Itzik.

The old man was again in front. The cold became drier, the day brighter; all of them walked on in silence. They came to the end of the street. The last two houses on either side were single-story but of brick, with flat roofs covered with bitumen, like the houses on Cracow Street.

The old man stopped, his sons and grandchildren behind him. From the courtyard on the left, which was fenced with a broken-down wooden fence, the sound of prayer could be heard. This was the synagogue of the butchers and animal traders.

"Good Shabbes!" the old one said to Feivel.

"Good Shabbes, good Shabbes," Feivel shouted.

Sabbath in a village. Engraving after pillati in a Polish illustrated magazine, 1876.
Courtesy of Beth Hatefutsoth Photo Archive, Tel Aviv.

The old man slowly entered the courtyard, followed by his sons and grandsons.

"Good Shabbes!" Shmiel shouted from afar to Dovid. His voice was tremulous, like the sound of a finger being pulled across a violin string. As he walked along the path, he kept looking back at Dovid.

The path was lower than the street, and in between the two ran a broad, frozen ditch. Dovid bent his head and ran after his father. When he reached the icy ditch, he stopped, measuring the distance across.

"Dovid!" Feivel said angrily, crossing the ditch.

Dovid spread out his arms to keep his balance, and slid along the ice. When he came to the end, he jumped back onto the street.

The street was filled with worshippers; it looked as though Jews were coming from every open gate and every byway. In this section were to be found most of the *batei medrash*, the *shtiblach*, and the main synagogue. The road here had been completely trodden down. Long icicles hung from the roof, and the frozen window panes reflected the light.

The town lay in deep snow and was cut off from the world. But in it the Jewish Shabbes reigned supreme. "Good Shabbes! Good Shabbes!" they wished one another. Their Sabbath greeting echoed through the cold air, like the fluttering of passing birds.

Dovid walked slowly with the stream of people and looked at the throng. Meanwhile, his father came over. Now they walked together, father and son, the old and the young; all types were in the procession, some tall, some short; some thin, and some fat; some walked slowly while others seemed in a hurry. As they walked it looked as if there were a single long chain, linking one to the other—a chain of Jews all moving in one direction. As they walked, their coats would sometimes open, showing the fringes suspended from the corners of their *talleisim*. They were all wearing either *shtreimels* of fur or velvet or simpler gleaming satin hats worn over satin caps. Jews of all ages and of all shapes and sizes moved slowly, majestically. They were going to *daven*, and on the way they gazed in admiration at the world that God had made.

There were also women in the throng of people on their way to the synagogue; they, too, wore their special Shabbes jackets and coats, under which you could see long dresses. Some women had *shaitels* that were combed straight back, while others had *shaitels* with a part in the middle. Grandmothers walked to the synagogue carrying *siddurim*. A large number of the grandmothers wore kerchiefs on their heads. They had their hands thrust deep into their sleeves, clutching their thick *siddurim* with Yisrael commentary under their arms.

Two tall, slim women, both in their thirties, Malka and Machtyeh, walked in the middle of the road. Malka wore a coat with pleats, her hands in a muff through which she clutched her *siddur*, with corners that were mother-ofpearl. A gray shawl was wrapped around her head. The corners of the shawl rested on her shoulders.

Machtyeh wore a beige coat and brown high-heeled shoes. She held her *siddur* in her hands. Her cream-blue flannel shawl was tied under her chin, the comers hanging in front. The two women had been friends ever since their childhood.

"That's the way it is," said Malka, and immediately added, "a very difficult winter." "Don't complain," said Machtyeh. Malka's blue eyes stared at her. "No sooner have I made the bed when it's needed again. As soon as one gets better, the other one gets sick," Malka insisted. "Don't exaggerate," Machtyeh told her. A little later, she said, "This year, thank God, my children have kept well. I'm waiting for a little sunshine. We have to warm the bones."

Her oval, full face smiled as she looked down. The women walked at a little distance from the men, but the children running around under everyone's feet linked the two groups together. The children ran back and forth, sliding on the ice, and every so often a boy would break off an icicle that hung from one of the roofs. One boy moved over to the side, formed a snowball, and aimed it at another boy.

Dovid, waiting for his father to catch up with him, made a snowball as well; then, making sure that his father could not see him, he threw it at a black crow on the roof. The crow flapped its wings and flew off, screeching as it did so. Dovid went back to his father and walked along at his side. A few steps further on, Feivel took Dovid by the hand.

"The authorities are around," said Feivel to his son. In the middle of the street, approaching them, was the police commandant of the town, a tall, thin man, his ascetic, elongated face divided by a long, thin nose. He walked without looking around. Only the eagle embossed on his nickel badge, which he wore on his dark blue cap, seemed to be looking at everything and everyone. Dovid managed to get a look at the lacquered peak of the officer's cap.

"Good Shabbes," said every Jew as he passed. The commandant, though, remained silent, not returning the greeting. His thin, blue-veined eyelids were almost closed. He looked angry. His uniform, with its nickel buttons, was encircled by a wide leather belt from which hung a narrow, long sword. He held the sword by the handle and pointed it ahead like a cane. He walked quickly, as if in a hurry. He seemed to want to get away from this part of the street.

Feivel moved to the right. He and Dovid hurried into the street leading to the synagogue. When they got to the corner, Feivel dropped Dovid's hand.

Dovid raced ahead. The street was very narrow. On one side of it a wooden fence marked the boundary of Michael's coal cellar. On the other side were two narrow, two-story gray houses. The windows and walls of the houses, built in a row, looked from afar like lamps that had been put out. At the end of the street was semicircle of level ground where the snow had been trodden down and was smooth, as if it were one solid piece of ice. Bunched together around this area stood a number of narrow one- and two-story homes, their roofs sloping and pointed, as though each was trying to climb up the other. The sun, looking like a metal disk, peeped over the roofs of the houses. In the middle, set apart from the houses, was the small *beis medrash.*

The *beis medrash* was a red brick building with houses on both sides. Its red bricks shone in the light. The long semicircular windows divided up its long walls, as though summoning the worshippers to enter. The wide door was open. The long glittering icicles hanging from the windows seemed to light up the interior of the building.

"Good Shabbes! Good Shabbes!" voices called out. The voices seemed to merge into a single sound that echoed through the open area around the *beis medrash,* where the people thronged. Shadows merged and then separated; every so often a figure would separate itself from the crowd of people to stand out darkly against the snow until it was swallowed up by the open door. A group of young boys was busy rolling a large snowball under the windows of the *beis medrash,* another group stood around a half-finished snowman.

Feivel walked faster, and as they passed the children playing he took Dovid by the collar and led him straight into the *beis medrash.* Dovid did not resist but did look around to see what the children were doing.

The light in the front lobby was gray. Much snow had been tracked in on everyone's boots, and now it lay on the stone floor, trodden down by countless feet. Worshippers milled around the inner door that led to the *beis medrash* proper. Whenever the door opened, the lobby was momentarily lit up. White icicles like goats' beards hung from the wash basin.

Feivel let his son go through the door first, touched the *mezuzah* with two fingers, kissed the tips of his fingers, and closed the door behind him.

12

OVERNIGHT, the air in the *beis medrash* had cooled, but it was still thick with the musty odor of old tattered books no longer usable and stored in the *beis medrash* to be disposed of later by burial. The white lime on the walls seemed to sweat, while the windows were all covered with ice. The ice on the windows was not smooth, but shaped itself into fantastic designs created by the thawing and freezing. The brass lamps hung from the brown wood ceiling. They were green with age. The color on the tiles covering the stove had worn off, and the cracks within the tiles looked like thin black veins.

The *beis medrash* was packed with Jews, relaxed and at ease, the joy shining from their faces. A hum of voices filled the air, like bees swarming about a tree in bloom. Jews with their *talleisim* draped around their shoulders and others with the *talleisim* pulled over their heads stood with eyes closed and swayed back and forth. Fragments of prayer drifted into the air, some from deep adult voices, others in the thin piping tones of children: "Lord, I love Your abode . . . ," "His name, 'Sovereign,' is proclaimed . . ." "The Lord is one . . . " A man close to the stove recited, "The Lord is with me and I shall not fear," and remained wrapped in thought.

Feivel started moving through the *beis medrash*, Dovid following him; they pushed their way through the crowd of people. As he passed the stove Feivel touched the lukewarm tiles, coming to a halt at the table where the Jews placed their coats.

Feivel unbuttoned his coat, hunched his shoulders, and pulled the coat off, laying it on top of the pile of clothes on the table. The corners of Feivel's *tallis*, which had been contained within his coat, now fell away, the four *tzitzis* remaining hanging in front and at the back.

"Time to start praying."

Feivel laid Dovid's coat on the pile as well. Then he started pushing his way through the crowd once more, followed by Dovid.

Feivel led his son to the table where they customarily sat. The long narrow table stood opposite the door. Around both sides of the gray table, Jews sat at their devotions. The table was old, the wood decayed. "Good Shabbes" said Feivel quietly, and nodded to the men sitting around the table. Feivel gave Dovid a gentle nudge, showing him where to sit.

Dovid sat down at the vacant seat at the head of the table. He bent down and placed his *siddur* on the table. Feivel also bent down, and stretching out his hands, opened his *siddur* and turned a few pages. "*Ma Tovu*—How goodly are your tents O Jacob, your dwelling places, O Israel . . . " began Dovid. His thin voice echoed in the chamber. Dovid swayed back and forth over his *siddur* as he prayed, but not to the same rhythm as the others who sat at the table. His lips moved fast, as if he were swallowing up the words. One could not hear the words he was saying, but one could hear the sound. Feivel observed his son. He turned away and looked at the congregation praying. He saw a large number of heads moving back and forth. Individuals with their *talleisim* over their heads paced back and forth. Some rubbed their hands together, others cracked their knuckles. Their lips moved incessantly. The murmur became louder. One could hear the sound of prayer echoing throughout the *beis medrash*. The words seemed to rise and swell over the heads of the congregants. The sound reached the ceiling and bounced right back, filling the *beis medrash*.

The door at the back kept opening and closing. More and more came to join the prayers. Each time the door opened, a burst of cold air accompanied whoever entered, but the warmth in the room soon swallowed up these cold gusts.

At this point, no *chazan* officiated at the reading desk. Its square shape was now very visible, the wood showing signs of great age. The two candlesticks on the reading desk, like the two columns supporting the *Shivisi* sign, were green with age and covered with wax.

The blue velvet *paroches* on the Holy Ark now seemed in the daylight to have been made of two different colors, the lower part darker, the upper part lighter. The two embroidered lions on the *paroches*, with their bared fangs, guarded the Mogen Dovid as before, within which was embroidered the word "Zion." But now the lions seemed to be smiling at the congregation.

Pesach the *shammes* stood with his elbows leaning on the *bimah*. His right, shorter foot was stretched as far as it could go so that he could stand up reasonably straight, but as a result his left shoulder drooped down. The front *tzitzis* of his *tallis* lay on the green velvet cover of the *bimah*. His *tallis*, yellowing with age, hung on his back like a stretched out curtain.

Every so often, the crowd shifted as someone else came in and made his way to his place. Some prayed in one place, while others paced back and forth. A mixture of voices, like an untrained choir, filled the *beis medrash*. Every so often one voice emerged above the others, then subsided back into the swell. Now the sound began to die down and there was a hush. Here and there an individual was swaying back and forth, but nobody was praying out loud.

The air became thicker, the warmth now suffused with the smell of old books, *talleisim*, and clothes. Men settled down in their places. After the preliminary prayers, recited individually, had been completed, the congregation was ready to recite the formal morning prayer.

Pesach the *shammes* stood on one foot and clutched the *bimah* with both hands. His head moved slowly, his eyes roved about the congregation: he sought the *chazan*.

A tall man with his *tallis* over his shoulders, Motte Blecher, moved among the crowd. He walked hesitantly, putting down each foot carefully, as if not trusting himself. The people moved aside, making room for him to pass. When he came close to the reading desk, Motte stopped. His large black eyes looked around. His long black beard was laced with silver. The Jews waited. Motte pulled his *tallis* over his head, and with careful steps moved over to the reading desk. He seized the two front corners of the reading desk with both hands, bent over, the top of his body covering the reading desk, then stood up straight, thrusting his head back, and sang out loudly: "*Mizmor shir*—A song of the dedication of the Temple, by Dovid . . . " His voice was mellow.

Joyfully, the entire congregation repeated the first words of the psalm and went on to read the rest themselves, taking pleasure in the communal act of worship, swaying back and forth with great emotion. The contact between the *tallis* and their clothing was like that of a summer breeze in an open field of wheat. The people all prayed, some hunched down with their heads between their shoulders and others moving their entire bodies. Here and there an individual said this or that word or phrase aloud with great emphasis.

A large head covered with a snow white beard moved to the front. The man walked with his hands stretched out in front of him. His thick gray brows seemed to block out his eyes. He seemed to be plowing through the crowd. His eyes were glassy; all he could see was darkness and light. As he walked, he prayed. The men in front of him moved to one side, allowing him through. Suddenly, he stopped. He had seen a shadow. The shoulder of one of the congregants was blocking him. "No evil will befall you," the man prayed audibly from Psalm 91 as the one blocking him moved aside.

The large man shuffled through the hall with his hands in front of him. He was afraid that he might fall. His eyes were vacant; his lips murmured as he walked. Two youngsters, of almost the same size, followed behind him. Each one held on to one of the back *tzitzis* of the man's *tallis*. "All by himself he caught the two thieves and brought them, bound, into the town," one of them declared. "No, three," said the other, objecting. The people crowded round to gaze at the two boys. "Idiots!" a thin man hissed at the children. Others also expressed their disapproval.

Pesach the *shammes* stood on his short foot. With one hand he held onto the *bimah*, while with the other he banged on it to silence the disturbance. "Praise the Lord, sing a new song to the Lord . . . ," the *chazan* said in a raised voice, one that carried above the others. The echo of the banging on the *bimah* accompanied his voice.

The two youngsters ran off and were swallowed up among the crowd.

Dovid pressed his feet against the wood boards that ran around the bottom of the table. With one hand he held onto the corner of the table and with the other he leaned on his open *siddur*. He stood up and remained standing, curious to see what was happening outside. Feivel placed a hand on his shoulder and gently pushed him down. Father and son continued with their prayers.

Motte the *chazan* coughed. He pulled his *tallis* over his head again and recited aloud, "Lord, in Your surpassing power, Magnificent One in the glory of Your Name, eternally mighty, awesome in Your awe-inspiring deeds," and here his voice swelled with pride, "the Sovereign, presiding upon Your throne, lofty and exalted."

Having completed the introductory psalms, the *chazan* was now ready to begin the Sabbath morning service proper. Switching to the unique Shabbes melody, he sang out, "*Shochen Ad*—The Eternal, the Exalted and the Holy One—that is His name . . ." The congregation repeated the words after him, each individual singing them in his own fashion.

As he recited the next words to himself, Motte's lips moved quietly. A little later, he sang aloud the beginning of the next passage: "In the assemblies of the myriads of Your people . . . ," and all the congregants began to recite the entire passage.

The people all stood and waited. The air in the *beis medrash* was somewhat thick, hanging like a mist over the heads of the people. The gray light of a winter day penetrated frozen window panes and reflected on the whitewashed walls.

The *chazan* stood with both feet together and then bowed forward. He straightened up and began the words of the *kaddish* prayer: "*Yisgadal veyiskadash*—May His great name be aggrandized and sanctified . . ." The Jews' faces were tense, their eyes sparkling. They appeared to be lost in wonder, although the familiar words of the *kaddish* were simply being recited by the prayer leader on this holy Sabbath day.

It was quiet in the *beis medrash*. The people all waited. They heard the sound of heavy boots marking time in place. Those at the table stood up; the *chazan* pulled the *tallis* over his head, bent down at the waist, and straightened up somewhat, his back still curved. As he did so, he closed his eyes and proclaimed, "*Borechu*—Let us bless the Lord who is to be blessed." The people all bent forward, and the *chazan*, along with the congregation, responded, "Blessed be the Lord who is blessed for all eternity."

The murmur gradually died down like a flame. The worshippers again began their swaying movement. A little later, a number of deep voices finished the paragraph directly before the *shema* prayer with the words "who has chosen Israel His nation in love." Soon, more joined them, the echo of the words reverberating in the *beis medrash*, like voices coming from afar. They all turned their heads to look at the *chazan* who was now about to pronounce the *shema*, the declaration of the Divine unity. The warm, moist air lay over their heads. The blue on the *paroches* was now discernibly lighter. Motte the *chazan* pulled his *tallis* even more over his head. He let his hands fall by his side, closed his eyes, and called out, "*Shema Yisrael*—Hear O Israel, the Lord is our God, the Lord is One." He stretched out the last word until he was breathless. Vizileh the baker, a short, thin man whose skin seemed to have been pulled taut on his bones, stood up. Vizileh's real name was Wolf-Ze'ev, but he had been dubbed Vizileh by the townsfolk. The children of the town even had a refrain they would sing about "Vizileh falling into the batter" at night. Everyone in town knew the story of how Vizileh had fallen asleep and had indeed fallen into a large tub of dough.

Sabbath

The *chazan* bent over the reading desk before again straightening up. He stretched his head forward, as if craning to read from the open *siddur*, and introduced the next section to be recited by all: *"Ezras Avoseinu*—Helper of our fathers . . . "

"And their children after them," Vizileh added aloud, repeating the prayer text. He was in a hurry, and one only heard the slurred ends of his words.

Vizileh would bring *challahs* each week for the *se'udah shelishis*, the communal third Shabbes meal, which would be eaten in the *beis medrash* just as night was about to fall and Shabbes was about to end. When a person from a different town needed a place to stay overnight, Vizileh would lodge him in his home and in the morning would bring him a *tallis* and *tefillin* so that he could pray. Vizileh was also known to drop off loaves of bread at the homes of people in dire need.

He tossed his head back, as if trying to rid himself of any alien thoughts that might ruin his concentration on the words of the prayers, but his *tallis* slipped off his head, remaining on his shoulders; his thin face, with its white, curly beard, looked as though it were chiseled in stone. He closed his eyes and exclaimed, "You are first and You are last, and except for You we have no king to redeem and deliver us." Vizileh sensed the quiet around him. He opened his eyes.

Pesach the *shammes* gave a bang with his fist on the *bimah*. He hunched his shoulders so that his short foot remained hanging. Then he looked all about him, as if the bang he had just given had scared him as well. The long hall was full. The whitewashed walls shimmered and sweated. The air was musty, hanging over everyone like a cloud. The dim pale light that managed to penetrate the frozen window panes shone on the people at prayer. The blue of the *paroches* was now a darker blue. From time to time, a voice rang out, interrupting the quiet. The last words of the silent *amidah* prayer, "Hamevarech es amo Yisroel basholom— . . . who blesses His people Israel with peace," were heard in the silence. One of the congregants cleared his throat.

One man raised his two toil-lined hands to move the *tallis* from his head; the man took a deep, audible breath.

Feivel took three steps back, marking the end of the *amidah* prayer. He waited a while and then returned to his former place. But he remained standing, at the same time glancing at his son. Dovid's *siddur* was closed, his finger between the pages; he was staring at the window. The men stood and waited. Their large, sad eyes were now at peace, their work-lined faces at rest. The *chazan* pulled the *tallis* over his head again and took a deep breath. With both hands he clutched the reading desk, and began his repetition of the *amidah* prayer out loud: "My Lord, open my lips and my mouth will declare Your praise."

13

THE LIGHT in the *beis medrash* had a gray hue. The rays of light that suffused the room were pale and weak. In the mix of light and shadow, the heads of the congregants were bright, as if lit up. The light from the windows fell on the Holy Ark. The Holy Ark looked as though it were moving. The edges of the *paroches* swayed back and forth, pushed by the currents of air in the room. The blue of the *paroches* was deeper, the bared fangs of the lions engraved on the *paroches* seemed to be sharper than before.

Soft footsteps could be heard. Shachna, a short, fat man with a long coat going down to the heels of his boots, walked over to the Ark. Shachna had short hands and small feet.

The congregants on both sides made way for him to pass through, dividing into what looked like two separate groups of people. Owing to Shachna's short size, the *tallis* he had pulled over his head trailed on the floor behind him. His long, white, pointed beard had a yellowish tinge, as if rusty. A pair of steel glasses rested at the very tip of his nose, and the left side of the glasses was tied to his ear with a piece of string. The frames themselves had been worn down by constant use, and his eyes looked over the glasses. Shachna, a teacher, was the only one in the entire *beis medrash* who wore a pointed *shtreimel*, indicating thereby his membership in the *Chassidic* sect of the Alexander Rebbi. The older boys studied Talmud with him, for he was a great Torah scholar. His sessions with the older students took place in the large *beis medrash*, but he preferred to worship with the common people in the small *beis medrash*. By long custom, he was traditionally given the honor of opening the Holy Ark.

Motte the *chazan* took out the great folio prayer book and placed it on the reading desk. He opened the *siddur*, turning the pages until he found the place. In the meantime, Shachna remained standing by the Ark. He pulled his *tallis* over his head, kissed the edge of the *paroches* with his finger, and pulled it aside in readiness for the opening of the Ark. "*Vayehi bineso'a*— When the Ark was to take its journey, Moses would say . . ." Motte sang out. At these words, Shachna seized hold of the two doors of the Holy Ark and pulled them open. "*Vayehi bineso'a* . . . " the congregation echoed and all bent forward. They straightened out again. Together with the *chazan*, they intoned, "*Boruch shenosan*—Blessed is He who gave the Torah to His people, Israel." The echo resonated in the space of the open Ark.

Shachna bent and leaned into the Ark; the shadows within seemed to come up to meet him. He closed his eyes, kissed the first Torah scroll of the row lined up in the Ark, then embraced it with both hands and lifted it out of the Ark. This particular scroll had a black velvet mantle, the black having faded with age to a grayish color. The Mogen Dovid on the mantle was embroidered with gold thread, and inside it was inscribed God's Ineffable Name. The Torah scroll seemed to dwarf Shachna as he carried it, walking erect and moving his lips in silent prayer. From time to time, he would utter a word or phrase aloud in his hoarse rumbling voice.

The congregants swayed back and forth in prayer, their faces somber. In their mind's eye, they could visualize the Levites in the great desert thousands of years earlier carrying the Holy Ark, with the pillar of cloud behind them and the pillar fire in front clearing every obstacle in their path so that the whole world lay open before them. The door to the *beis medrash* opened. The cold air rushed in to mix with the overheated air in the hall. Yankel the *feldsher* had arrived wearing long, black striped trousers, shoes with laces and rubbers over them, a well-fitted black coat with a fur collar, and a black hat with a crease in the middle.

"*Brich shemei*—Blessed be the name of the Master of the Universe . . . " intoned the *chazan,* reading from his *siddur,* and the congregation read the entire paragraph after him.

Shachna walked on majestically with the Torah scroll in his arms, taking small, measured steps. The congregants moved aside, making way for them. Shachna's eyes were closed; he could sense, from the pressure of bodies around him, which way he should walk. The Jews bowed slightly as the Torah scroll passed, each of them reverently touching the mantle with one of his *tzitzis* and then kissing that *tzitzis*. From time to time, there was a denser group, and more hands stretched across to be able to touch the mantle.

Hurriedly, Yankel pulled a black silk *tallis* bag from his pocket, took out his *tallis,* and crammed the bag back into his pocket. He spread the *tallis* out and threw it over his shoulders, at the same time reciting the blessing. The *tallis,* narrow and with blue stripes and a silver neckband, was small on him—the local Jews referred to it as "the Prussian *tallis,*" Prussia being notable for religious laxity. Yankel prayed along with the rest of the congregation. His black, thick eyebrows stood out from his clean-shaven face.

The crowd that had come to kiss the Torah mantle as it passed now began to disperse, each person to his own place, and the room seemed to become cooler. The men stroked their beards or rubbed their hands together, resting after the morning *Shacharis* service, resting and waiting.

Motte the *chazan* now stood up straight, his task completed. He seemed to have grown taller. He kissed his *siddur,* and with both hands pulling his *tallis* back off his head, moved away from the reading desk with a sigh.

From all sides one heard the cry of *"Yasher ko'ach! Yasher ko'ach!* — May your strength increase!" the customary greeting to a person who has done well. The cry echoed back and forth.

Yaakov the *ba'al koreh* walked bent over to the *bimah,* holding the decorative fringe around the top of his *tallis* as if straining under a heavy burden. He and Shachna stood on opposite sides of the Torah scroll, preparing it for the reading. The *ba'al,* tall and lean, stood in contrast to the diminutive Shachna. Pesach the *shammes,* the beadle, his *tallis* worn haphazardly over his shoulders, limped down the steps from the bimah.

Yankel the *feldsher* moved into the crowd, people nodding to him and moving aside to let him through. Yankel was a village healer whose father, Velvele the *feldsher,* had practiced his art of letting blood before him. In an emergency, when someone in town became very ill, they would call for Yankel. He smiled back at everyone, moving to the head of the table and sitting down next to Feivel. Dovid, seeing Yankel, moved away immediately, his child's eyes showing fear, and he looked up at his father.

The *ba'al koreh* on one side and Shachna on the other, stood opposite one another on the *bimah.* The Torah scroll, written on pieces of parchment sewn together, was attached to two wooden staves, the *atzei chaim.* Now the *ba'al koreh* and Shachna each held one of these staves as they rolled the Torah scroll to the correct place for the day's Torah reading. The Jews stood about and waited, each hoping to be called that day for the Torah portion. During the course of the reading, eight men would be called up, each to "read" a portion of the Torah, although, in fact, the portion was read out aloud for him by the *ba'al koreh.* Being called up to a "reading" was considered a singular honor. Each man in the *beis medrash* was afraid to look the others in the eye as all waited. Some nervously fingered their *tzitzis,* while others rubbed their foreheads, as if trying to remember something.

The *ba'al koreh,* his broad forehead wrinkled, now had moved the Torah scroll to the place where the reading for the day would begin, but out of re-spect for the Torah scroll he touched it with his *tzitzis* rather than his bare hand.

Shachna peered around at the congregation.

Finally, he announced, "Let Reb Asher, son of Ephraim the Kohen, as-cend." All held their breaths. It became very quiet. The silence, though, lasted only a few moments, and then people began stirring again.

A large head gave a shake; the deep-sunken eyes under the prominent cheek bones looked around in astonishment. Asher did not believe that Shachna could have meant him. He pushed his shoulder forward and tore himself from his place; those near him cleared a path.

Asher seized hold of the wooden barrier around the *bimah* and climbed the steps leading to it, hastily taking his place before the Torah scroll. After pulling his *tallis* over his head, he took hold of one of his *tzitzis*, placed it on the spot to which the *ba'al koreh* was pointing, and then kissed the *tzitzis*. Standing up straight, he closed his eyes and began to recite the blessing: "*Borechu*—Bless the Lord, who is blessed," he said slowly, concentrating on the meaning of the words. "Blessed is the Lord, who is blessed for all eternity," the entire con-gregation answered. When Asher had completed the blessing before the read-ing of the Torah, all answered "Amen," and the *ba'al koreh*, bending over the Torah scroll to squint at the text, began reading aloud: "Jethro, the priest of Midian, the father-in-law of Moses, heard . . . " As he read, he swayed back and forth as if walking to and fro, his head bent over the Torah scroll. Asher stood ramrod stiff throughout the reading, as if afraid to move, his big eyes fol-lowing the words on the parchment as they were read by the *ba'al koreh*.

The people listened, their faces showing a barely discernible smile of their satisfaction. Each of them had shed his weekday woes; all were at the far-off desert with the Israelites, whom Moses had freed from captivity, and they were thrilled that Jethro had come to Moses and brought Moses' family with him. They saw before their eyes how Moses told Jethro all about God's might and witnessed Jethro's amazement at the wonders that the Jewish God had wrought. The congregants were as deeply involved in all this history as if they themselves were actually taking part in the events.

When the first portion had been read, Asher gripped both *atzei chaim*, closed his eyes for better concentration, and recited the concluding blessing, thanking God for having chosen Israel and for having given them the Torah. He opened his eyes, looked at Shachna, and gave him a smile of deep appreciation for the honor granted him.

Shachna clutched the *bimah* with both hands, as if he was leaning on it, and looked around at the people. He turned away and called out the next name: "Let Reb Shraga-Feivel, the son of Meir the Levite, ascend." A thrill passed through Feivel's body; he trembled, his eyes sparkled, and a grave expression came over his face. Those near him moved away to let him through.

Feivel was alone in his glory. With one hand he gathered together the borders of his *tallis*, and with the other he took Dovid's arm and pulled the boy over to him. Feivel took long strides, Dovid running behind him. And now he was standing in front of the Torah scroll, his *tallis* hiding his face. He pulled the upper part of the *tallis* over his head and covered his son on the left side with the lower part.

Dovid, feeling his father's hand on him, closed his eyes and leaned his head on Feivel. Feivel, taking the *tzitzis* fringe with his right hand, touched the place where the second Torah portion would begin. As soon as he had recited the opening blessing, the *ba'al koreh* went on with the reading, Feivel swaying along with him, his eyes following along the text being read word for word.

After the reading was over, Feivel seemed to lean backwards; then he stood up straight, closed his eyes, and recited the concluding blessing.

"Let Yosef, the son of Yerucham, ascend," announced Shachna.

A thin man standing at the side shook himself and put out his hand, as though wanting to swim through the crowd. Feivel turned his head, and his *tallis* slid off, resting on his shoulders. Dovid crawled out from under the *tallis*, gazing at his father with his small black eyes. Feivel gathered together the two front *tzitzis* of his *tallis* and seemed to inspect them, rather than look anyone in the face.

Yosef, son of Yerucham, was in a hurry but was only able to take small steps. When he ascended the *bimah*, he closed his mouth and seemed to hold his breath. Feivel moved to one side, and he and Dovid left the *bimah*.

Yosef bent low over the scroll, his lips almost touching the letters. The black letters on the yellowed parchment seemed to blind him for a moment; then he stood up straight, closed his eyes, and recited the blessing. His hands were at his sides.

The *ba'al koreh* proceeded to the third part of the weekly portion, and when he had read it, Yosef recited the concluding blessing. As he finished, the people, who had been motionless until now, seemed to relax, moving this way and that. They were glad that Moses had sent Jethro on his way.

"Let Reb Akiva-Tzvi, the son of Matisyohu, ascend." For a while, the silence in the *beis medrash* seemed to freeze. Jews turned their heads and looked up; no one moved from his place.

"Nu! nu!" There was an impatient cry from a few people: "Harsh-Kiba!" This name was the more familiar Yiddish equivalent of Tzvi.

Harsh-Kiba shook his head back and forth, as if he had just been woken up. With both hands he gathered together the corners of his *tallis* and started pushing his way through to the *bimah*. He had not realized that Shachna had called him up. Among the locals, he was known as Harsh-Kiba the wagoner, the one who drove people to the train station. He was the only cart driver who attended the *beis medrash* rather than the cattle dealers' synagogue. Harsh-Kiba pushed his way through the hall, and Feivel, who had not yet moved far from the *bimah*, moved aside to let him through.

Dovid seized his chance. Glancing at his father to make sure that Feivel was not looking, Dovid darted away, and within a few seconds was swallowed up in the crowd. Feivel actually saw Dovid running out, but did not call him back. Instead, he returned to his place, where he remained standing.

Harsh-Kiba almost ran up to the *bimah*, as if someone was chasing him. There he remained standing, pulling his black cloth jacket about him, and then, after rubbing his eyes with his stubby fingers, he pulled his *tallis* over his head.

The *ba'al koreh* moved closer to the table and bent over it. The upper part of his body seemed to be suspended above the Torah scroll as he took his *tallis* and moved it over the parchment. His brow furrowed as he began reading: "On the third month, after the Children of Israel had gone out of Egypt . . . "

The people moved about restlessly, as if they were about to make their way through the desert where the Israelites had been and were approaching Mount Sinai.

Harsh-Kiba stood by the Torah scroll with his hands folded, his feet together, not moving, his small eyes sharply focused on the lines of text being read so as not to miss a single word.

Shachna laid the palms of his hands on the table and rested his head on his hands, being too short to lean on the table. This time he did not need to look around for someone to call up; he knew exactly whom he would call for the special honor of the fifth reading. Shachna let his hands drop, turned to the spot where the person whom he had selected was standing, and called out: "Let"—the rest he said in one breath—"Reb Dov Ber ben Mordechai ascend." Those standing behind the *bimah* hurriedly made way for him to pass. They all looked at Dov Ber; he was well-known in the village. Dov Ber occupied the other half of the same wooden house where Yaakov the *ba'al koreh* lived. He and his wife and their three children sewed shirts; his two sons traveled from one market town to the other to sell the shirts.

The two neighbors looked at one another and remained silent as they stood in front of the open Torah scroll. Dov Ber stretched out his foot and bent over the Torah scroll.

Between the stove and the *bimah* stood two men, both following the reading in the *chumash* that they shared. "Dov Ber has a letter from his son in

Eretz Israel," whispered the one on the left to his neighbor; he looked back at the *chumash*.

The others who were nearby crowded around the two men, pricking their ears to hear further details.

"The Jewish National Fund gave him land and he has become a farmer," the man said even more quietly, and again looked into the *chumash*. The people around them remained standing open-mouthed, their eyes sparkling. They seemed to see before their eyes the "land flowing with milk and honey."

The *ba'al koreh* had now reached the account of the giving of the Torah on Mount Sinai, pronouncing each word distinctly and with great deliberation. The people seemed to hold their breath; they stood and looked at one another as though entranced, hearing and seeing the momentous events unfold before them. The *ba'al koreh* continued with his reading; Mount Sinai was covered with smoke. His voice trembled; a large vein throbbed on his throat. The people drew closer together, as if standing at Sinai, and held their breaths.

Dov Ber sighed with satisfaction as he looked around him. His left eye, which had squinted from birth, seemed to be laughing with joy as he glanced at the congregation. He bent over, touching the spot on the parchment with his *tzitzis*, which he then put to his lips. He closed his eyes as he recited the concluding blessing, his black beard held high above the scroll.

The tension relaxed; the people stood waiting. Most knew that they would not be called up for the sixth *aliyah*. Only one of the more prominent members of the synagogue would receive this portion; the few people in this category were seated at the second table, and they coughed discreetly as they waited to see which of them would be chosen.

Shachna held on to the *bimah* with both hands and looked down, but he saw and heard everyone.

"Let," he called out joyfully as the hall became deadly still, "Reb Dov the baker, son of Yaakov, ascend." He looked around, as if teasing the congregation.

All the muscles in Vizileh's face seemed to be working. He squinted and pulled his *tallis* over his eyes, hiding his face from the crowd, and hurried over to the *bimah*.

Those who were in his way moved to the side; they looked at him and grinned. Those who had thought they might be honored with the coveted sixth *aliyah* looked down and seemed to withdraw within themselves.

From outside, from behind the wall, there was a commotion of some kind; everyone looked to see what was happening, but the windows were covered with frost. Zalman the tanner, a tall, broad-shouldered man, looked through a corner of the window that was still clear. He used his fingernail, reddened from the tanning, to scrape some more ice off the window pane. The children outside had finished their snowman. Feivel stood on his tiptoes, craned his neck to see, and then turned away chagrined. He noticed that the children had placed a stick in the snowman's hand.

Vizileh touched the scroll with the edge of his *tallis* and then put his lips to the *tallis*; his toil-lined hands seized the *atzei chaim*. Then, swaying back and forth, he recited the blessing in a somewhat muffled voice.

Yaakov the *ba'al koreh* bent over the Torah scroll and began to read in his strong, clear voice: "The Lord came down upon Mount Sinai to the top of the mountain and called Moses" (Exodus 19:20).

Between the stove and the bookcase stood a group of men, arrayed in *talleisim*, everyone wrapping his *tallis* about himself in his own fashion. One wore his like a toga, another had it folded over his shoulders; others had their *tallis* wrapped around their heads like a kerchief, with the fringes hanging over their shoulders.

"They say that the new commandant is not among the worst," one of them remarked. "Who cares?" said another man, tall and broad-shouldered, his hand resting on the bookshelf. "He can cause trouble!" a third chimed in, his voice emerging from the *tallis* thrown over his head. "Esau!" said the second man, using the epithet traditionally applied to those who hate the Jews.

"I am the Lord your God, who took you out of the land of Egypt, from the house of bondage," the *ba'al koreh* continued, as though playing with the words. His head was tilted to one side. The group near the stove was now more attentive; each hurriedly adjusted his *tallis* as they fell silent, each listening to the words of the *ba'al koreh*, who swayed forward and then straightened up. He craned forward and continued his reading: "Remember the Sabbath day to keep it holy."

Vizileh bent over the Torah scroll; the words of his concluding blessing came out in a rush, indistinctly, as though he was chewing his moustache. His teeth were small and narrow, as if they had been filed down.

Shachna stared at Vizileh's work-stained hands, which together clutched the wooden rollers. Again, Shachna did not need to look around; he knew whom he planned to call up.

Those people who had thought that they might possibly be called up earlier now tried to ensure that no one would look at them. Those sitting around the table bent down even lower and peered around as though waiting for someone.

A few of the men had their eyes closed and shook their heads, as if continuing the reading; others stood looking around, and there were those who had pushed their *talleisim* off their heads so that they could see who would be called next.

Vizileh finally released his grip on the *atzei chaim.* He looked around him, as if just waking up. Shachna placed his left hand on the table of the *bimah* and thrust his head backward. Yaakov the *ba'al koreh*, tugging at his beard, bent over, as if peering into Shachna's mouth.

"Let," the word was dragged out, "Reb Menachem, son of Moshe, ascend," Shachna announced. His hoarse voice could be heard throughout the hall.

A thin man who seemed to be swathed in his *tallis*, sitting in the right-hand corner of the hall, turned around and looked out from beneath his *tallis*; his path to the *bimah* was clear. The people had already moved aside and were following him with their eyes.

As soon as he ascended the *bimah*, Menachem let his hands fall to his sides; his *tallis* opened up. Menachem had a thin, long face, a broad arched brow, a long black beard with some white hairs in it, and thick, gray sideburns. He was the only tile manufacturer in the village. Everyone knew that he was among those who arose each midnight to recite the special lamentations for the destruction of the Temple and the exile of the Jewish people. Menachem closed his eyes and recited the opening blessing, then stood motionless, not swaying at all but saying the words quietly to himself word for word. His face looked like a mask, only his eyebrows and cheekbones being prominent.

"Feivel!" Grunem called quietly. "In my village, there's a chance of a little business deal," Grunem added, still quietly, as it letting Feivel in on a secret. "Shabbes! Shabbes!" Feivel, angered, muttered, and dismissed Grunem with a motion of the hand. Grunem looked down ashamed, pulled his *tallis* over his forehead and edged to the side. He did not want anyone else to notice what had happened.

Shachna looked all about him, seeking someone to call up for *maftir*, the last *aliyah*, and with it the prophetic reading of the week, the haftorah, but he was in no rush. He had not yet decided whom to call. He took note of all the important people who had hoped to receive an *aliyah* earlier. Those who felt themselves fit for the task glanced away or buried their heads in their *chumashim*. None of them was sure that Shachna meant him, but they did not want the others to note their eagerness.

"The blind one," Shachna mumbled. The words were swallowed up in his beard. He was evidently referring to Ber the Big One. But the *ba'al koreh* placed his left hand behind his ear, as though straining to hear, and winking with one eye, announced playfully: "Let Reb Shachna, the son of Tzaddik, ascend." In his voice one could sense that he was having his fun. He let his hands fall down and his *tallis* began slipping off him. He stood looking around at the congregation. Shachna bent his head down and his mouth opened, a round face expressed amazement, and his gray eyes danced and sparkled. Those who had been hoping that Shachna would call them up took a deep breath. They bent down and hurriedly pulled their *talleisim* over their heads. Shachna shrugged his shoulders. His *tallis*, now spread out, hung on him like a shirt. He moved close to the reading desk, gripping the rollers tightly. He drew himself up tensely, closed his eyes, turned his head a few times, and recited the preliminary blessing.

"You shall not make for Me silver gods nor shall you make golden gods for you," the *ba'al koreh* read. He completed the reading; Shachna closed his eyes and again held the *atzei chaim* as though hanging on them, and then, thrusting his head back, he recited the concluding blessing. As soon as he ended, he placed his hands on the *bimah* and squinted at the people. He did not use his glasses, which remained on his forehead. The men near the *bimah* moved away. None was interested in having Shachna notice him now that the main honors had been distributed. Many people even turned away, holding their breath.

Shachna leaned on his hands and began to say something. His glasses slipped off his forehead, but he grabbed at them before they fell. Finally, he announced: "Let Shmuel, son of Yaakov, ascend." "Shmiel! Shmiel!" a few people repeated, as if chasing after the man. Immediately afterwards, Shachna announced: "Let Shraga, son of Elimelech, ascend." Shachna called the two, one after another, in accordance with the custom, but he dashed off the words, half into his beard. The two men who had been called started moving forward. Both were tall and strong, and both walked swiftly, as if wishing to meet one another. Shraga came first, and as he walked he pushed the *tzitzis* of his *tallis* under his *gartel*. He continued with his hands crossed over his chest.

Both men, Shmuel and Shraga, held the railing of the *bimah* as they climbed onto it. When they were on top, they came to a halt, briefly staring at one another. Yaakov, the *ba'al koreh*, moved away to the far end of the *bimah*. Shmuel moved over to the Torah scroll, wrapping his fingers tightly around the *atzei chaim*. He then bent his knees, and as he straightened up, picked up the Torah scroll, holding it vertically. His sleeves slipped up to his elbows, and his hands remained uncovered. Shraga looked at Shmuel nervously, afraid that he might lose his balance while holding the Torah scroll. "And this is the Torah which Moses placed before the Children of Israel . . . " Yaakov recited, and everyone else in the *beis medrash* echoed him.

Shmuel clung tightly to the Torah scroll while he held it aloft, showing it to the congregation.

"It is an *aitz chaim* to those who cling to it, and those who support it are happy," the people continued. They swayed back and forth and from side to side, as if they wished to run over and grab the Torah scroll. A number of them lifted their hands in the direction of the Torah scroll, their *talleisim* remaining hanging like wings.

Shmuel moved backwards, holding the scroll as if it were a child; Shraga followed after him very carefully, as if afraid that he might step on Shmuel's toes. Shmuel, feeling the bench behind him with his feet, finally sat down. Shraga, whose task it was to close the scroll tightly and bind it, spread his feet and shook himself; he wanted to test that he was standing firmly. His work-trained, thick hands were not used to work of this kind.

Shraga raised his head; Yaakov the *ba'al koreh* bent down, and picking up the cloth *gartel* used to bind the Torah scroll and the velvet cover of the Torah scroll, handed both to Shraga. Shraga took the two items; he placed the Torah cover on the bench and used the cloth *gartel* to bind the Torah scroll. He took one end of the red velvet strip, which was already green with age, and tucked it between the two parts of the rolled up Torah scroll. He then started, slowly and carefully, to wind the *gartel* around the Torah scroll. When he came to the end of the *gartel*, he tucked it under the previous loops and then placed the velvet covering over the Torah scroll. As he finished, he bent down to see if it was firmly bound and the scroll covered. This done, he touched the covering with the tips of his fingers, put his fingers to his lips, and sat down next to Shmuel. Shmuel also brushed his lips against the Torah as he eased it against his breast.

Yaakov now bent down. He reached underneath the table on the *bimah* and brought out a *chumash*, which he then proceeded to open. Leather strips of old binding hung from the *chumash*. Shachna shifted his *tallis* on his shoulders and closed his eyes. There was a rushing rustle of people in movement throughout the hall as people settled down in their seats for the reading of the haftorah. Shachna recited the blessing: " . . . Who chose good prophets, and looked favorably upon their words which were uttered in truth." He then bent over the table, pushed his hand underneath the *chumash*, and held the left cover; his glasses slid down to the tip of his nose; he squinted at the text and proceeded to read from the sixth chapter of Isaiah, "In the year of the death of King Uzziah . . . " As he came to the end of the chapter, Shachna closed the *chumash* with one hand and with the other lifted the table cover. He placed the *chumash* inside and took out the *siddur*. The *siddur* had been printed in Lublin and included the prayers for the entire year. The edges of the pages were gray, while the blue cloth in which the volume had been bound was already a darker color, the sharp corners of the pages worn away by constant use. Shachna placed the *siddur* on the table, touched a finger to his lips to moisten it, and began to turn the pages with the moistened finger until he found the place. "Have mercy on Zion, for it is the source of our life," he shouted out, twisting his head from one side to the other.

Shmuel and Shraga sat and looked at Shachna. From time to time, Shraga's bottom lip trembled, but each time he overcame it, compressing his lips as though he were swallowing a word. Shmuel held the Torah scroll close to himself, checking to see that he was holding it properly.

Shachna finally tore himself away from the *siddur*, raised his head, and concluded with the words, "Blessed are you, O Lord, who sanctifies the Sabbath."

14

Yaakov, tall and thin, stood once again at the reading desk and began reciting the additional prayer service reserved for Sabbaths and holidays. *"Yekum purkan*—Let help arise from Heaven . . . "* he sang out in a voice that carried over those of everyone else. A hum of voices murmuring the prayers echoed through the hall. Fathers and grandfathers all looked for their *siddurim*; they could all find their way in any *siddur*, a skill they had already learned in *cheder*, but some of the words were still strange to them.

Feivel closed the *siddur* and removed his *tallis*, placed his *siddur* inside it, and then placed both on the table. He turned up his collar and hunched up, as if already feeling the cold. He went over to the door. " . . . With all of Israel, their brethren, and let us say Amen," a loud voice cried out, accompanying Feivel. In the meantime, Yaakov walked over slowly to the reading desk and recited aloud the memorial to the martyrs, concluding, " . . . the Lord resides in Zion." He then placed a hand on the desk. Shachna closed the *siddur* and began walking very slowly and deliberately with the Torah scroll. He bent over, closed his eyes, and clasped the Torah scroll in both hands. Straightening out, he clutched the scroll even more tightly.

The door opened again and Feivel came back into the synagogue followed by Dovid, whom he had just brought back inside. Dovid's cheeks were red with cold, as were the tips of his nose, ears, and fingers. Dovid looked down at the ground, straightening his cap on his head as he walked.

Grunem moved aside to allow Feivel and Dovid to pass. "Come by after *havdoloh*," Feivel said to him, and went on. "Your kingdom is an everlasting kingdom," sang out Yaakov. As he recited the words, he banged both fists on the reading desk, so that one of the wax-encrusted candlesticks jumped and a light metallic ring reverberated through the hall. Yaakov remained leaning on his fists, his head rocking back and forth over the reading desk.

Dovid turned the pages of the *siddur* with his thumb, searching for the place. Feivel spread out his *tallis;* with both hands he took hold of the upper border of the *tallis* and threw it around him once again. His lips began murmuring the prayers. Feivel glanced at his son, pointing with his finger to show Dovid the place the *chazan* had reached.

The door kept opening and closing; worshippers who had been outside in the street came back now, hurrying for the *Musaf* service; every now and again there was the snapping sound of a *tallis* being shaken out and put on.

"A song of Dovid," Shachna recited, opening his eyes. He turned around slowly, as if he was about to turn a full circle where he stood, then he walked slowly away from the *bimah.* Behind him, Shachna carried the Torah scroll back to the Ark; he walked with his eyes closed but knew the way. His *tallis,* flying in the air as he walked, seemed to carry him along like the sail of a ship in the wind.

Those with children brought them over. The children stood on tiptoe to reach the Torah scroll, and as it passed them they kissed the outer mantle. The men, for their part, touched the mantle with the corner of their *tallis* and then reverently kissed that corner. Often, after reaching out for the Torah with their *tzitzis* in their hands and then laying their *tzitzis* over their closed eyes, their hands trembled.

Feivel pulled his *tallis* over his head, leaving his face uncovered. He thrust his head back and forth as if it was a separate entity rocking over his body.

After returning the Torah scroll to the Ark and then pressing the tips of his fingers over his lips, Shachna closed the doors and pulled the *paroches* across. The tongues of the embroidered lions now seemed smaller and they seemed to be smiling at the people.

The *chazan* pulled his *tallis* over his head and recited the *kaddish:* "May the name of the Holy One, blessed be He, be exalted and sanctified . . . " It was quiet in the hall as the congregation recited the silent *amidah* of *Musaf.* Jews were busy pulling their *talleisim* over their heads, allowing the folds to fall back over their shoulders; they untied their *gartlach* and retied them more tightly about their waists; those who had been sitting now stood up. The tables, which could not be seen before because of the bodies pressed around them, were now visible. Fathers looked around to check that their children were near at hand; the children stood bent over their *siddurim*. The older boys swayed back and forth, like their fathers, but being unmarried wore no *talleisim*. In that gathering, they stood out as though they were in a state of undress, naked.

The silent prayer ended and the *chazan* grabbed the two ends of the border of his *tallis*, closed his eyes, and chanted, "I shall call in the name of the Lord; ascribe greatness to our God." Then, placing both palms on the reading desk, he swayed back and forth. The cold outside forced its way through the cracks and overcame the silent atmosphere within. The warm breath of those assembled in the *beis medrash* seemed to chill under the onslaught; you could feel the fear of God in the air, the greatness of their faith, as the assembled Jews, enclosed within the four walls and under the wooden ceiling of their sanctuary, beseeched their God. Those who had completed their prayers took the required three steps backward—leaving, as it were, the divine presence—and remained standing for a few moments before moving back to their former places. Every so often another person was heard uttering aloud the final words of the silent prayer: " . . . and peace be upon all of Israel, and we will say Amen."

The *chazan* coughed, moistening his dry throat. He bent over the reading desk and said, "I shall call in the name of the Lord; ascribe greatness to our God," and added, "Our Lord, open my lips, and my mouth will declare Your praise."

When the *chazan* reached the blessing for the resurrection of the dead, "Blessed are You, our God who revives the dead," all sighed. The *chazan* coughed. "Let us revere and sanctify You," he continued, reciting the first words of the *kedushah* passage. The entire congregation moved; those whose *tallis* had not been on their heads hurriedly pulled them over, and all responded with the words, "Holy! Holy! Holy! is the Lord of Hosts . . . " At each

Jews returning from the synagogue on a winter Sabbath, Chorostkov (Khorostkiv),
Eastern Galicia, 1917. Photograph by G. J. Willie. Courtesy of Beth
Hatefutsoth Photo Archive, Tel Aviv, and G. J. Fogelson.

mention of the word "holy," they lifted themselves on their tiptoes, as if trying to draw closer to the Almighty.

The *chazan* bent down and then straightened up, continuing the prayer. Finally, he concluded the *kaddish* with the words, "He who makes peace on His heights will grant peace to us and for all of Israel, Amen."

"Amen!" the whole congregation chorused, and all expressed their appreciation to the *chazan* for having led them in prayer. They could breathe easily once more, as though a burden had been lifted from them.

The *chazan* tossed his head, clutched at the borders of his *tallis* with his hands, and proclaimed, "It is our duty to praise the Master of All . . . " All began reciting the *aleinu* prayer. Some of them were already sidling up to the table where the coats had been piled up. Some used their *gartel* to tie their *tallis* around them, hurriedly pulling their coats over the *tallis*, and moved toward the door.

"Good Shabbes! Good Shabbes!" The doorway was jammed full of people; the cold from the outdoors forced its way inside; waves of cold and hot air collided. Feivel held Dovid by the hand and pushed his way through the door. The two breathed in the fresh, cold air. The entrance was bright with the light reflected from the snow outside; the lobby itself was a dirty gray, with mingled light and shade.

"Good Shabbes! Good Shabbes!" The area around the *beis medrash* echoed musically with the two words. The dry cold carried away the echoes on the wind. Feivel walked swiftly. The wind blowing through the folds of his *tallis* seemed to spur him on. Some of his *tallis* stood out of his collar at the rear; one corner hung out at the back. The sky was gray; a frozen mist blocked out the sun; the morning frost had still not melted. Jews went home to eat.

15

THERE was a sudden crack, as if someone had just pulled the cork out of a bottle. Yachet, who sat at a bench away from the table, lifted her head; the sharp odor of burning coal filled the house; the glowing coals in the stove burned more brightly.

The two little girls looked up at their mother and returned to their game. In the corner, between the two walls behind the door, Zlotele and Rivkele were playing. They had marked off six squares in the wood shavings on the floor. Taking turns, each closed her eyes, placed her foot inside a single box, and asked the other, "Am I OK?" When her sister told her she was doing fine, she gingerly stepped into the adjoining box. Each tried to make it across the squares and reach the corner. Whenever anyone stepped on one of the lines, she had to start all over again.

Yossele stood to the side and watched his sisters playing.

The glow of the fire cast shadows on the metal sheet covering the stove, its heat slowly warming the house. The cold retreated before the hot air, and the room itself became lighter as the sun penetrated through the windows.

Yachet rested. She heard the blood flowing in her veins, experienced a lovely sense of tiredness, heard the quiet around her. She glanced at the children, rested her fist on the table, leaned on her elbow, and then slowly stood up.

Yachet gathered together the coffee mugs from the table, placing one inside the other. She held the crooked tower of mugs in one hand, and with the other she picked up the empty coffee pot by its handle. She carried the dishes over to a basin, straightened up and walked, with slow careful steps, to the alcove. She stood poised at the entrance, giving herself up to the feeling of fullness and lassitude. She opened the door and entered. It took her a little while to adjust to the dim light. The darkness within blurred her vision; a sweet smile spread over her face; her eyes were moist, her long lashes fluttered. "Zlotele," Rivkele said suddenly, and remained standing with a foot inside one of the boxes. The sisters looked at one another and became aware of the quiet in the house. From the alcove, they could hear the sound of beds being made up.

"Enough! Mommy will soon come out. She'll be angry," said Zlotele. She got up and went over to the table. Rivkele followed her silently. Yossele turned his head, following his sisters with his eyes. The girls were restless in the empty room. "Let's go and look out of the window," said Zlotele to her sister. "Fine," answered Rivkele. The girls picked up the bench between them and carried it to the window; Yossele followed them. "Come," said Zlotele. She bent over and took Yossele's hand, then picked him up and seated him on the bench. The girls then sat down on either side of him, resting their elbows on the window as they looked outside. Rivkele pressed her nose against the window pane. They stared out. Yossele also wanted to see what was happening. The door to the alcove moved as Yachet came through it. She looked at the children, her oval face calm and peaceful. The girls did not turn around but remained staring through the window. They sat quietly: neither of them wanted their mother to call them right then.

"Tfu, tfu," Yachet spat twice to ward off the Evil Eye. She walked over to the pail in the corner, removed the hand towel covering it, and tied the towel around her waist. She wanted to keep her Shabbes dress clean. Yachet poured in half a basin of water and placed the pots inside it. Then she placed the dirty plates and silverware inside the basin and began to wash them out.

The windowpanes were frosted over, and one could not see through them. Only at the spot where Rivkele had laid her head had the frost melted. Elsewhere, the frost on the window panes had shaped itself into flowers and twigs.

"The people are coming home from the synagogue. The policeman is going around and telling the *goyim* not to beat the Jews. The policeman has a sword and a big black dog," Zlotele told her sister, as if she had seen all of this through the window.

Rivkele moved her head away from the window.

"On Shabbes the Jews stay home and the *goyim* don't beat them."

Every time Yachet dipped the dishcloth into the water, a plop could be heard. The house became warmer, the air milder. Yachet washed the dishes, straightening her back from time to time; she was somewhat too tall for the low basin. The drops of water glistened like tears on her long, thick fingers.

Yachet shook the water off her hands into the basin, picked up a towel, and dried the plates. As she finished each plate, she placed it on the bench.

When Yachet finished drying the plates, she hurriedly dried off the silverware. As she dried each fork and spoon, she placed it on the pile of plates. When she had finished this, she did not squeeze the water out of the towel, as on Shabbes this activity was considered to be work. She poured the water from the basin into another pail, placed the wet dishcloth in the basin, and returned the basin to its place. She took off the towel she had wrapped around herself, wiped her hands on it, and put it away. After straightening out her *shaitel*, she bent down, her face flushed, and with both hands picked up the pile of plates and carried them away. A little later, she turned to the children.

"Children, what can you see?" she asked them.

"We're going for a walk," said Zlotele, not tearing her face away from the window.

Yachet smiled, her eyelids trembled. She glanced sideways at the stove; the light of the fire burning inside it could be seen through the cracks in its side. Yachet looked around the room and started walking slowly, putting down one foot and with the other gently spreading the wood shavings evenly over the floor. On Shabbes, she did not use the broom to sweep.

"See, Rivkele?" Zlotele asked, and without waiting for an answer she began to relate what was happening outside: "Yankel the *feldsher* is walking along with his medicine case; it looks as though someone must be sick." Her eyes were wide open with fear. Rivkele pressed her nose even more closely to the window so she could see the healer with his box.

Yachet remained standing by the bed. She smoothed out the eiderdown so that the bed would look rectangular. She twisted her head even further, as if resting it on her shoulder, and looked at the other bed; it looked smooth and even.

The children looked through the windowpane and remained silent; both girls were afraid of Yankel. They were afraid to look around. "Let's go and play ball and jacks," said Zlotele suddenly, and she got up from the window. "On Shabbes?" Yachet asked her.

Yachet went over to the stove. Both girls turned their heads, following their mother's movements. Yachet now bent down, took the chopping board and chopping knife from behind the stove and a towel from the cupboard, and she placed all on the table.

Zlotele jumped down. She picked up Yossele and placed him on the floor. Rivkele watched her carefully; she, too, jumped off the bench. Zlotele thrust her shoulders forward as though preparing to run, but she remained standing.

"Bring back the bench," said Yachet to the two girls. They picked up the bench and returned it to the table. Yachet used the towel to wipe down the chopping board and knife. The chopping knife had many uses: Feivel would use it for breaking up coal, splitting tinder or wood, or banging in a nail. The children stood gaping at the sharp implement; it was off-limits to them. "I'm going to prepare the onions," said Yachet smilingly to the children. She wanted to calm them down. The little girls felt more at ease. Yachet went away to the cupboard and the girls quietly followed her. With one hand, Yachet took down a tin basin, dented on one side. With her other hand she picked up two hard-boiled eggs and placed them in the basin. Reaching under the shelf, she brought out three large onions and then placed the little pot containing salt inside the basin. She then went over to the alcove. "Mommy is going to get the meat," said Zlotele, nodding her head.

Yachet came out of the alcove, leaving the door open. She walked past the children and over to the table. The children joined her there. Yachet placed the basin on the table. Zlotele lifted up her brother and sat him down on the bench. The sisters again sat down on either side of him.

"Children, sit quietly," Yachet told them, her eyes smiling. She placed the piece of meat on the chopping board, picked up the two eggs, and broke one egg against the other. A loud crack was heard as the shells fell away.

Yachet moved her hands over the basin. With her fingers, she finished peeling the eggs, the shells falling into the basin. Yachet placed the eggs on the chopping board and, holding the knife firmly, sliced the eggs with short rapid movements.

Both little girls strained to look; the yellow and white pile on the dark chopping board grew bigger. Yachet placed the knife back on the chopping board.

The little girls looked on, amazed at their mother's dexterity. Yossele stood up on the bench to see, while his sisters held him.

Yachet stretched out her hand to pick up an onion. It was round and had long dried roots attached to it, like a scraggly beard. Yachet cut off the roots and removed the outer layer, which crackled like paper. She did the same with the second. The third onion, which was oval and long, was much larger than the first two. Its peel had already cracked by itself, and it came off easily.

Yachet again picked up the chopping knife. She wished the blade was longer. She picked up an onion and cut it up; onion rings fell on to the cutting board and the pungent odor filled the air. Yossele leaned on his sister's shoulder and sat down again. The children looked at what was happening, their eyes sparkling. Yachet's eyes turned red. She sliced the second onion, which was plump and was green at the stalk, as though it still had some growing to do. She severed the green stalk and then placed both onions on the cutting board. This onion was harder. As she cut, the slices started building up on the cutting board and the smell became even sharper. The children sat with their eyes tightly shut. Yachet's eyes were watering, but she was already into the third onion; as she sliced it, the rings fell into her hand. She wiped her eyes with her sleeve and looked at the children. Their eyes were watering also, the tears running down their cheeks. Yachet moved to the other side of the table. In one hand she held the knife, which shone with moisture, and with the other she took the end of her dress and wiped the children's eyes.

Yachet went back to the chopping board. Walking, rubbing her eyes with her sleeves a second time as she went, she began cutting up the piece of meat. She cut it lengthwise, pulling the knife toward herself. When this was done, she put away the knife, picked up the meat, and threw the meat onto the onion pile.

"Oh!" she sighed as she leaned backward, but she did not move away. With her hand, she picked up two pinches of salt, one after the other, adding them to the pile on the chopping board. She put away the salt pot and moved the bowl from the table. As she walked, she scooped up the onion peels, taking care not to let them drop. She did the same with the egg shells and then threw both into a pail.

Having wiped out the bowl, Yachet returned and placed it on the table. She then began chopping up the mixture on the chopping board. Yachet's right shoulder was raised. She pounded rhythmically with the chopping knife, but taking care that the blade never touched the chopping board. The children saw how the pile kept changing. One time, a few little bits of meat flew away from the chopping board, another time, the yellow and white pieces of the eggs spread over everything else, and another time, onion rings covered the board. The pieces on the board became smaller, and the chopping became more intense. The blade of the knife hit the cutting board, and from time to time Yachet used it to push everything on the board into a pile, and then continued chopping.

Yachet peered at the cutting board like a chicken looking at a bowl of water. Now she chopped even faster, as if in a hurry to finish. The pile was now a homogenous mass. Every time the knife came down, the cutting board itself sprang up as if dancing.

Yossele stretched out a hand. His other hand remained resting on the table. He wobbled for a second, as if losing his balance, but in the meantime managed to reach out and grab a piece of onion.

"No, you scamp!" Yachet shouted at him, but her eyes were smiling. Yossele pushed the hand with the onion into his mouth. His cheeks puffed out. The warmth permeated the house and was accompanied by the smell of the Shabbes onion. Yachet cleaned off the onion still clinging to the knife blade and put the knife aside.

The children sat and watched every movement of their mother. Yachet now used the knife to push the mixture into the tin bowl. Finally, she scraped the last few pieces of food from the cutting board directly into the bowl. Again using the knife, she smoothed the mixture down on the bottom of the bowl.

The children sat, fascinated. They wanted to see how their mother divided the mixture up into square portions.

Yachet put away the knife, holding the bowl in her lap; then she entered the alcove, carrying the bowl with the onions far away from her as if gazing with pride at her work.

Presently, she came out of the alcove, moving more slowly and carrying her own *siddur* under her arm. When she reached the table, she let her arm loose so that the *siddur* slipped onto the table. She did not want to handle the *siddur* while her hands were smeared with food.

She went to the basin, where she wiped off her hands, each finger individually. With two fingers, she adjusted her *shaitel* once more, then picked up the *siddur*, kissed it, and moved over to the window.

The little girls watched her. Zlotele sprang off the bench, picked up Yossele and placed him on the floor. Rivkele sprang down after her. All three ran over to their mother and stood around her in a semicircle.

Yachet opened the *siddur*, moistened a finger, and began to turn the pages. The edges of the *siddur*, where the pages had been turned, were yellow. She looked into the *siddur* and finally found the page; then, with her fingers, she wiped off the corners of her mouth and began reciting: "May it be Your will, our God and the God of our fathers, You great and strong and revered God, that You may be filled with compassion for us, for Your sake and for the sake of the holy Psalm and the divine names mentioned there, and for the sake of its verses, words and letters, and because of Your holy name."

The children stood with their hands down and looked at their mother in awe. Yachet's face was aflame, her brow wrinkling and then unwrinkling. She moved back to the *siddur* and continued: "'I will heap upon you blessing without end'—shine upon us the light of Your face and inscribe us in the book of sustenance and provision, this year and every year, us and all our families as long as we live." Yachet paused and remained deep in thought. She prayed, but her prayer was also praise. She raised the *siddur* even closer to her and went on: "And even if I am not worthy to pray for myself, and all the more so for my husband and children, I trust in You, who are gracious and compassionate to the thousands."

Yachet let her hands fall to her sides. Now she looked at the *siddur* from above, and raising her elbows, continued: "May my tears not be in vain, may Your strict judgment be tempered with mercy, and may the Redeemer come this year. May God grant that we and our children see the holy Temple rebuilt in our time. As for me, Yachet, the daughter of Fraidel, together with all pious women, may I live to pray there, through the merits of Sarah, Rebeccah, Rachel, and Leah, and may Mother Leah entreat for us and for all of Israel." Yachet touched the *siddur* to her lips. She closed her eyes and concluded: "Speedily in our days, Amen."

Yachet swayed back and forth, opened her eyes and moved the *siddur* away from her lips. The skin on her full face was taut. For a short time, she looked without seeing. Her mouth felt dry as she moved her tongue along her gums. She kissed the *siddur* and closed it, and placed it on the window ledge. She turned around toward the children and embraced them. They moved closer to her, pushing to sit in her lap.

Rivkele tossed her head to one side. "Mommy, let's all go into the street." Yachet was busy straightening the tablecloth.

"Yes, let's go out for a walk," Zlotele echoed her sister's idea.

"Children," their mother said, turning to them. She remained standing with her hands at her sides. "It is cold outside, so cold that your ears and noses will freeze," she warned them, crouching over as if she felt the cold. Now Yachet went over to the cupboard. She bent down and took out two *challahs*; then, closing the cupboard door, she picked up the *challah* cover and walked back to the table. As she walked, she said to herself, "On Shabbes, God makes the worst frosts." The children watched her and walked behind her.

"That's because on Shabbes the Jews are at home, they don't have to go out to buy or sell," Yachet continued. She held the *challahs* in front of her, as if they were resting on her bosom. At the head of the table, where Feivel would sit, Yachet placed the *challahs*, unfolded the *challah* cover, and covered the *challahs*. Yachet moved away a little from the table, inspecting the *challah* cover, which had on it the words "*Shabbes Kodesh,*" the Holy Shabbes, embroidered in orange thread.

"Thank God," she said, and went back to the cupboard again. The little girls ran after her. They wanted to hear what story their mother would tell them this time. Yachet moved the stack of plates to the end of the shelf, picked up the forks, the spoons, and the kitchen knife, placing these on top of the plates. She added the salt shaker and then picked up the whole pile. She went over to the table, talking as she walked. She taught the girls that when there is a severe winter with a lot of snow, the summer will yield plentiful crops. Carefully placing the plates on the table, she added, "The snow warms up the fields."

The mother pushed the stack of dishes into the center of the table. She placed the kitchen knife underneath the *challah* cover and put the salt shaker on the table. Picking up the silverware, she placed it next to the dishes. The metallic sound of the forks and spoons striking the table echoed through the room. "Mommy, tell us more," Zlotele pleaded. Her plea went unanswered; Yachet merely nodded her head as she walked around the table. As she did so, she pushed all the benches over to the table.

She looked at the table: it was ready. It was quiet in the room. The house was now pleasantly warm, the whitewash shining on the walls. The little girls looked at their mother, hoping that she would tell them more, but they could already smell the different foods.

"Mommy! Mommy!" Yossele cried out, reaching out to her with his hands; he wanted to be picked up. Yachet merely bent down, kissed him on the forehead, then straightened up, and with both hands patted the girls' heads. "Children, I am going out to bring the *cholent*. Zlotele, you are to see that no one goes near the fire," she said. "Today is Shabbes," she added.

Yachet covered her head up with her kerchief. She hunched up, as if already feeling the cold throughout her body. "My darling, look after the house," she told Zlotele as she went over to the door. She left the house, hurriedly closing the door behind her.

Yossele started crying. "Mommy, Mommy," he called out after her. His eyes filled up and a tear fell and hung on his cheek. Zlotele went over to him and rested his head against her body. "Be still," she hushed him, just as her mother had done earlier. Rivkele sat down and looked at her sister and brother. "Let's play," she said. She thought for a while and then added, "hide-and-seek." She pulled Yossele toward her. Yossele looked at Zlotele and calmed down. Rivkele did not move. All she did was look at her sister. Zlotele took Yossele to the corner, between the bed and the window, and let go of his hand. "My eyes are closed. Go and hide," she said, as she pushed Yossele away from her. She covered her eyes with her hands, rested her head on the wall, and asked, "Ready?" Yossele ran to the other side of the bed and hid in the corner. Rivkele crawled into the corner near the stove. She sat down and called out, "Ready!" Zlotele uncovered her eyes and began to walk around slowly, as if afraid to put her feet down. When she reached the center of the room she stopped and began searching everywhere with her eyes. Rivkele raised her head. "Rivkele!" Zlotele cried out. She ran over, touched the bed, and began counting: "One, two, three." Both Rivkele and Yossele crawled out of their hiding places. Yossele remained standing in the middle of the room. Rivkele went over to the bed. Now it was her turn to cover her eyes and stand where Zlotele had stood.

Zlotele took Yossele by the hand and whispered to him, "Crawl underneath." Yossele crawled under the table. "Ready?" asked Rivkele. Zlotele tiptoed over to the corner near the cupboard and crouched down. Rivkele heard her footsteps. She turned around. "Zlotele!" she called out, and touched the bed. Zlotele ran out and remained standing.

"You cheated. I don't want to play any more," she shouted at her sister. Rivkele looked at her, afraid. She had no idea what she had done wrong. Yossele sat under the table and looked on. "You first saw Yossele," she argued. She stood with hunched up shoulders, as if hiding before her sister. "No, I saw you first! I saw you first!" Rivkele screamed back, gesticulating with her hands. Yossele crawled out from under the table. The children remained standing, looking at one another, enveloped in the warmth of the house. They remembered that they were home alone. The low room now appeared to them enormous and empty. For a while the children stood, listening. Time seemed to go on forever, and the house frightened them. They anxiously awaited their mother's return. Rivkele remained silent. She stared at her sister; her glance was childlike, fearful. Zlotele, too, became uneasy. She glanced at the door and said, "Let's play catch." "Yes," Rivkele answered quietly and unwillingly, and began to run around the benches and the table, Zlotele chasing after her. Yossele stood and sucked his thumb as he watched his sisters racing about the room.

The girls chased one another. Whenever Rivkele passed a bench, she touched it with her hand. This way, she made it easier for herself to run. At first, the girls ran slowly, but later, after they had circled the table a number of times, they tried harder to get rid of their fear at remaining alone. They ran and breathed hard. Zlotele ran behind her sister but made no attempt to catch Rivkele. She did not want the game to end.

Suddenly, Rivkele came to a halt, out of breath. Zlotele, also out of breath, touched her. Rivkele rested her head in her hands; she was dizzy. When they had both caught their breath, Rivkele cried out, "Run! Now I'll chase you."

Zlotele started running. They ran slowly in the opposite direction. The light in the room was dim. Only by the window was the light brighter. The girls ran after one another but without any real effort. From time to time as they ran, a knee would give, but the child regained her balance and went on running.

The door opened slowly. Through the open door, along with the cold, Yachet pushed her way into the room, closing the door behind her with her foot. She stood there out of breath. She had been running, and her face was frozen; she looked to see what the children were up to. Her kerchief hung down on one side, and only the shoulder on the other side was covered. The tips of her ears were icy cold. She was carrying the pot by its handles with her two hands. "Shabbes," she cried out angrily. Yossele took his thumb out of his mouth. The girls remained standing, their heads bowed in shame. A little later they stared at one another with laughing eyes. They were overjoyed that their mother had returned. The wood shavings around the table had been pushed aside, and a path had been trodden round the table and benches.

Yachet went over to the stove and placed the pot with *cholent* on the very edge. She did not, heaven forbid, want the pot to be warmed directly by the fire. The girls smelled the delicious odor of the *cholent* and ran up to their mother.

Yachet bent over the pot, Her hands were warming up. Now she wanted to untie the string that held the paper cover on the pot. The children surrounded her. The bow had been dried out and it was difficult to untie. Finally, she was able to remove the paper along with the string. She sniffed and exclaimed, "I should be as fortunate as the *cholent* is delicious." The sweet, fatty odor of baked potatoes filled the house. Yossele began smacking his lips. Zlotele clutched at the edge of the stove, raised herself on her tiptoes, and looked into the pot. Yachet's nostrils flared. She quickly closed up the pot with the paper; then she stretched out her hands and embraced the children. The children snuggled up to her.

They heard heavy steps accompanied by lighter steps. Yachet pulled the kerchief from her head, hurriedly folded it up, and threw it on the bed. The kerchief landed on the edge of the bed, with one of the corners hanging over the side.

16

THE DOOR CREAKED, as if trying to resist, and finally opened. Dovid entered the room first, accompanied by the cold. The cold wandered about the room, as if trying to drive out the warmth.

Feivel remained standing in the open door, his head bowed, as if trying to peer into the room. Seeing his family standing around the stove, his black eyes sparkled. He raised a foot and put it down, as if leaping into the house, and banged the door behind him.

Both father and son looked bundled up in their heavy coats. Their ears and noses were red with the cold. Yachet looked up at Feivel. Without thinking, she pulled her dress over her and looked downward. The children fell upon their father, hanging on to the flaps of his overcoat. "Children, enough!" Feivel said, and slowly moved away from them. The children remained standing in the empty space, their hands hanging down.

Feivel and Dovid unbuttoned their coats, doing a kind of dance and waving their arms about so as to allow their coats to fall off their shoulders. Feivel turned around; his face shone. He was still wrapped in his *tallis*, and his beard lay on top of the *tallis*.

"Make *kiddush*, you must be famished," Yachet murmured to Feivel. Feivel nodded. He took two paces, stretched out his hands, removed the *tallis*, and placed it on a bench. He turned and went over to the water basin. Feivel picked up the ewer and dropped it into the basin. The splash of the water could be heard. Yachet pushed her shoulder through the entrance and hurried out of the alcove. She placed a pot on the table, and on it the dish containing the chopped eggs, meat, and onions. With three fingers, Feivel removed the *challah* cover and raised it up in the air. The cover bunched together like an umbrella. He put the cover aside, reached over, and covered the *challahs* with the palms of his hands. He closed his eyes, swayed back and forth over the *challahs*, and began reciting, "Remember the Sabbath day to sanctify it . . . " He raised both *challahs* up in the air, as if weighing them, and then replaced them on the table. He thrust the knife point into one of the *challahs* and turned the *challah* around against the knife blade. The *challah* was now cut in two. Taking hold of the lower piece, he cut off a slice. The rest of the *challah* lay on the table. He put down the knife, dipped the edge of the *challah* into the salt, and took a bite.

Zlotele picked up Yossele and sat him on the bench. Dovid and the girls sat down, each in his or her place, where they had sat on Friday night.

Yachet was bent over the table dishing out the food. Using a fork, she portioned out the fish, placing the portions in the dishes that she had prepared earlier. As Feivel chewed, he cut slices for the other family members. First he dipped a slice in salt and laid it down next to Yachet. He cut four more slices, placed them in a pile, and then proceeded to give one to each child.

Yachet stood up. For a short time, she inspected the portions on the different plates. Tipping the pot with fish at an angle, she emptied its contents into a single plate. After putting away the pot, she used the fork to share out the fish. She pushed the first plate over to Feivel; he looked at the plate and then at Yachet. Yachet looked down shyly, her eyelashes fluttering for a brief moment, and then she went back to portioning out the fish.

It was quiet in the house. All that could be heard was the metallic sound of the forks as they made contact with the plates. The two candlesticks, encrusted with melted wax, remained on their tray on the table, guarding the Shabbes table. Feivel looked at Yachet and bent over. He pushed the bench away from himself and stood up; then, raising his cap as if greeting someone in the street, he straightened his *yarmulke* underneath the cap and went into the alcove. The children remained sitting quietly; they knew why their father had gone into the alcove.

Feivel returned walking slowly and carrying the bottle of brandy. The glass on top of the bottle wobbled, ringing out. Feivel had left his cap in the alcove, and now wore only his *yarmulke* on his head. The girls smiled. The sound of the glass made them happy.

Feivel removed the glass from the bottle and placed it on the table. Then, removing the cork, he began to pour from the bottle into the glass. Feivel leaned back and tossed the liquid down his throat. Holding the button in the center of his *yarmulke*, Feivel raised the *yarmulke* a few times, as if trying to cool his head. A little later he broke off a piece of *challah*, placed it in his mouth, and swallowed it whole. He rubbed his hands together and smiled at everyone.

Feivel shook his head a few times. He bent over his *siddur* and began singing: "Blessed is God day after day; He will bring us deliverance and relief. Each day we bless You, O God. You will bring us joy and deliverance, and we will rejoice in Your name."

Dovid leaned closer to his father. One side of the bench went up into the air, and it remained resting on only two legs. Dovid clutched at the table. Feivel pushed the *siddur* over to him as Dovid picked up the tune: "He will raise up a horn for His people; all His followers will praise him." His alto voice echoed through the home.

"La . . . ," a pleasant, woman's voice hummed in the background. It was Yachet, singing along as she stood by the water basin. She was washing each plate separately. Zlotele stared at Dovid, then looked at Rivkele, and pretended to be conducting the singing with her finger. The girls opened their mouths and began to sing along with their father.

Yachet hung the towel over the basin. She picked up the dishes and forks she had just washed and leaned the pile against her stomach. She carried the pile back to the table, walking lightly and casually. Now Yachet spooned out the onion mixture to each one on a second plate. The children bent over the plates and began eating. Yachet picked up the empty bowl by its rim, bent down, and slid it into the pail. She straightened up and sat down on the bench.

After eating her portion, Yachet went to the stove; she bent over and removed the paper covering of the *cholent* pot. The paper had become brown and dry from the heat; as soon as the paper was removed, a cloud of thick smoke enveloped her. Yachet turned her face away for a short time and then again bent over the pot.

"A great *cholent*," she said, squinting, her eyes crinkling with pleasure. Taking hold of the rim of the pot with two fingers of each hand, she pulled the *kugel* out of the *cholent* and placed it on top of the stove. Yachet walked over to the table carrying the pot by its handles. She took her time and moved cautiously, as if carrying a glass of wine. Suddenly, she let go of one handle; the pot remained hanging by the other as she reached out for an old piece of cloth. Placing the cloth on the table, she put the pot down on top of it. The *cholent* steam spread, remaining suspended over the table.

Yachet took her spoon and thrust it into the *cholent*. With her other hand, she picked up Feivel's plate. Scooping out some of the stew, she ladled it into Feivel's plate. Every potato looked different, depending on how it had been peeled. Some looked square and others round, some long and others broad. The large potatoes, which had been cut in pieces, looked like pyramids and trapezoids. The pieces of potato became a single heap on the plate. Yachet looked at the plate and placed it in front of Feivel. The entire plate was filled to the brim with the brown, shiny potato pyramid. She pushed the other plates into the center of the table and began spooning out *cholent* to the other members of the family. The steam from the pot rose, and Yachet's face became moist; her skin shone. She remained standing with the spoon in her hand, checking to see that all were eating. Only then did she spoon out a portion for herself.

Feivel ate quickly. Each time he placed a spoonful of food in his mouth, he bent over the plate, wolfing down the food. His lips barely closed, and his jaw worked incessantly. He cooled down the hot potatoes in his mouth, chewed each bite, and swallowed it. His plate was already almost empty, with only a few potatoes still lying on the side.

The children ate hunched over their plates. They looked for small potatoes, which they would be able to put into their mouths whole. They picked up each potato with their spoons, lifted it up off the spoon with their teeth, and slid it into their mouths. The hot potatoes burned them. They hardly chewed the potatoes, but rather mashed them against their teeth. Each time they swallowed they stretched out their necks, as if choking.

Yossele held his spoon in one hand over the plate. Bent over, he nibbled at the potato in his spoon. Every so often he bent toward the spoon, took a bite and hurriedly swallowed it, as it was too hot for him. Yachet ate slowly. She took the large, cut up potatoes for herself. She had almost been sated by the smell alone as she had spooned out the different portions. The table with the family sitting around it was enveloped in the fatty, sweet smoke of the *cholent.* The rest of the room seemed empty.

Feivel laid down his spoon and pushed himself away from the table. He bent toward the table and stretched out his hands. With one hand he picked up the glass on top of the brandy bottle, and with the other hand he uncorked the bottle. He filled the glass again, leaned back, and drank with closed eyes. Yachet looked down: she did not want Feivel to see her smile. Feivel replaced the glass on the bottle. He clapped his hands once and then rubbed them together, as if he were cold.

Feivel took the *siddur* and placed it on the table in front of him. With his thumb, he opened it to the middle and began singing gustily. The melody was that of a march, and one could almost feel the steady rhythm of drums: bom! bom! bom! His voice was somewhat hoarse. Yachet gathered the plates together on the table. Whatever potatoes were left were returned to the pot. As she worked, she hummed along with Feivel. Picking up the pot with one hand, she carried it into the alcove.

Yachet came back in. She placed the pot with meat at the edge of the table, on the spot where the *cholent* pot had stood. Yachet reached deep into the meat pot with a fork and speared three pieces of meat. She reached over to Feivel's plate and placed the meat on it. She moved aside to check the portion. The small, long pieces of neck meat were black and dried out, their sides curled. Yachet placed a piece of meat on each plate. The children waited without moving from their places; they were tired, their eyes beginning to close. The warmth in the home was suffused with the smells of the different dishes. "Eat, children!" Yachet said. She remained standing with her hands folded in front of her; the fork in her hand seemed to be poised to repel any onslaught. Zlotele sighed and pushed out her stomach. Dovid had stopped eating. None of the children could manage any more. The spoons all lay on their plates. "Don't you want any more?" Yachet asked fearfully. Her large black eyes were now even larger. The little girls looked at their mother. Their look was one that begged their mother to allow them to leave the table.

"God's gift," said Yachet, and she added, "It's a sin to leave it over." She looked at the little girls: "Thank God," she said quietly a little later, and she, too, sighed. She was delighted that her children were full. The pieces of meat in the plates lay waiting for someone to touch them.

Feivel speared a little piece of meat and carried it over to Yossele's mouth. Yossele turned his head away. Yachet sat down with her feet at the side of the bench, as if she intended to stand up any moment. She plunged her fork into the pot, speared a small piece of meat, and withdrew the fork. She turned the fork over, and the curled ends of the piece of meat looked like the ears of some household pet. Yachet bent over the table and bit into the meat, holding the fork over the plate. She ate slowly, but with relish.

Yachet remained seated with her elbows on the table. She rose from the bench as if in a hurry. She leaned over the table and let go of the fork in her hand. "God willing, tomorrow you'll want to eat again," she said, stretching out her hands. She collected the meat from each plate and returned it all to the pot. She replaced each plate in front of its owner, as the girls looked at their mother. The girls' eyes were large, round, and sparkling.

"Those who didn't eat the meat won't have the *kugel*," said Yachet turning her head, teasing the children.

The children looked at one another and smiled.

"Yes, Daddy will have the whole *kugel* himself," she said as she left the table.

Yachet did not go to the stove. When she was still some distance away, she reached out to it and picked up the *kugel* pot. The coals in the stove glimmered; the flames had already died out.

"A *kugel* fit for a king," said Yachet.

"And you're the queen," muttered Feivel into his beard.

Both looked down. A little later, Yachet took her fork and glanced at Feivel. She poked the fork into the space between the pot and the *kugel*.

Dovid and the girls pushed their plates over to their mother, still holding them.

Yachet pushed the fork around the edge of the *kugel*. She peered into the pot to see how big it was and how she should divide it up. She picked up some of the *kugel* with her fork and placed it in front of Yossele, who promptly grabbed a handful and stuffed it into his mouth. Yachet added two more forkfuls of *kugel*, glancing at the little boy's plate and then at those of the other children. Having given Dovid his portion, she worked faster because she knew how much there was to share out.

Yachet conveyed the portions carefully to the different plates, taking care that nothing fell off the fork. Then, bending over the pot, she put two forkfuls of *kugel* on her own plate and looked to see what remained. She added a soft piece of crust to each plate. Then she picked the pot up with one hand, and with the other scraped off whatever was still left, emptying it into Feivel's plate.

The children ate slowly and looked into their plates, savoring each bite and looking for the raisins in the pudding. The warmth in the room was palpable as it mixed together with the odors.

Everyone at the table was lethargic from eating well. Feivel stretched out his hand and pulled the *siddur* toward himself, opened it with both hands, and turned the pages slowly as if each page weighed a ton. Suddenly, he stopped, relaxed, cleared his throat, and sang one of the *zemiros* of Shabbes: "*Yom zeh mechubad*—This day is honored above all other days . . . " The children joined in. Dovid sang along in his alto. The little girls tried to sing the words.

Yachet had one hand pressed to her heart and with the fingers of the other she beat time on the table.

"This day is honored above all other days," repeated Feivel. "La, la, la, la . . . " Dovid carried the tune with his alto. He sang in a higher key than his father, his voice wavering a little from the strain. "This day is honored above all other days," the two finally ended in chorus.

Yachet leaned on her elbows and stood up slowly. She took a step forward, leaned on the back of the bench with her hand, and looked at the children. Their cheeks were all red, their eyes sparkled, and their faces were moist.

"Tfu," Yachet exclaimed, as if spitting out—her way of warding off the Evil Eye. She moved closer to the table and set to work again. With one hand she gathered the forks and with the other she stacked the plates on the table. She held the pile of plates far away from her, not wanting to soil her Shabbes dress. She walked slowly, stiffly, staring at the forks, willing them not to fall down. Then she bent down, placed the dishes and forks into the bowl, and stood up again. She returned to the table and began collecting up the pots. The children at the table laughed. "Children, you've just finished eating," Yachet pleaded with them. She picked up the dish of meat and took it into the alcove. Dovid placed his hand on the table and slid it over to his father, teasing him. Feivel looked carefully at the hand, looked away, and suddenly slammed his hand down on the table. But Dovid had been too quick. Feivel's hand hit the table instead. "Oh!" screamed Zlotele; she thought her father must have been hurt.

"Now your turn," said Dovid to his father as he bent closer to the table. Feivel placed his hand on the table and looked away. Dovid exploited the moment. He slammed his hand down on that of his father. Feivel did not snatch away his hand; he wanted Dovid to win. Zlotele stretched forward, looking at how her brother's small hand lay on her father's large hand. "Daddy, again," said Dovid. Feivel leaned on the table as though he were going to flatten his hand once more. Just then, the door to the alcove squeaked and Yachet walked in briskly. "Enough," she said in mock anger. Everybody at the table pretended to be afraid. Yachet looked down at the floor: "I have to clean the table and we have to get some sleep," she explained, and started working. She gathered the empty pots from the stove and from the floor next to the table. When she straightened up, her face was red. Her face was flushed more from being upset with herself than from any physical effort on her part: Why had she been angry at the children? She took the pots and placed them under the shelf. She turned around to see if the children were staring at her, and then she went back to what she was doing.

Feivel shoved the bench away with his feet and stood up. He moved into the middle of the room, followed by Dovid. Yossele clambered down from the bench and ran over to his father, who stooped down and picked him up. The little girls also stood up and went over to their father. Dovid clutched at his father's arm with both hands; Zlotele did the same, clinging to Feivel's other arm. Rivkele stood staring at her father; there was no place left for her to hold on to, but Feivel bent down and picked her up. "Children, are you holding on tight?" Feivel asked, and started turning around, a human carousel. Zlotele squealed in fear. Yossele tugged at Feivel's beard and laughed. Feivel straightened out his *yarmulke* on his head and smoothed out his beard. To the children, he was their hero.

"Dovid, *mayim ach'ronim*," exclaimed Feivel. Dovid was reluctant to let go. Yachet looked at Dovid; he was clearly tired. She let her hands drop and moved to the table.

"I'll bring the water myself," she said, taking a glass and going over to the water pail.

Feivel picked up the glass of water and poured a little over his finger tips. Then he closed his eyes and began reciting the grace after meals. He clapped his hands from time to time, and the sound splintered the silence in the room. Yossele and Zlotele looked at their father. Yossele smiled, thinking that his father was playing with him. Zlotele looked at her father's lips as he murmured the words; she would have liked to understand what her father was saying.

Yachet placed her hand on the table, leaned on it, and stood up. Then she bent over the table, spread out the *challah* cover, and placed the remaining *challah* in it, making a bundle of the whole. On the bundle she placed the knife. Then, picking up the bundle with both hands and holding the knife tightly, she went over to the cupboard.

"Dovid, go to sleep," said Feivel. Dovid ran over, opened the door, and disappeared into the alcove.

Yachet gathered together the linens on the beds. She placed the blankets on the bench, pounded the pillows to rearrange the feathers in them, and placed the pillows on both sides of the bed.

"Well, who's going to be first in bed?" Feivel asked the children. Feivel turned around slowly. He was full and found it tiring to move about; he walked slowly to the alcove.

The children copied their father but moved more quickly.

"Each of you must put your clothes in a neat separate pile," exclaimed Yachet. Rivkele threw her dress over a bench.

Yachet now went over to Yossele, wiped his face and hands, and placed the towel on the table when she was finished. Then she placed Yossele on the bench and removed his outer clothing.

Zlotele and Rivkele both sat down and took off their shoes. Yossele tried to do the same, so as to help his mother. Two thuds sounded as the two shoes fell to the ground. Both girls stood up in their underwear, and a little later they both jumped into the bed. Yachet lifted up Yossele and laid her cheek on his head. As she carried him over to Zlotele, she patted his head. "Mommy, come to sleep," said Zlotele as she moved to make room for Yachet. Rivkele raised her head. She wanted to see if Yachet was indeed going to lie down in the empty space next to her. Yossele cuddled up to Zlotele. He placed his hands on her. Their eyes slowly began to close.

Yachet looked at the children. They were breathing easily as they slept. She reached under the pillow and took out a white head kerchief. Removing the *shaitel,* she looked around to be sure no one was looking, then hurriedly placed the *shaitel* on a bench and pushed it underneath the table so that it could not be seen. In its place, she quickly tied the kerchief around her head and unbuttoned and took off her dress. She made sure to hang the dress neatly on the back of one of the benches, and then continued undressing. Holding on to a bench with one hand, she removed her shoes. Tiptoeing, she went over to the bed, lifted up the corner of the blanket, and quietly crawled in next to Rivkele. She remained lying down, her body straight, looking at the ceiling. She could hear the quiet in the house and feel the warmth that suffused her entire body. Slowly, she turned onto her side.

Feivel remained standing at the door, his eyes drooping with weariness. He thought that Dovid was still undressing, but Dovid was already in bed, tossing and turning, fighting the blanket, and laughing. Feivel untied his *gartel*, unbuttoned his shirt and trousers, and took them off. Then, sitting down at the edge of the bed, he took off his boots and crawled in underneath the blankets. Feivel placed his hands under his head and closed his eyes. The warmth enveloped his body. The quiet and the darkness of the alcove contributed to his weariness.

The last coals in the oven were uttering their dying gasps as they turned to ashes. The light in the house was dim. In a house without a clock, this was Shabbes afternoon, and everyone slept.

17

YACHET lay with her eyes open, both her hands outside the blankets. She turned her head to look at the stove, noting that the fire was out. The air in the room was damp, dark, even though it was still early afternoon. The frozen window panes cut out the sunlight; one could hear the breathing of those asleep.

Yachet crawled out from underneath the blanket, stood up, picked up her dress, and pulled it over her head. She then removed the kerchief from her head and replaced it with the *shaitel*, ladled out a little water to pour over her fingers, and walked, taking small steps, to the center of the room. Passing the bed, she took her shawl, spread it out, and threw it over her shoulders.

She went over to the cupboard and took out a high, narrow, tin pot, which she had prepared earlier. She wrapped herself tightly in her shawl and went to the door. She turned her head: everyone was sleeping. Then she turned the door handle and the door sprang open. Rivkele sat up, her sleepy eyes following her mother. She woke Zlotele. Yossele woke up too and cried out, "Mommy!" He sat up in the bed, looking for his mother. Rivkele embraced and soothed him.

"Mommy will be back soon. She went to the baker to bring the tea." Zlotele sat up. She bent over the bed and pulled her shoes toward her, lowered her feet directly into her shoes, and remained where she stood. Zlotele then picked up Yossele and carried him over to the bench, where she sat him down and began to dress him. Rivkele crawled off the bed, walked to the table and sat down on the edge of the bench so as not to crease her dress, and began dressing herself. Leaving Yossele sitting, Zlotele went over to her sister, and without saying a word raised Rivkele's feet and wiped off the wood shavings clinging to them; then she returned to attend to dressing her brother.

Meanwhile, Feivel began to dress while Dovid dressed himself at the foot of the bed. He grabbed his trousers with both hands and worked his legs into them.

Dovid went to the water basin. He drew a little water in the ladle and used it to pour water on the tips of his fingers. He walked to the bed and bent over. His sisters continued to dress themselves; they knew what Dovid was looking for. Dovid stood upright, his face red with exertion. He was holding something in his left fist as he went over to the table.

Feivel now stood up, stretched his arms, bent over, and straightened the bedding, lifting up the pillows and tugging at the blankets this way and that.

He then turned toward the cupboard and took out his hat. He wiped the brim with his hand and put the hat on his head. Feivel remained standing on one side of the door and looked to see what was happening in the living room.

"Where is Mommy?" he asked, even though he knew that she was at the baker, as she was every Shabbes afternoon. "She went to the baker to bring the tea," Dovid answered, and went over to the table. The edge of the tablecloth was carelessly draped over the table. Time after time, Dovid tried to get his top to spin properly, but he had carved it himself from a piece of wood and it was not properly balanced. Each time he let go, it toppled over.

Feivel picked up the ladle and dropped it into the water pail. Feeling the weight of the water in the ladle, he pulled it out. The water splashed over the edges of the ladle.

Zlotele looked at her two younger siblings. She went over to Yossele and ran her fingers through his hair. Yossele kept turning his head—he wanted to see what Dovid was doing. Zlotele went over to Rivkele. She now did the same to Rivkele's hair. Rivkele lowered her head to make it easier for her sister. Rivkele's longish hair looked as if it had been braided.

Zlotele ran the fingers of both hands through her hair—on Shabbes, combs were not used in Feivel's home—and let her hands fall to her side. She turned her head, as if looking for a mirror. A little later she went over to the bed and stood on tiptoe to be able to reach higher. She ran from one side of the bed to the other, fluffing up the pillows. Afterwards, she straightened out the blankets. She could not make the beds properly—her hands were too short—so she looked for help. "Rivkele, come here," she called out.

The two girls, one on each side, took hold of a bench and carried it over to the bed. Zlotele climbed onto the bench and started fixing the eiderdown. She labored heavily, pulling it first this way then that. Every so often, surreptitiously, Feivel gave a tug, not letting Zlotele know that he was helping her.

The door sprang open and Yachet stood in the doorway. Her cheeks were red from the cold, her shawl no longer tightly bound about her, her hands laden with the tea canister. Yossele ran over to his mother. "It's boiling hot," she said to him, pointing to the canister with her finger. She went to the cupboard, brought out tea and sugar, dropped them in, and then hurriedly covered the pot again. Yossele carried the mugs over to the table, along with a large spoon. The spoon gave out a loud metallic clang as it hit the table. "My little doves, come to the table," said Yachet.

Yachet stirred the pot of tea a few times. After pouring the first mug, she brought it up to her own mouth; the smell was delicious. She put down the mug and took the spoon out of the pot. She picked up the pot by its handle, holding its cover in her other hand so that it would not fall. One after another, she poured out four mugs of tea. "Who wants a *kichl*?" she asked, not looking up. No one answered. The tea was light brown. As she had poured the tea, tea leaves had also flowed into the mugs. Yachet picked up the pot again. It was discernibly lighter. She now filled Feivel's large mug.

Feivel sat down and slid his feet under the table. His lips murmured the Shehakol blessing: " . . . at whose word all exists." He raised the mug to his mouth, bending his head at the same time.

Yachet's lips seemed to tremble as she quietly murmured the blessing. She lifted the mug to her mouth and sipped the liquid, and only afterwards did she sit down. The children were all holding their mugs, their eyes peering over the rims; they drank audibly, drinking and swallowing mouthful after mouthful. Sometimes they had to stop to catch their breath, and then they would raise their heads from the mugs.

Feivel absentmindedly combed his beard with his fingers. "Yachet," he said aloud as if calling her. Yachet glanced at him and stood up. She knew what Feivel meant because this was his regular practice on Shabbes after tea. She gathered up the mugs on the table, hooking a finger into each one, and carried them over to the basin. "Dovid, my precious one, time to hear what you learned this week," said Feivel as he turned to his son.

Dovid bent over, pulled open the drawer under the table, and took out the *chumash*. The *chumash* was bound in brown leather, worn and shiny with age and use. Yachet brushed off the tablecloth, picked up the teapot, and carried it to the cupboard. Dovid opened the *chumash* and leafed through the pages until he found the place. He sought the second portion read that morning in the *beis medrash*. The pages of the *chumash* were yellow with age, the corner of the page he sought folded over ready to use.

Dovid bent over the chumash and began reading in Hebrew: "*Vayehi mi'mochoras*—It came to pass on the next day that Moses sat to judge the people, and the people stood before Moses from the morning to the evening." He glanced at his father, as if asking a question. He then translated the verse into Yiddish. Then he went on: "*Rashi* tells us that this was on the day after *Yom Kippur*, the day after Moses had come down from the mountain."

Dovid bent over to the *chumash* again. Swaying back and forth over the *chumash* as his father did when he studied, Dovid continued: "Moses' father-in-law saw all that he was doing for the people, and he said, 'What is this thing that you are doing with the people? Why do you sit by yourself and have the people stand before you from the morning to the evening?' And *Rashi* says," and here Dovid gesticulated with his thumb as his Rebbe did when teaching him, "'A judge who judges the people is God's agent.'" Yachet moved closer, remaining standing behind Dovid. "And Moses said to his father-in-law, 'Because the people come to me when they seek God.'" Translating and explaining this, Dovid added, "When the people come to me to seek God, should I run away?" Feivel leaned forward. Seizing Dovid's cheek between two fingers, he pinched the cheek.

Dovid squealed and grimaced, rubbing his cheek, which was now red.

Yachet turned away and spat three times to ward off the Evil Eye, rubbing her eyes each time with her thumbs. She shook her head, her lips trembled, her head swayed from side to side, and she uttered a wordless prayer. She glanced at Feivel, two tears hanging from her eyelashes.

"Give him some Shabbes treats," said Feivel to Yachet, full of pride. He leaned over the table and closed the *chumash*. "Shabbes treat, Shabbes treat," the little girls cried out in delight. Yachet turned away slowly, as if her feet were unable to support her, and went over to the cupboard. Dovid opened the drawer, placed the *chumash* inside it, and closed it. Feivel stretched out his hand and reached for the *siddur*, and wetting his right thumb on his lower lip, began turning pages. Soon he found the right place, bent over the *siddur*, and began reciting "*Borechi nafshi* — My soul, extol the Lord." He swayed back and forth over the *siddur*.

Yachet moved away. When she came back, she held a small package wrapped in green paper in her right hand and a little bag in the other.

Yachet unwrapped the package first. In the creased paper stood eight hard candies and four jellies — the portion which the storekeeper would include in her order each Thursday. She then opened the little bag, which contained peanuts.

Feivel bent back and looked at the four portions. Each portion consisted of two candies, a jelly, and four peanuts. "Children, take them," Yachet told them. "My jelly is bigger than yours. It's got six corners and yours only has four," Rivkele teased Dovid. "My candies have the prettiest colors," said Zlotele. "Mine are prettier," Rivkele answered her. Zlotele addressed Rivkele, but she really meant Dovid. Yossele sucked on a hard candy. He clutched the other tightly in his hand. His lips were sticky. The children ate the peanuts, but the sweet taste of the candies still lingered in their mouths.

Dovid stood up and went over to the stove. He took out the top from his pocket and twirled it with two fingers. The top spun twice and fell on the stove. Dovid picked up the top and inspected it. He realized that it could not spin properly because the tip was not rounded. "Feh!" said Feivel as he looked at Dovid. He did not want to interrupt what he was reciting. Dovid picked up the top and shamefacedly went over to the window. He wanted to see, in the light from the window, if it was not really round enough.

"Dovid, let's go and pray the *minchah* service," Feivel said to his son. Both father and son went over to the door. Feivel took their coats off the hook. Dovid picked up the *siddur* lying on the table. Unbuttoning his coat, he placed the *siddur* inside it. Half of the *siddur* was now inside his coat and half outside. "Good Shabbes," said Feivel as he walked toward the door. "Good Shabbes, a good year," answered Yachet, and she nodded her head.

The quiet warmth in the room filled the entire cavity within the four walls. The warmth was palpable, but the room looked empty.

18

DOVID was first out in the street. The cold made him catch his breath; he swung his hands around, as if ready to take off, and ran ahead.

Feivel clutched at the doorway and stepped into the street. His nostrils tightened up at the sudden onslaught of the cold. The transition from the warmth of the house to the cold in the street seared his lungs. He looked around, following his son.

Dovid ran on, tossing his head from side to side like a young colt just released from its reins; the snow crunched underfoot.

"Dovid!" Feivel shouted. The dry cold carried the sound of his voice, the echo reverberating in the quiet of the street. Feivel started walking faster. A little later he caught up with his son. The street was empty, the frost sharper. The huts seemed to be rooted in the snow. Feivel turned left. He walked between two huts and took a short cut, coming out onto a large, snow-covered square. Dovid followed his father. This empty lot was narrow and long; low, squat huts lined both sides. The lot was the path used by those who lived in these huts. The snow-covered roofs sparkled. The sky above looked like a sack with holes in it.

"Good Shabbes!" a high, female voice pierced the cold quiet. "Good Shabbes!" Feivel answered hurriedly.

Sabbath

Typical Jewish house in Konstantynow, Nad Bugiem, Lublin Province, Poland, 1936. Courtesy of Beth Hatefutsoth Photo Archive, Tel Aviv, and Shmuel Goldring.

A short, thin woman, her head covered in a heavy kerchief, crossed Feivel's path. The kerchief seemed to be a burden to her. Feivel slowed down and allowed the woman to pass by. She entered the door across the way.

"The leech!" cried Dovid, fear in his voice. He nestled closer to his father.

Far in the distance, Yankel the *feldsher* was walking slowly; in his hand he carried a long, round bag with a nickel lock. "Good Shabbes," Feivel greeted those who passed him. The street was filled with Jews. The voices of people who had clearly rested echoed back and forth: "Good Shabbes! Good Shabbes!" The cheerful echo of the words cut through the gray cold. Each gate and door disgorged more worshippers on the way to the synagogue, coming together in the street or walking faster to catch up with their friends. All were on their way to take part in *shalosh se'udos*, a communal meal.

"Marvelous!" Feivel sighed with pleasure. "Dear fellow Jews!" he said joyfully to himself. Then he added, "May no ill befall us!"

Feivel and his son walked along with the stream of Jews. Here and there one could see a curious woman peering out of a window—a grandmother, a mother, or a young girl.

Jews bundled up in their coats, their hats pulled down tightly on their heads, strolled in leisurely fashion. They did not feel the cold; the warmth of their homes, from which they had just come, was still with them as they made their way through the streets. Each one seemed to occupy the breadth of the street, as if it all belonged to him. Their beards were neat, combed out. Unhurried, they walked along the street, bringing with them the Sabbath, to which they were about to bid farewell, in their stately progress.

The street through which the Jews walked to the *beis medrash* was the widest in the town, double the width of the average street. Feivel did not turn immediately into the synagogue street but walked on a little further; he wanted to remain a little longer with the stream of his fellow Jews. He turned in a block later, along a street of homes with thatched roofs. This route was all uphill, narrow at the foot and widening at the top of the hill. Looking down from the top, it was like seeing the street through a magnifying glass.

Dovid started past the homes at a run, but was forced to slow down and lean forward, as if he was climbing stairs. The road had icy, slippery patches; he held on to the fence as he climbed, but he looked back to see the different groups of Jews below. Down below, he could see the springs where the people came to draw water. During the winter, the water was cold and clear. People whose eyes bothered them would come to this spot and apply cold water compresses to their eyes. The water flowed from the springs to the lake, passing by the *mikveh*.

Feivel stood and waited for his son. "Dovid!" he called again, and started moving faster. Dovid crept carefully off the ice, as if tiptoeing, and followed his father.

Sabbath

The snow on the ground in the center of the road had been cut through by wagon wheels, but the snow at the sides was untouched. On the left side of the road were some narrow, seemingly low-built, emaciated houses, their fronts as well as their walls covered with snow. The winds driving in from the open fields had carded the snow here. The walls were all frozen, the wind danced in the spaces between the houses; from time to time, a particularly fierce gust would strike the windows, like a hungry bird pecking with its beak. On the other side of the street were the crates used by the Jewish fish merchants to store their carp for the Shabbes needs. Further up was Isser's tannery; the smell of the leather could be sensed from far off. The tannery itself was all but hidden, only its roof visible above the snow. On the other side stood an old wooden fence, the fence of the old graveyard.

The street ran past the *beis medrash*. In the empty square in front of the *beis medrash*, Feivel stopped to straighten up and regain his breath. The *beis medrash* area was filled with Jews coming in from every side street. They now seemed to be in a hurry, as if each wanted to overtake the other. The trodden snow was gray, the skies becoming darker and the contours of the different houses beginning to merge into one another. Friends nodded as they greeted each other with "Good Shabbes!" The dry air picked up the greeting, as the people disappeared one by one into the entrance to the *beis medrash*.

The frozen courtyard was filled with dancing, elongated shadows. Feivel pushed the handle to the front door open with both his hands, butted the door with his shoulder, and waited for Dovid to enter first. The sudden warmth seemed to slap them in the face.

19

THE *beis medrash* itself was packed. From every corner one heard voices, which seemed to merge and ascend, echoing off the ceiling; the echo rang in the people's ears. A thin, gray fog seemed to envelop the heads of the people.

Short, feeble rays of the sun shone through the semicircular, frozen windows, as if engaged in battle with the fading light. In the great hall itself, the light was mingled with the gray—the day was fighting a losing battle with the night. The brown wood ceiling was low, as if resting on the heads of the people; the benches and tables seemed to be emerging from the gloom. Only the narrow, tiled stove stood out clearly inside in the semi-darkness against the white plaster walls.

The air was warm with the breathing of the crowd. Some people were still wearing their coats. Periodically, draughts of cold air infiltrated through the door or one of the windows. The people were jammed tightly together, as if leaning on one another. All of them together formed the community. Some Jews were still busy pushing their way through to empty places; others sought a place simply to rest their feet—while the others parted to let them through.

All were busy reciting *Tehillim*. One heard snatches of verses coming from here, there, and everywhere, as if the people were talking to one another: "The tribes of the Lord," "Our help is from the Lord," "Happy are those who fear the Lord and who follow in His ways." One of the men swayed back and forth over a tattered *siddur* and recited, "*Al naharos Bavel*—By the rivers of Babylon we sat, yea, we wept." A deeper voice, audible above the others, continued the verse: "As we remembered Zion."

Feivel removed the *siddur* that Dovid had kept under his coat. As soon as he had taken it, Dovid slipped away, disappearing in the throng. Feivel followed him with his eyes, trying to see where he was headed, and then pushed his way through the crowd to the same table where he had prayed in the morning. Dovid had found himself a place in the corner between the stove and the bookcase.

"Odd or even?" a boy asked him, brandishing his clenched fist. The eyes of the older boys sparkled. The boy who had asked the question opened his fist, showing another boy the single button he had in his hand. Dovid stood and looked; he had left his buttons at home.

The door opened. Vizileh seemed to dance into the *beis midrash*. The door closed by itself. He was breathing heavily, both because of the cold and because he had rushed to the *beis medrash*. His thin face was blue with cold. His coat, originally black but now green with age, was buttoned up; years of flour dust had worked their way into the very fabric. Vizileh held the lapels of his coat in his hand, with the fur on the outside. His mouth was open and showing his bottom teeth; his white beard trembled.

Pesach the *shammes* stood leaning against the door waiting for him. He started forward, his short foot first, and stretched out his hands. Vizileh let go of his coat flaps, spilling the five *challahs* he had brought with him into Pesach's hands. Both of them then moved in the same direction.

The psalm recital continued, the words seeming to flow together into a single murmuring sound. Sometimes the melody was louder and stronger, at other times quieter. Even though the *beis medrash* was packed, there were those who could not remain still but paced back and forth as they recited the verses, moved by the power of the words.

Vizileh stood bent over the *bimah*, his long white beard skimmed the reading desk. His half-closed eyes squinted into the Talmudic anthology, *Ein Yaakov*, which he was reading; he hummed the text quietly, as if not wishing to disturb the psalm-singers.

Vizileh lifted his head, closed the volume he had been reading, and presently banged on the *bimah* with the palm of his hand to signal that the service could now begin. The echo rang through the warmth of the *beis medrash*. Those who had been moving about stood still, while those who had been sitting raised their heads. They closed the volumes of *Tehillim* and the hum died down. A man who was close to the reading desk sidled up to it so that the people would not see him. He removed a *tallis* from the shelf inside the reading desk, spread it out with both hands, and threw it over his shoulders. He then leaned on the reading desk. It was Yisroel Dovid the watchmaker. "*Ashrei*—Happy are those who dwell in Your house," cried Yisroel Dovid in a loud voice, so that all should hear that the *minchah* prayer had begun. He adjusted the *tallis* round his shoulders and continued praying.

The light coming from the windows was now very weak. It remained hanging on the wall behind the window. The hall became steadily darker. Yisroel Dovid stood clenching the *tallis* in both hands, as if afraid that it might drop. The murmur of prayer died out as all finished reciting the psalm. Shachna went over to the Holy Ark while Yisroel Dovid stretched out his neck to look around at the people; from his perch high up on the *bimah* he could only see their heads; he pulled the *tallis* over his head.

Shachna opened the *paroches*. "Hersh Tzvi!" he called out, and then added, "the strap maker." Leaning over, he then took out a *tallis* from behind the Holy Ark. At this summons, a man with his hands outstretched pushed his way through the crowd. When he came to the Holy Ark, he remained standing. Shachna handed him the *tallis*.

Shachna proceeded to open the two doors of the Holy Ark, at the same time bowing reverently. The Torah scroll was encased in a red velvet cover, upon which was a gold breastplate. "*Brich Shemei*—Blessed be the name of the Master of the Universe," the *chazan* recited. Hersh Tzvi stretched out his long hands and picked up the Torah scroll, holding it near his head, and started walking. He climbed the steps of the *bimah*, followed by Shachna, whose body, as he climbed, swayed like a sack of flour. As he walked, he held on to the railing with both hands, his steel-framed glasses resting precariously on the tip of his nose. Hersh Tzvi slowly placed the Torah scroll on the table, taking great care, as though afraid lest he accidentally break something. Shachna and Vizileh came closer, bent over to kiss Torah scroll, and then, taking hold of the *atzei chaim*, they rolled the parchment to the correct place. "Here it is!" said Shachna, pointing at the place with his finger. "Let Reb Ozer, son of Menasheh the Kohen, ascend!" he announced. He had already decided upon the three people he intended to call up for the *minchah* reading.

The man who had been thus called hurriedly took a *tallis* that was hanging on the railing, threw it over his shoulders, and hastened to his task. Placing his feet together and closing his eyes, he recited the blessing before the reading. Vizileh touched the Torah scroll with his *tzitzis* and then put his lips to the *tzitzis*. He moved a little to the side so as not to hide the text from the view of the man who had been called up. "If he comes alone, he shall leave alone," intoned Vizileh, "if he has a wife, his wife shall leave with him" (Exodus 21:3). Close to the *bimah* stood a circle of congregants listening attentively to his account of the manumission of slaves.

"A Jew in exile is worse than the slaves of olden times," said Chaim, a man with a long face and deep, black eyes. The others looked at him expressionlessly. "May you be pardoned for ingratitude!" retorted Eli, a tall, broad-shouldered man. "But the gentiles hate us," Chaim continued. The other Jews again remained silent. "One must have faith in the Almighty," Eli eventually murmured. The others nodded in agreement.

Ozer recited the concluding blessing of the Torah reading. Shachna raised his head and announced, "Let Reb Chanoch, the son of Yaakov the Levi, ascend." A corpulent man ran up to the *bimah*. Ozer removed the *tallis* from his own shoulders and handed it to Chanoch, who wrapped himself in it and recited the blessing.

Vizileh stooped over the Torah scroll again and began reading. At the end of the reading, Chanoch touched the Torah scroll with his *tzitzis*, which he placed to his lips, and recited the concluding blessing.

"Let Reb Asher, the son of Moshe, ascend." Asher, a man of medium height with a long, sparse beard, climbed the steps of the *bimah* with great deliberation, clutching the railing with one hand. As he reached the top, he turned around so that all could see him. Chanoch handed the *tallis* to Asher and moved over to the side. Asher held the sides of the *tallis* and closed his eyes as he recited the blessing.

Vizileh coughed. Seizing both of the *atzei chaim*, he bent over the Torah scroll and read, "If a man strikes a man and he dies, he shall surely be put to death . . . " A group of men stood between the stove and the door and listened to the reading. A man with a long, emaciated face said, "Who cares in the slightest if Jewish blood is spilled? There is no law and order." Those near him turned to him. "The baron turned his dog on Boruch," he added. The man wiped his lips with his tongue and went on: "The dog tore his coat and Boruch barely managed to run away. The baron just stood by and laughed." The man spoke slowly, quietly so as not to disturb the reading.

Vizileh read on: "If a man steals another man and sells him, and he is found in his hand, the man shall surely be put to death." Asher stood at his side, not moving a muscle. Shmerl the furrier, who had related the story of Boruch and the baron, spoke again. "The baron sent his agent to Boruch's home; he wanted to pay him." Shmerl's voice dropped even lower, as if divulging a secret. "But Boruch didn't take the money." Vizileh ended the reading and Asher recited the concluding blessing. Vizileh wiped his palms and took a firm grip on both *atzei chaim*. As he raised the Torah scroll on high, his *tallis* slipped onto his shoulders: "*Vezos Hatorah*—And this is the Torah . . . "

Vizileh carried the Torah scroll over to the bench and sat down. Shachna followed him, raised his short hands, rolled up the parchment, and replaced the velvet cover. Vizileh then carried the Torah scroll off the *bimah* while Shachna, following, pushed his glasses back to his eyes.

A number of wrinkled, muscular hands reached over and reverently touched the velvet cover, as if greeting it as it passed. Vizileh bent over and replaced the Torah scroll in the Ark. Shachna then pulled the *paroches* across to cover the entire ark. The *paroches* was a dark blue, heavy curtain, touched with the gray of evening. The golden lions on it shimmered.

Now came the sound of a strong hand striking the table a number of times, whereupon silence descended on the entire hall; the *chazan* pulled the *tallis* over his head.

Heavy boots were heard moving over the floorboards as the worshippers took up their positions for the quiet *amidah*; the *chazan* swayed back and forth. Silence hovered over the heads of the worshippers. The Divine Presence could be felt in the air; the worshippers prayed with their eyes closed.

As the different people completed the silent prayer, one could hear their boots shuffling quietly backward as they tried not to disturb the others. When they came to rest, they tossed their heads to the right and to the left, as if looking about, but their eyes were still closed. They opened them only as their prayer came to an end.

It was quiet again in the hall. The shadows in the corners became longer and longer. The yellow letters on the Holy Ark seemed to achieve a momentary brightness in the evening twilight.

20

THE *chazan* removed his *tallis*, folded it to a quarter of its size, and stuffed it into the shelf of the reading desk. He then turned and began walking in the same direction as the others, who were hurrying to wash their hands for the meal, the door opening and closing as they passed through to the wash basin.

A number of men with long beards sat down at the tables, leaving room for those who had gone out to wash. Some sat down on the benches near the *bimah*; some, their hands clenched behind their backs, paced back and forth; while others stood leaning against the wall near the stove and waited. Pesach the *shammes* stood near the wall and collected the volumes left on the tables. He took the pile of books and carried it back to the bookcase. There was a low bench to the side that Pesach moved to the head of the table. Feivel pushed himself through the open door and into the dusk of the entrance hall. In the street, opposite the door, stood a large wooden barrel encrusted in snow, around which were three metal hoops. The water that had spilled from the barrel had already frozen into ice.

Meanwhile, Pesach the *shammes* came close to the table. In his right hand he carried the *challah*s, and in the left a handful of salt. As he reached the table, he opened his arm and allowed the *challah*s to fall onto the table. He allowed the salt to fall in a little pile on the tablecloth. Then he bent down and brought out two kitchen knives.

The children slipped back and forth between the adults. They wanted to show how quickly they could run without bumping into anyone; other children ran around the tables playing tag. A few of the boys stood around the table watching Pesach *shammes* prepare "*Sholeshudes.*"

A boy with a round face and rosy cheeks called out, "Pesach!" Pesach looked at the boy; the boy pointed at him with his finger and said, "There!" "Wretch!" Vizileh, who happened to be passing, shouted at the boy; the boy ran off. "Pesach!" Vizileh called out, as if gripping the name in his clenched teeth. Pesach did not look around. He stood and sliced the *challah*s. Each slice was then cut into smaller chunks and a pile of these now lay on the table. Vizileh picked up two uncut *challah* loaves and placed them at the head of the table, covering them with the edge of the tablecloth. He then laid the second kitchen knife next to the two *challah*s.

The door was constantly opening and closing as the men came back from washing their hands, bringing the cold with them. The hall was now distinctly cooler than before; those who had been outside stamped their feet and rubbed their hands to warm their fingers. They wiped their hands on the towel hanging by the door. The gray towel was wet, and some men did not bother using it, rubbing their hands together instead, as though pulling off their gloves. Feivel also returned to the hall. He did not have to close the door, because there was another man behind him. Feivel inhaled the warmer air, walking slowly as he wiped one hand on the other.

Everyone, including Feivel, passed by Pesach, took a piece of the *challah*, dunked it in the salt, and sat down. They carried the *challah* pieces carefully, like rare precious gems.

Feivel walked slowly, pushing forward with his shoulders so that he should not need to use his hands. He looked at the corner to find his son. In each hand, he held a portion of *challah*. One of these he handed to Dovid. Dovid placed his *siddur* underneath his arm and picked up the *challah*, while Feivel stood quietly next to him.

Pesach went on cutting the *challah*s.

"Yoel!" called out Vizileh, pursing his lips. Vizileh sat down. Yoel's neighbors looked at him as he responded to Vizileh's invitation, sliding into the space between the table and the bench at the head of the table and sitting down. The others waited. Yoel now uncovered the two *challah*s lying on the table, laid his hands on them, and recited the blessing: "*Hamotzi*—who brings forth bread from the earth."

There was the sound of many jaws working as mouths opened and closed to bite into the *challah*. Yoel cut one of the *challah*s in half and then cut a thin, small slice for himself, dipped it into the salt, and bit into it. As he chewed the bread, his thick beard flapped. He went on cutting the loaf and distributing the pieces, each time turning the *challah* on the sharp knife edge and handing out the cut slices with the point of the knife. He, Yoel the bag mender, who lived in a cellar, who could see only people's feet from his cellar windows, was now presiding at the head of the table, handing out *challah* slices to Shachna the teacher, Yaakov the *chazan*, Vizileh the baker, and Menachem, the man who arose to pray at midnight! He also handed a slice to his neighbor, Motte the tinsmith. When he had finished, he cut the remaining *challah* into smaller pieces, which he piled at the center of the table. Those standing around the table reached over the heads of those sitting down in order help themselves.

Presently, the *shammes* carried over a small metal plate to Yoel. The plate had a little water in it. Yoel dipped his fingertips in it and rubbed his hands together.

"*Rabosai, nevoreich*—Masters, let us recite grace."

"*Yehi sheim*—May the Lord's name be blessed from now unto all eternity," all answered together. Feivel was louder than all the rest; it was the first time on this Shabbes that he was reciting the grace with a quorum.

Yoel closed his eyes, repeating the words of congregation and adding: "*Bireshus rabosai*—With the permission of my masters, let us bless Him of whose food we have eaten."

The people swayed back and forth and responded: "*Baruch she'achalnu*—Blessed be He of whose food we have eaten, and whose goodness sustains us." Yoel bent over the table, repeating the words.

It was getting darker outside. Yoel concluded the grace with the words, "*Oseh Sholom*—May He who makes peace in His high places make peace for us and for all of Israel, and say Amen." He looked at the *chazan*. Yaakov *chazan* struck the table with his palm and began singing a hymn of praise. All joined in. The people pushed in closer to the table, forming a ring around Yaakov.

The first melody was fast and catchy, but now the mood became more somber. The new melody was slow and without words. Grandfathers, fathers, children, and grandchildren were all singing; some tried to outdo the others, but the tune kept them together. All members of the congregation were caught up in the wordless melody, which captivated them. The echo resounded through the *beis medrash*, echoing off the walls and ceiling. The day was dying out, light and dark merging into one.

Pesach the *shammes* stood in a corner near the stove. He closed his eyes, tossed his head, and began praying the evening *ma'ariv* service by himself. Now the singing became louder; the air was filled with song. The *chazan* sang the words of a melody with the people humming in the background. But suddenly it became quiet; the singing stopped. Inside the *beis medrash* it was becoming dark. Against the background of the whitewashed walls, the shapes of many heads swayed back and forth. Suddenly, a gentle voice in the congregation began another melody without words: "Ay, ay, ay, ay." The entire congregation took up the tune: "Ay, ay, ay." They swayed in rhythm with the melody. Each Jew was in his own personal world, but they all felt happy being together. There was the felt kinship of being with the others. Here and there, one voice could be heard singing louder than the others. The voices were filled with longing; the Jews wept without tears as they bade farewell to Shabbes. From time to time, a pair of strong hands was clapped together, the clapping accompanying their longing. Feivel stood with his eyes closed and swayed back and forth, humming the melody to himself. Dovid stood bent over, his head resting on his father. They swayed together.

Pesach tossed his head back and forth. Night was peering in through the windows. He stretched out his hand, took out the matches that were kept behind the stove, and moved away.

The people swayed and sang. The melody now was softer. Pesach remained standing at the reading desk. The sound of a match being lit was heard as he struck it against its box. The little flame burst forth, sending shadows scurrying throughout the *beis medrash*; he squinted at the sudden light, his eyes opening and closing alternately. Then he took out the two candles that had been prepared before Shabbes and lit them. Once they were burning, he placed them in the candle holders on the reading desk. Then he pushed his way through the crowd until he came to the great kerosene lamp that hung in the middle of the *beis medrash*. He climbed up on a bench, removed the glass panel, and lit the lamp. The congregation squinted at the light in their eyes; shadows began dancing up and down the walls.

Berele, the only upholsterer in the region, stood up near the reading desk. Closing his eyes, he intoned the opening words of the *ma'ariv* service: "*Borechu*—Let us bless the Lord who is to be blessed." The people all bent forward and responded: "Blessed be the Lord who is blessed for all eternity."

The candles on the reading desk flickered, the shadows on the walls responded accordingly, shrinking and then expanding to their original shape. The Jews all prayed together, the rustle of their clothes serving as an accompaniment to their prayers. The flame in the kerosene lamp reached higher and higher, as if unwilling to remain confined to the glass. The *chazan* coughed. He leaned on his hands and pronounced aloud the words of the *kaddish:* "*Yisgadal veyiskadash* — May His great name be aggrandized and sanctified . . . "

The people swayed gently, as if readying themselves to leave, but they remained where they stood. Only the shadows on the walls moved back and forth. A black point detached itself from the lamp flame, a shadow was cast across the stove; the heads swayed about, as if they had no support. Feivel seemed to look fixedly into the distance; he saw the villages where he would be tramping, day after day, throughout the coming week.

The weekday really was beckoning at the door. Jews on the benches near the *bimah* moved back and forth slowly, their coats hanging down. They sat as if someone had removed the table in front of them. The door opened again, letting in the cold of the street and bringing the weekday in with it.

"A good week! A good week!" the Jews wished one another as they pushed their way to the door. "A good week! A good week!" Feivel answered. He pulled Dovid by the hand. The front entrance was as dark as a coal cellar as they crossed the space to the outer door. They remained standing on the street, momentarily dazzled by the whiteness of the snow. "Come, then!" said Feivel, tugging at Dovid's hand. Home they went, accompanied at first by shadows, but later those, too, disappeared as on they walked in the dark.

21

YACHET stood not far from the stove. The children snuggled up to their mother, and she to them. The long living room seemed empty, as the ice on the window panes became thicker and the house became darker, although outside it was still day.

Yachet straightened up on her feet and seemed to grow taller. She looked straight ahead but felt the children at her side. "Children," said Yachet, "come and catch me." The little girls looked at her. Yachet started running. The little girls smiled. "Zlotele," said Rivkele, and she, too, began running.

Yachet held Yossele in her arms and ran around the table. The little girls chased her, and Yossele laughed joyfully, his hand around his mother's neck. Yachet ran round the table a few times. The girls chased her but could not catch her. Suddenly, Zlotele turned in the other direction and caught her mother. Yachet stood, out of breath. The little girls, too, had to catch their breaths. Yachet sat down on the bench and the girls moved closer to the table, where they remained standing. "Mommy, tell us a story," Zlotele pleaded. Yachet nodded in agreement and sat Yossele down on her lap; the little girls rested their elbows on the table. "Children," said Yachet, "I'll tell you the story about fish for Shabbes." Both girls clapped their hands joyfully.

Yachet swayed back and forth, as if praying. She began: "One Friday, just before Shabbes, a Jewish man was walking about in the market looking for something. All the Jews of the town knew him and he knew them all. They asked him, 'Nochum, how are you?' 'Thank God, fine,' he answered, and he looked to the side. He didn't want them to see his face. He felt weak, for, as everyone knew, he had just been sick. His children lived across the ocean in another country.

"The man kept looking until he came to a fish store. 'Nochum, wait!' Meir the fish merchant said. Meir turned around and went back into his store.

Nochum remained standing with his head down. Meir soon came back and pushed a package into Nochum's hands. 'Have a good Shabbes!' he told Nochum, and went back inside his store. 'May you, too, have a good Shabbes, and may God pay you,' Nochum told him. 'Good Shabbes,' Meir answered from the store. Nochum looked down, because he was ashamed. He started for home, hurrying on his way. With his last few coins, he bought *challahs* from the baker and ran home. His wife, Beile, sat with her hands folded, waiting. 'Beile, I've brought *challah* and fish! Make Shabbes!' he shouted happily. Beile jumped up from the bench. 'God is merciful,' she said, and started working quickly because it was almost Shabbes."

At that point in the story, the door opened and a woman came in, hurriedly closing the door. She looked at Yachet and the children and remained standing at the door.

"So Beile started cooking," Yachet continued. Neither Yachet nor the children had heard anyone coming in. The woman stood looking at Yachet and the children and smiled. Her head was covered with a brown hat; a hatpin, with sparkling stones glittering in it, had been stuck through it. She wore a black dress and black laced shoes.

Yachet leaned forward and went on with her story: "The fish was a pike from a large pool; Beile prepared it, scaled it, cut open the stomach, and took out the entrails. A little stone fell out on the table." Yachet bent over the table, drawing out the words: "Beile picked up the little stone and looked at it. 'Nochum, a diamond!' she cried out frightened. 'A diamond?' Nochum asked. He couldn't believe it. Both of them, Nochum and Beile, remained speechless. But it was already close to Shabbes. 'Beile, make Shabbes,' Nochum told his wife, 'and after Shabbes I will bring the diamond back to Meir.' Nochum and Beile had a happy Shabbes," Yachet concluded.

Zlotele gave a shout of joy. Both little girls banged their hands on the table. Rivkele did not understand the moral; she was simply copying her sister. The woman who had been listening now broke in: "Good Shabbes," she said, and laughed. Yachet turned her head, and the children followed her gaze.

"Reche, good Shabbes! How are you? Come, sit down. When did you get here?" said Yachet wonderingly. "Aunty, aunty," the little girls exclaimed happily. Yossele stretched his hand out to her, as if he wanted her to pick him up. Reche lived across the road.

Reche nodded her head happily, glad to be with them. The shawl around her shoulders became loose. She placed the thick, small, leather-bound volume that she had been carrying underneath the shawl on the table. Reche removed the shawl, folded it, and placed it on the bench, sitting down next to Yachet. Yachet turned to her and came near for a better look at her friend. Reche gave a sigh of contentment as she felt the warmth of the home; she reached over to Yossele and patted his cheek; Yossele tried to grab her hand.

Reche turned to Yachet and asked her, "The children are all well?" "Thank God," Yachet answered. "Did you have a joyful Shabbes?" Reche asked again. "Fit for a king," answered Yachet.

Reche looked at Yachet; Yachet cast her eyes down and took Yossele in her arms.

Reche wiped her lips with both her hands, a smile spreading over her face; she understood Yachet's modesty. "I also have news," said Reche, as if imparting a secret: "I received a letter from my Hersh Dovid." "Really?" said Yachet in wonder, curious as to the letter's contents. The girls looked at Reche. They could not understand what their mother was talking about.

"He is earning a good salary and is keeping up his *Yiddishkeit*; he has sent us a package."

"*Naches* from children."

"God should help all the Jews." A little later, Reche went on: "Now I must think about marrying Leah off." She swayed over the table and added, "Ephraim, her fiance, is a good provider. He is a master shoemaker, you know, and all the rich folk come to him." The women remained silent, shaking their heads. A little later, Reche said, "My husband has already been to the post office to ask how long a package from America takes. Yachet, have you already read this week's portion?" Without waiting for an answer, she went on: "I've finished it. Let's go over as much as we can manage before it gets too dark."

The light from the street still entered through the windows. Reche opened up the *chumash* she had brought and pushed it in front of Yachet; both bent over the book. Reche swayed back and forth, and in a singsong fashion began, "'And Jethro heard,' says King Solomon, in Proverbs, 'that a wholesome tongue is a tree of life.' That means that the tongue is a cure for the soul that sins. Sins, on the other hand, are diseases to the soul, when one doesn't truly believe in God."

Yachet held Yossele in her lap and swayed back and forth with him. The little girls stood next to one another, Zlotele with her hand propping up her chin, Rivkele with her head resting on her sister's shoulder. Reche looked up and continued: "Thus we find about Abraham, about whom our Sages relate: 'He had a precious jewel hanging around his neck, and whenever anyone who was sick saw it, he became well. When Abraham died, the precious stone passed over to Isaac.' In other words, our Sages tell us that good news came from his throat, for Abraham persuaded people to believe in God and serve Him."

Yachet sat listening attentively and breathing hard; Yossele banged the table with his hand. Zlotele pulled her chin away from her hand. "Quiet!" she said to her brother. Yachet picked up Yossele's hand and held it. Rivkele, astonished, stared at Reche. Reche bent over the *chumash*. Pointing with a finger, she went on: "When Abraham died, he left no one to persuade others to worship the true God, and he had the precious stone hung around the sun. In other words, when one wants to know that there is God in the world, one should learn it from the sun, which rises in the east and sets in the west. Therefore there must be a God, who directs the sun."

Reche continued, her singsong voice wavering. The little girls had their hands on the table. They looked at Reche and listened. Reche squinted, looked into the *chumash* again, and said, "The same is true for the good words of Moses: when Moses told Jethro of all of God's wonders, Jethro recognized the truth. This we see in the verse, 'Jethro heard all that God had done for Moses and Israel.'" She said the last few words with great deliberation, as if trying hard not to make any mistakes. At each word, she nodded her head. Reche raised her head from the *chumash*. She was no longer able to make out the letters.

The sudden silence interrupted the smooth flow of the Torah portion. The dark of the night was spreading onto the walls. As one looked at the tablecloth, one could see that the day was setting. A frozen shine covered the windows.

"I'll leave, before it's night," Reche said. She brought the *chumash* up to her lips and reverently kissed it, and then stood up. Reche went over to the door. Yachet and the girls followed her. Close to the door, Yachet overtook Reche and opened the door for her. A dry, dark cold pushed its way through the open door.

"May God be merciful to you," Reche said, leaving. "May God help all Jews," Yachet answered.

Reche bowed her head. She hurriedly left the house. "Can you see?" Yachet shouted out after her. "Yes! Yes! Close the door!'"

"Children, come!" Yachet called them. She went over to the table with them. The cold air that had been let in was now circulating throughout the house.

"Mommy," Zlotele called out, and pulled Yachet's dress. All remained standing in front of the table at the spot where the tray with the candle sticks stood. "Mommy, what did Aunty Reche read you?"

"My darling, that there is a Jewish God and that a Jew must always believe in Him," Yachet explained.

It was quiet in the house. A little later, Zlotele again asked her mother:

"And who wrote her the letter?"

"Her son in America. He is a smith there. He sends them fancy clothing. Aunty Reche is marrying off her daughter Leah." "It's dark," Rivkele cried out. "Shabbes is over," Zlotele said regretfully. She again grabbed her mother's dress.

Yachet looked out the window. With both hands, she embraced her daughters and began reciting the supplication: "O God of Abraham, of Isaac, and of Jacob, protect Your nation of Israel from all evil for Your sake. The beloved Sabbath is departing. May the week which follows be one of perfect faith, of faith in the Sages, of love for our fellows, of clinging to the Holy One, blessed be He, that we may believe in Your Thirteen Principles and in the redemption—may it come speedily in our days—in the revival of the dead and in the prophecy of Moses, peace on him. May the week that arrives be one of health and of good fortune and of success and of blessing and of mercy; and for children, life and sustenance, for us and all of Israel, and let us say Amen." Her voice trembled. Her words echoed in the dark.

Yossele wrapped his hands around his mother's throat and clung to her. The little girls clung to her dress and stared at her. "Children, sit down," Yachet said, and started moving. She shuffled with her feet on the floor, clinging to the table with her hands, taking care not to bump into anything. With her knees, she directed the girls to the bench. She remained standing at the bench. She picked up Yossele and seated him on the bench. "My darlings, look after your brother," she said.

The girls moved over to him, and each took one of his hands.

Yachet left the table. It was dark in the house. The girls closed their eyes. Zlotele sang to herself:

Under Yossele's little crib
Stands a pure white little kid
The kid went to trade
What will its trade be?
Raisins and almonds.

Yachet went over to the cupboard and lit a candle. She squinted and called out to the children, "A good week!" Both little girls covered their eyes with their hands: "A good week!" they answered their mother.

Yachet took the glass off the kerosene lamp and turned the wick up. Soon, she had it burning.

"A good week! A good week! A good week!" Yachet said quietly three times, and sighed. She bent down and picked up Yossele again.

Yachet and the children turned their heads and listened. Heavy footsteps were searching for the path, while light footsteps followed. The handle turned and the door opened.

Yachet cupped the flame with her hand and turned her head to the door. The children did the same. The cold again found its way into the house. Feivel pushed Dovid through the door ahead of him and followed, closing the door immediately. "A good week!" he called out, blinded by the light. "A good week," Dovid echoed him. He was shielding his eyes with the palm of his hand. The light blinded him as well. "A good week! A good week!" the mother and daughters answered. "A good year," Yachet answered.

Dovid sprang forward, as if suddenly released of a burden he had been carrying. He took off his coat and threw it on the bed. Feivel unbuttoned his coat, went over to the wall, and placed his coat on the hook in the wall. He turned around and looked at his family.

Dovid brought over the flask with the remaining wine, the wine goblet, and the spices.

Feivel went over to the table. He picked up the corner of the tablecloth and exposed the wood underneath it. He placed the goblet on the wood and filled it with the raisin wine. Yachet left the table. She came back carrying things in both hands: in one hand she held the ladle, and in the other she held Yossele. Feivel put down the empty flask and took the ladle from Yossele. He added a bit of water to the goblet. Dovid took the matches from the tray and lit one. He lit the special *havdoloh* candle and put the matches down. Yachet picked up Yossele so that he could see better.

Feivel held the goblet in his right hand, swayed back and forth, and began: "*Hinei*—Behold, God is my savior, I will trust and not fear." The melody was essentially a cheerful one, but with an undertone of concern and pleading. Feivel swayed back and forth as he recited the words. Dovid held the candle high over his head. The flames flickered. Feivel's and Yachet's shadows danced on the walls, along with the smaller shadows of the children alongside them. The candle dripped. One could smell the melted wax. Feivel swayed and proclaimed aloud, "The Jews had light, joy, delight, and esteem." Feivel spilled some wine on the table as he recited the blessing, "Creator of diverse kinds of spices." Feivel did not have a special container for the spices they used. Now he recited the blessing, "Who created the lights of fire," and he held the fingernails of each hand, in turn, up to the light of the candle.

Dovid dipped the candle in the wine that had been spilled. Feivel then poured the remaining few drops of wine on the candle. Finally, the candle went out. One could smell the burned wick. Feivel dipped his fingers in the wine on the table and then rubbed a little of the wine onto his forehead. Now Feivel sang, "*Hamavdil*—He who separates between the holy and profane, may He forgive our sins . . ." The melody was monotonous, but Feivel stretched out the last word of each verse. Dovid sang the words along with his father. The girls shook their heads in rhythm. Feivel and his family sang the song: Feivel and Dovid sang the words while Yachet and the girls hummed the melody.

Not only Feivel, but Yachet as well, wanted him to delay as long as possible taking his walking stick from under the bed. Feivel's face shone, his red beard glowing in the light, but the two wrinkles on his forehead were again prominent, as on every weekday.

GLOSSARY

aitz (atzei chaim): the Tree of Life, situated in Eden. The tree of life is traditionally associated with the Torah, as indicated by a prayer recited on the Sabbath morning, which likens the Torah to "a tree of life to all who hold fast to it."

aleinu: a portion of the daily prayer in which one bows before God, thanking him for distinguishing between the Jews and other nations.

aliya: an honor extended to worshippers in the synagogue, in which they are called to ascend to the podium where the Torah is being read and to recite blessings.

amidah: a central portion of the service, termed the "Shmone Esrei" (the eighteen blessings), which is recited silently while standing.

amud: reading desk of the cantor.

ba'al koreh: an expert Torah reader who reads aloud from the weekly Torah portion using the traditional melodic intonations.

beis medrash: prayer and study house; a small orthodox synagogue.

bavarke: milk mixed with boiled water and sugar.

bimah: a raised platform or pulpit in the synagogue, from which the Torah is read; a reading table.

challah: braided bread eaten on the Sabbath and on festivals.

chazan: cantor.

cheder: class of young boys studying religious texts.

cholent: a stew of meat, carrots, and other vegetables cooked on a low flame and traditionally served on the Sabbath.

chumash: the Pentateuch; a volume containing the five books of Moses, occasionally including a supplement with the additional reading portion appropriate for each week.

feldsher: old-time barber-surgeon; healer.

gartel: belt, especially a cloth belt, worn by men during prayer outside of their clothing, symbolically separating the upper and lower parts of the body.

gemara: derived from the Aramaic verb "to learn," this term refers to the second part of the Talmud, consisting of discussions and amplifications of the Mishna (first part of the Talmud, which deals with the whole range of Jewish legislation and religious ethical teachings).

goyim: Gentiles, non-Jews.

havdoloh: a small service conducted at the conclusion of the Sabbath and holidays, in which Jews differentiate between holy days and the regular weekdays. The havdoloh prayer is recited over a cup of wine, a candle, and sweet smelling spices.

hekdesh: the shelter where paupers and those without a roof over their heads lodged.

kaddish: a doxology in Aramaic recited by mourners during the first eleven months after the death of a parent, child, or sibling. Traditionally, sons are sometimes referred to by their parents as "the kaddish."

kedushah: literally means holiness, yet also refers to a section of the Shmoneh Esrei prayer in which the cantor leads the congregation in a responsive prayer stressing the holiness of God.

kichl, kichlach: cookie(s).

kiddush: a small ceremony in which a blessing is recited over a cup of wine for the purpose of sanctifying the Sabbath and holidays.

kishke: stuffed derma.

kugel: a casserole usually made with noodles and/or vegetables, or a pudding cooked within a cholent.

lokshen: noodles.

ma'ariv: evening prayers, recited after sunset.

maftir: the person who concludes the reading of the Torah and introduces the supplementary reading portion, termed the haftara, which is read thereafter.

melamed: teacher in the cheder.

mezuzah: a parchment scroll that is attached to the door post on the right side of the entrance to a Jewish home and to the entrance to any of the rooms within the home. The inscription consists of several verses from Deuteronomy.

mikveh: bathhouses; pools of clear water for ritual purification.

minchah: the afternoon prayer, to be recited before sunset.

moydeh ani: an early morning prayer to be recited upon awakening in which one expresses thankfulness to God for restoring him to the condition of wakefulness.

Musaf: additional prayers recited after the Torah reading on the Sabbath, holidays, or the new moon.

naches: to derive joy or pride from someone or something.

paroches: curtain in front of holy ark.

rebbi: teacher of Talmud in a yeshiva; also charismatic leader of Hassidic sects.

shalosh se'udos (or **se'udah shelishi**): the third of the obligatory Sabbath meals usually eaten in late afternoon after prayers.

shaitel: wig worn by orthodox Jewish women after marriage to conceal their hair from the eyes of strangers.

shammes: the caretaker of the synagogue and its religious paraphernalia.

shaygetz: male Gentile.

shema: "Hear O Israel, the Lord our God is One," the most important Jewish prayer, recited several times daily.

shtetl: Yiddish diminutive for *shtot*, meaning town used to refer to small communities of Jews in eastern Europe.

shtiblach: small, one-room synagogue.

shtreimel: a fur hat worn by Hassidim.

siddur: a prayer book containing the daily prayers, the Sabbath prayers, and the holiday prayers in their specific order.

tallis: a traditional prayer shawl worn by men during the morning prayers. Ritual fringes are attached to each of its four corners in accordance with biblical law. Traditionally, the tallis has been white with stripes of black or blue.

tefillin: phylacteries, or parchment inscriptions encased in two small leather cubicles attached with straps to the arm and the head during the morning weekday prayers.

Tehillim: the book of Psalms.

tzimmes: a stew of carrots and radishes.

tzitzis: fringes attached to the four corners of the prayer shawl, functioning as visible reminders of God's commandments. The *tzitzis* appear both on the *tallis* as well as on the tallis koton.

yarmulke: skull cap, or head covering worn at all times by observant Jews, and worn by all Jewish men during the performance of religious functions.

yeshiva: Talmudic academic seminary.

zemiros: Sabbath songs.